Adam's about to discover how much drama a mid-life crisis can be. He's obsessed with Mannix, the nude model in his art class. But Adam has been married to Wade for nearly two decades, and they don't have an open relationship.

Little do they know that Fabien, a warlock from the Afterlife, has secretly cast a spell of lust on Adam and his potential toy-boy.

As things begin to heat up, Adam's guardian angel, Guy, steps in. But what's the best way to save the relationship? Should Guy subdue Adam's wandering passions or instigate a steamy threesome?

Drama Queens and Adult Themes

Actors and Angels, Book 2

Kevin Klehr

Published by
NineStar Press
PO Box 91792
Albuquerque, New Mexico, 87199
www.ninestarpress.com

Warning: This book contains sexually explicit content which is only suitable for mature readers, and infidelity.

Print ISBN #978-1-947139-14-5
Cover by Natasha Snow
Edited by Jason Bradley

Acknowledgements

I'd like to thank a fan of my writing, who I've never met personally but helped me in the direction this novel took. Thanks to T.J. Burzynski, who read its prequel in one day, and gave me advice on an earlier draft of this book. I listened.

Thank you too, Angus, Nicky and Clinton, who have encouraged me to write, along with Krys, Bernie, Mary, my Mum, and the many others in my life who have kept me on this path.

And a general thanks to all my friends who've contributed dialogue to this twisted plot. Without your enlightened musings, this story wouldn't have the sense of humor it has. You all know who you are.

Thanks to Ethan, Jason, Adrian, J.P., and Val who have helped make this novel see light. It's nice to have a supportive and professional team.

Huge appreciation goes to my partner in crime, Warren, who has told me time and time again to just keep following this passion. He is my love in life and fiction. And yes, darling, I'm listening!

And lastly, thanks to Dad, who watched me silently put words to page.

Prologue

I'VE LOST TWO friends. One was in my adolescence when I was trying to master the art of flying. He was everything I wanted to be. Confident, charismatic, and someone people wanted to be around. I feared he tired of me as he tried to teach me to soar. I never reached for the skies, physically or emotionally. I think that's why he disappeared. Thankfully, I found him again recently.

The other did teach me to soar, though not through flying. He taught me how to love myself, even though I'm still mastering that skill. He taught me that some dreams are worth pursuing, which I learned through observing his actions. But he was mortal, and that's what mortals seem to do. Eventually, I had to bid him farewell as he began his new life as a new person.

And yet it's ironic that the person who touched me the most was that random soul. I never pined for him. I never wished to share his love. He was just a friend; a good friend. Which is why I'm writing this.

If anyone ever reads this, I want them to understand why I intervened in his life. I want them to understand why I broke the main rule that we, on this side of mortality, are never supposed to break. I want them to understand, because I need an explanation. Personally, I don't understand my actions myself.

Extract from Guy's Journal
Guardian Angel Class One
Head, Afterlife Welcoming Committee

Chapter One

ADAM

He stood wearing a velvety white towel and an eager grin. Either could've disappeared at my whim. I smelled the freshly laundered lemon scent of the towel combined with the odor of his body sweat, which I was dying to lick from his forehead. I'm always a sucker for a devil-may-care attitude. It makes me weak at the knees in an instant, but in this case, I was already reclined in my gleaming white tub, so there was no danger of losing my balance. The water filled to the brim, and I knew that when he joined me, he would splash the tiles below.

I'd only known him for half an hour, and already I was under his spell. Was he a young man of style, or was he a man of simple tastes? Did he have a daytime career that gave him the world at his fingertips, or did he simply have the freedom of freelance engagements?

Time slowed as his luxurious towel fell to the floor. His body was not toned like a swimwear model. His features would never inspire a dozen wet dreams. It was his everyday physical qualities that were driving me wild. That tuft of silky chest hair that traced its way to his belly button. He even had a little flab. Not too much, just a tad. To me, it signaled a man of zero pretense.

But as the towel was now on the floor, his upper body wasn't what I was focusing on. He lifted one leg and eased himself into the water. The other leg followed as instinct lured my face toward his luscious...

"At some point, Adam, you do need to put pencil to paper," said my art teacher. He had crept up behind me.

My wayward daydream vanished. Hopefully, I'd find it again before bedtime. I blushed and so did the nude model. I quickly drew a line, but it wasn't in keeping with the young man's form.

I was startled at my own behavior. A man of my age wasn't supposed to act like a starstruck teenager. My instructor gently gripped my hand and guided my pencil to create a more natural line.

The model winked at me as some of the other students chuckled. Another budding male artist with bleached-blond hair nodded in my direction, smiling slyly.

"Okay, I admit it. My mind was somewhere else, and I apologize to the model," I said.

All eyes in the room were on me.

"I'm flattered," the model replied.

"It's not like me to act like this, seriously."

"Can I get you a glass of water?" asked the teacher.

"Thanks but I'll get one myself. I think I need a walk. I'll catch up on my drawing as soon as I get back."

I rushed out of the classroom. This was all too weird in my situation. I was in my early forties and still madly in love with the man I'd shared my life with for the last eighteen years. We had a healthy sex life, even though I fantasized more than I'd like to admit. In fact, any dreamy man wandering past my view would arouse my animal instincts faster than a straight guy in a room of lipstick lesbians. But this young man posing for art class had my tongue dragging so close to the floor I was licking it clean. I was definitely not ready for a midlife crisis, or so I thought.

I sat on a seat in the corridor. Was I capable of having a discreet fling? I lightly slapped myself on the cheek, waking up to how ridiculous this question was. Why would he want to have an affair with an old fart like me?

It was the middle of winter, and I could already feel chilled air on the tip of my nose. I stood up and headed for the bathroom. I splashed warm water on my face. I stared at the mirror, giving my reflection some sound advice.

"Adam, get a grip. You don't know this guy, but suddenly he's invaded your thoughts. Yes, I know he looks really cute up there with nothing but that devilish grin and a pair of turquoise socks, but come on now, he can't be more than thirty!"

"Seems like you're smitten," alleged the bleached-blond student.

He had wandered through the door and was heading for the urinal.

"Were you standing outside long?"

"I heard you down the corridor. Nothing to be ashamed of, really. This is my fourth class, and I've had to draw that same model once before. He hasn't got the perfect body, but boy has he got the perfect attitude. Alluring, and if there is a god, available."

The blond zipped up his fly and wandered to the sink next to me.

"I agree, but I usually don't go around acting like a schoolgirl with a crush."

"Enjoy it. Not all their models have that much charisma."

We escorted each other back to art class where the other students had made headway on their drawings. I focused on the model's socks in an attempt to concentrate on my artwork, rather than the young man's prominent feature. Soon the ankles were added before my pencil carefully outlined his masculine legs.

As I traced up to the hip, I sighed as I studied his most manly asset. How should I draw it? Would the teacher fail me if I portrayed it erect? After all, a great artist should display his own feelings on the sketchpad.

I decided to skip his crotch and draw his chest. His slightly defined chest. Not too developed, but not devoid of shape either. The small tuft of dark hair in the center of the upper body was outlined with great care. Outlining shape was one thing, but defining the type of chest hair someone had was another. A trail of thick small lines was carefully added to the picture from the torso to the navel.

"Okay folks, pencils down."

The teacher wandered around the room giving us feedback. The charming model reached for a pair of frayed blue jeans, which were neatly folded over the back of a chair just an arm's length away. He pulled them up and carefully buttoned the fly around his naked assets, as he clearly hadn't brought underwear.

"We'll have him back in a couple of weeks if you want to complete this particular drawing," said the teacher.

He gave me a cheeky look.

"How far did you get?" asked the model.

He grabbed his dusty-pink T-shirt and snuggled into it tightly.

"Not as far as I would have liked," I replied.

"Let's see."

He strolled over to my unfinished work. I was anxious by the thought of only a patch of denim between me and the model's private bulge. I concentrated on my artwork and tried not to let the man's proximity lead me to more wicked thoughts. Who was I kidding?

I had to divert my attention to our teacher instead, who was heading my way. He was a funky, retired chap. Black thick-rimmed glasses, peppered hair, and beard with a gentle face. The kind of man who'd take long walks with his wife in the park and watch Sunday arts programs on television.

"For the short amount of time you spent on this, you did pretty well for a newcomer," he said. "But what are these strange lines to his side?"

"Um, I had this desire to add wings to my subject."

"Wings?"

"I know it's odd, but you did say at the beginning of class not to be constrained by what we see, and that we all see characteristics differently."

"Yeah, but wings? Are you picturing our model as some kind of angel?"

"Why not? I'm seeing caring characteristics."

The young man gave me a saintly smile. The teacher stroked his chin before pointing to the socks I'd drawn.

"Are my ankles really that shape?" the model asked.

He bent over to take a closer look. I wanted to bury my tongue in the nape of his neck and lick off any imaginary sweat.

"Yes, that's the shape of your ankles," the instructor replied. He gestured toward a student near the window. "Ian over there did a better job on your ankles, but Adam really did well on your socks. The way the shape of the feet peep through the cotton is not something I expect from a first-timer."

"Thanks," I replied. "I used to do a little sketch work last year but only amateur stuff. Still life from things around the house. A clock, fruit, dirty laundry, that sort of thing."

"Bring in your drawings next week. I'd like to see them." He spoke up to address the class. "Now let's check out Ian's work, and Carla's. Ian knows his ankles, and Carla's good with faces."

We walked over to look at Ian's sketch as the other students followed. Ian's careful study of the model's feet almost made them look bare. Carla captured the man's cheeky smirk skillfully, making that feature alone the highlight of her image. The budding blond artist did his best work with the chest and hips, although they were considerably more masculine than they needed to be.

We all made the rounds, admiring and commenting on the other artworks before ending back at my attempt. There were unanimous compliments about the socks, sparking the suspicion that I must have a foot fetish. Like anyone, I had my kinks, but sucking toes was not one of them. There's something about a tinea marinade that just doesn't float my boat.

"You know, Adam, maybe you're onto something with the angel wings," said Carla. "I would have put a wry smile and devil horns on him, just because I think he's cheeky. But you see him as virtuous."

"Divine, maybe, but not virtuous," I replied.

Everyone strolled back to their easels to pack away their portraits except for the appealing model. He stayed to chat. He even helped me roll up the drawing as I studied the way his skillful hands worked with a cylindrical object.

"I'll be back here in a couple of weeks if you want to finish the picture. They use me at least once a month."

"Getting naked doesn't bother you?"

"I have open-minded parents. They used to take me to nudist beaches when I was a kid."

"Only child?"

"Only child."

"Spoiled?"

"A bit. Still am, I suppose, even living away from home. Mum's always dropping off baked dinners or cookies for me and my flatmate. You'd think we can't fend for ourselves."

"I'm Adam," I said.

I raised my hand, and he shook it firmly.

"Mannix. Please don't ask what my parents were thinking when they came up with that name. On marijuana or something."

"I like it."

"I want to change it, eventually."

"What to?"

"At this stage, I haven't a clue."

"Keep it. It sounds like the name of a secret agent."

"Yeah, a pretty lame one at that."

Mannix handed me my picture as I beamed at him, probably resembling a lonely bachelor with a crush on an enigmatic porn star.

"I'm honored you were taken with the subject matter," he teased.

"Between you and me, Mannix, that's never happened to me before. I'm sorry if I was staring."

"Not blowing my own trumpet or anything, but Adam, you wouldn't be the first." He winked, which kind of made me feel embarrassed. "Do you need a lift somewhere?"

"It's okay. I have my car."

Instantly, I regretted this admission of car ownership. Could I grab those words from the air and stuff them back in my mouth? My beautiful partner, Wade, was not going to be home for at least another hour and a half, and maybe, just maybe? I snapped back from my adolescent thoughts and sighed.

"Do you want a nightcap before going home?" he asked.

"Yes!" I replied with the zeal of a henpecked man about to get a lap dance. "I mean, sure. That's a good idea. Whatever you want. Drink. Good suggestion."

"Is that bar on Clarence Street on your way home?"

"As a matter of fact, it is."

It was actually in the opposite direction.

"Looks like we've got a date."

He walked ahead of me before helping get my pencils and my sketch onto the passenger seat of my car. It was a ten-year-old modest two-door hatch, which Wade and I had bought secondhand. We both used to drive it before my partner fell in love with a flashier sedan he'd found at a dealership.

I thanked Mannix as he walked to the opposite row of vehicles parked at the neighborhood center. The beep of the automatic lock made a sporty little mini double blink its headlights.

The young man eased into his understated luxury car with unassuming confidence. I was a sucker for material items I couldn't afford, especially this type of tasteful indulgence. Mannix teased his engine before letting his vehicle make its way out of the car park.

I sat there for a minute or two, wondering if I was doing the right thing. After all, I was only going for a drink. Wasn't I? Guilt was rising through my body. I could see Mannix climbing over me into that imaginary bathtub again. His basket of goodies inviting this old wolf to sample.

I turned the key and started my engine. As I made my way to the street, my thoughts alternated between Technicolor adultery and refined G-rated friendship. Did Mannix have an ulterior motive, or was I full of wishful thinking? It wouldn't be hard to hide this fling from Wade, even if we just decided to meet up on another night when I was supposed to be at art class.

No, bugger it. Why wait? There was a bathtub waiting at home, and Wade was at his salsa lesson and wouldn't be home for at least another hour. The tub would be filled to the brim, a bottle of champagne, two glasses, and a Northern soul compilation drifting in from the lounge room.

But then, I wondered what would happen if Wade's dancing partner, Tim, didn't need a lift home. He'd be home early. How would I have explained my need to bathe? Perhaps the other students attacked me with their charcoal crayons. Maybe the teacher hated my work so much that I was berated to the point of needing to soak up the tension.

I pictured Mannix on our sofa when Wade came home. I would try several coded words to let my husband know that a threesome was on my mind.

But this wasn't our style. We didn't invite costars to our bed. In fact, like most long-term couples we went through phases of being either solely devoted or acting more like two confident individuals. In recent months, we'd behaved like old souls who knew we couldn't live without each other. We'd hold each other before we fell into slumber and awake needing to possess each other again. But it might have been fun to share that experience with Mannix.

I pulled up in front of the pub, still reeling from my own errant imagination. I took one deep breath to jolt myself back to reality. It didn't really work. My sense of guilt magnified while I pictured that bathtub again and Mannix's soft lips cruising toward my own.

"Adam, are you okay?"

My gaze darted to the person who was knocking on the windscreen. It was Mannix, curious to why I was taking so long to get out of my car.

Chapter Two

Mannix

I liked being admired by this clumsy guy. It'd happened before, but with Adam, it was like having Ted Schmidt from *Queer as Folk* have a crush on you. You love the attention, but you're in two minds just in case he got needy.

He was anxious as I opened his car door and casually led him through the entrance of one my favorite pubs. A classic old watering hole that had been half gentrified before the previous owners ran out of money. Upstairs was sparse, metallic, and new, while downstairs the classic fixtures had been mostly restored.

We sat at the bar and ordered drinks as I let him talk about his husband. He overemphasized how much he was in love, in a monologue that would bore anyone into a coma. He did make me smile, though. He made me sort of feel special at the same time. Knowing that I was the one who had turned him to jelly even though there wasn't a snowball's chance in hell I'd sleep with him. At some point, I interrupted his ongoing declaration of love to a man named Wade and stumped him with a question about why he was preoccupied in his car.

"Seriously, there was nothing on my mind."

He feebly raised his eyebrows and sipped vodka and cranberry.

"I know we've just met, but it might help you to talk about it. Even to a stranger."

I sat on the stool, resting my elbow on the bar while attempting my best faraway expression. I couldn't help myself. I liked being a tease.

"Really, it's nothing. I was just going through a shopping list in my head while I was sitting in my car."

"At this time of night?"

"Shops are open late."

I knew it was bullshit, but I was mischievously enjoying watching Adam squirm with my line of questioning.

"Okay, what do you need to buy?"

"Furniture polish."

"What? You're doing housework tonight?"

"Yeah. Wade and I are into role-play. We take turns at dressing up like the French maid."

"Adam, you don't strike me as the kind of person who can walk in heels."

"True. I'm more of your well-worn house cleaner. Slippers, nightgown, cigarette in mouth, and attitude. It really gets Wade going when I demand that he keep his feet off the coffee table."

"So what's really on your mind?" I asked.

I shouted another round of drinks. One more vodka for my awkward mate and a scotch and Coke for myself.

Adam paused a while. That distant expression that I saw in his car came back. He no longer reminded me of Ted Schmidt. He was now an older Michael Novotny during his relationship with Ben. Confident but still a bit too self-aware. This was when I first found a hint of sex appeal in his style. Maybe he was better at faraway looks than I was?

"Adam, your drink," I said.

"Sorry, I was just noticing the room."

"With your eyes focused in one spot?"

"Okay. Caught out. I'm having a weird night."

"It's just a friendly drink in a pub."

"It's more than that. Mannix, I'm a happy self-assured human being who's at a stage of life where the world makes sense. There's no mystery. No mountains to conquer. No questions to ask. And yet, tonight, I made a total fool of myself."

The barman gave Adam a wink as he polished beer glasses with a checkered tea towel. He'd seen me here before hitting on good-looking girls or guys, many times. This was where I took my dates at the start of the night. But the barman was reading this wrong.

"Maybe you need a bit of serendipity in your life," I said.

"Make no mistake, my life isn't predictable. We're busy socially. Plus we're both involved with amateur theater, so that keeps us busy. And to top it all off, we're still very much in love with each other."

"But you don't like it when there's a spanner in the works."

"Spanners come with life. I just don't like them when I can't nut out why they're there in the first place."

Adam gulped down the rest of his drink and then rolled a solitary ice cube around his tongue.

"Hey, you saw a younger man naked tonight," I said. "It doesn't happen every day. I found it flattering."

We giggled as my infatuated artist-to-be called out to the bartender for another round of drinks.

"Adam, just a Coke for me. I have to work tomorrow, plus we're both driving."

"Good thinking. I'll go for a lemon squash."

He ordered the drinks.

"Acting, eh? Any parts for a guy like me? I need something to take the boredom out of my daytime job."

"What's your daytime job?"

"Call center."

"Yep. Sounds like you're in desperate need to revive your imagination."

"My imagination?" I said. "It packed its bags and ran away from home."

"There's a new show being cast next month. I can get you a script to read if you like? You can decide if you want to audition."

"Are you directing it?"

"No. I've got my hands full rehearsing a piece written by our theater president."

"Oh, so you're acting?"

"Again, no, I *am* directing this one."

"What's it called?"

"*Midsummer Mayhem.*"

"Um."

"Trust me, the play is better than the title."

"I'll have to take your word for it. What's it about?"

"It's about an eccentric couple who play wicked games on guests for fun. So it seems on the surface they're a happy, if not odd, couple. But there's a young man next door who sparks the wife's interest."

"Is it steamy? Like, is there any sex onstage?"

"I'm not sure you'd want to see our theater president naked. We're trying to get people into our theater, not send them running and screaming from their seats." Adam laughed before giving himself a playful slap on the cheek. "Mannix, do you ever get aroused when you're posing for art class?"

"You were slapping yourself as a precursor to that question?"

"Something like that."

I stared at Adam for several seconds. Was this man loony, eccentric, or just incompetent in the art of flirting?

"Maybe if I was an exhibitionist, I'd get turned on," I replied, "but filming myself and uploading to amateur porn sites is not my thing."

"What if there's someone you fancy among the students?"

"You know, strangely it hasn't happened. I've fancied a student or three, even went home with one of them, but as for embarrassing myself while posing, no. I'm usually going over my shopping list."

He grinned.

"Oh well, I'll just have to let my imagination fill in the blanks. Did I just say that?"

"Yes, Adam, you did. Besides, I know you have imagination. You were going to put angel wings on me. What was that about?"

"I'm a bit obsessed with angels."

"Do you believe in them?"

"Kind of. I'm sure they exist. As a kid, I had this—"

"Yikes!"

I let go of my glass. It bounced with a thud on the beer-stained carpet.

"That was a very *manly* reaction. What is it about angels that freaks you out?"

I didn't answer. It was the outside world that had freaked me out. People wandered past the windows in slow motion as the eerie sound of a cat screeching amplified in my head. The bartender stopped wiping the bench.

"You okay, mate?" he asked.

I rubbed my eyes.

"Um. Yeah. I think so."

Adam crouched to pick up the glass and placed it back on the wooden counter while exchanging concerned looks with the barman.

"Adam, my 'manly behavior,' as you put it, has nothing to do with angels. Don't look at me strangely, but I think I've seen a ghost."

"A what?"

"Maybe the ghost wants a drink," said the barman. He began wiping down the benches again.

"Look, I don't believe it either. But this guy in a white shirt and glasses was watching us."

"Why is that strange?"

"At first, I thought it was someone's reflection in the window because I could still see the traffic moving through him."

"But there's no one but us and the bartender."

"I realized that when I squealed like a girl."

"White shirt and glasses, you say?"

"Watching us. Almost studying us."

Adam headed for the door and stood at the entrance.

"Mannix, there's a buxom blonde woman walking a small dog with clipped short hair coming in that direction." He pointed to his left. "There's another woman in a smart black jacket and washed-out jeans going the other way. From this distance, I can't tell if she's wearing glasses."

"No jacket and definitely no jeans. I think he had black trousers."

"No one around with that description."

Adam strolled back inside.

"He disappeared when I coughed up my Coke. Look, I'm not even sure if I believe it myself anymore. It was just the fact he was staring at both of us that worried me." I looked back at the window. "Would you mind walking me to my car? It's just around the corner from yours."

"Do you think you know him?"

"Never met him before in my life, although strangely, I feel I should know him even though he was sort of old-fashioned."

"Like grandpa who wears pulled up socks with sandals?"

"No. Like from a different century. A beard and mo, but not in the way you'd trim them now. Red hair, freckles. Shirt cut loose, tucked into well-fitted trousers. I can still see his image in my mind."

"And you don't normally believe in ghosts?"

"Well, not usually."

"Why not? If I believe in angels, why can't you believe in ghosts?"

"I think you're both a bit weird believing in things that don't exist," said the barman.

"You're quite shaken, aren't you?" Adam asked.

"I think it's time to go."

Like an old friend, he escorted me to my Mini, then gave me a prolonged hug to calm me down. We exchanged phone numbers and said something about going to dinner together. Adam was keen for Wade to meet me, and I was equally keen to meet the love of his life. He gave me a peck on the cheek before I climbed into my car. He shut the door for me before heading to his own vehicle.

Such a sweet guy. Sensitive, artistic with a goofy quality. I imagined taking Adam by the hands and leading him onto the crisp white sheets of my own bed. I pictured him kneeling on the mattress while he unbuttoned his shirt down to his belly button. His smooth chest hairs would be caressed by my hand, while my other hand would cup the back of Adam's solid neck, slowly coercing us to touch lips. The kiss easing us to lick parts of each other's bodies.

I hit my brakes hard. I'd just noticed the pedestrian crossing. The teenage girl who was halfway across bolted to the other side. I yelled out an apology only to be greeted by a rude hand gesture. I continued traveling cautiously, though puzzled at how these steamy fantasies entered my head. He was a nice guy, but not really my type. I stopped at the traffic light before images of Adam nestling his bristly beard into my neck took over.

Chapter Three

IPAN

In the context of everything you've read thus far, our part of the story is going to seem out of place. Like someone had accidentally mixed up the pages of two accounts that have nothing whatsoever to do with each other. Let me assure you, this is a very significant part of the tale.

What type of a name is Ipan, you're probably asking yourself. Sounds like a court jester or a lord of the dark perhaps? Let me point out here and now that in this part of the yarn, I'm the good guy. And although this part of the story takes place far from the mortal world of Mannix, Adam, and Wade, it's where this story truly begins.

It all started when I was visiting my fellow warlock, Fabien, who insisted I come and take a look at his new spell.

Let me put Fabien into words. Mischievous. Self-centered. Lack of empathy. You get the picture. He resides in a large tent made of a glossy black material. A color that matches his soul at times. There are all sorts of macabre fixtures like a stuffed tiger's head sitting on top of a caged armadillo. His furniture squeaks or creaks constantly. Plus there's that musty bachelor odor that occurs from lack of dusting.

I was often wary of Fabien's spells and asked him what tomfoolery he was up to as I studied the layout on the table in his marquee.

"No tomfoolery," he replied. "Just a social experiment."

We considered his collection of wooden dolls and magic tokens. One carved redwood artifact had a strong jawline and a naked body. His head jagged into little spikes at the peak.

"Does he wear too much hair gel, Fabien?"

"It's a crown."

"Is he a prince of some sort?"

"I was thinking more of a king in his own world. He's young. He's at an age where he believes he's invincible."

"A teenager?"

"Add about ten to fifteen years, Ipan."

The other figurine's face only had a set of eyes, which stared back at the younger man like a jeweler pricing a precious ring for a customer, knowing it was an item he couldn't afford.

"Remarkable work on his eyes, Fabien. Are you going to carve the rest of his face?"

"I intended to, but somehow I stopped at the eyes. They seem to say it all."

"Like I said, remarkable work."

This particular sculpture was more rounded than the first, so I deduced he was older. His right hand clutched a real set of old keys. Grime had settled on their shiny outline as dust would settle on vintage wine bottles.

But even more curious was the use of cooking ingredients. Sprinkled over both of them was a mixture of cayenne pepper and ground chili powder. The younger man's figurine had a pinch of nutmeg added to the top of his spikey head, while the older gent was covered in cinnamon. I slowly circled the table.

"Fabien, the cayenne and chili are for passion, aren't they? And the keys represent someone who needs to let go of a materialistic outlook. Too many possessions locked inside the house for security. He's someone who needs to reconnect with chance."

"Correct. Champagne tastes, lemonade pockets. He wants it all, but needs none of it."

"But I don't understand the sweet spices."

"It's simple," replied Fabien. He took off his glasses and cleaned them with the base of his shirt. "Think of cinnamon donuts or maybe cinnamon on toast. Childhood favorites."

"I still don't read your meaning."

"The older man, let's call him Adam, is sprinkled with cinnamon to make him seem sweet to the younger man."

"Ah, I see. And the younger man has a dash of nutmeg to appeal to the established gentleman. Something that might be added to hot drinks. A scent that's not sickly sweet like the cinnamon, but pleasant enough for adult tastes. What would his name be?"

"He calls himself Mannix."

I bent down and studied the layout carefully, making sure that nothing was added that might complicate the magic charm.

"It's lovely," I said. "Two single people about to fall in love. I'm proud of you. Simple passion with no complications." The corner of Fabien's mouth turned up, but he straightened it immediately. "What have you done?"

"Nothing that would usually complicate the lives of gay men."

"One of them isn't single," I alleged. He nodded. "At a guess, it's the older chap, isn't it?" He nodded again. "Is he in an unhappy marriage?"

"No. He's quite settled."

"I see." I turned away from the malicious sculptures. "So you *are* up to mischief!"

"Ipan, look at it this way. Adam is set in his ways. He needs to feel young again. Mannix is just the injection of youth he needs."

"Time and time again I'm sickened by your desire to use mortals as your own personal playthings. Are you out of your mind? The man is in a relationship. He doesn't need another!"

"He's getting boring. Trust me, he *needs* an affair. He's a twenty-first-century gay man, after all. What's he doing in a monogamous relationship? He needs to live a little."

"Boring or not, there are ways you can add spice to his life without an affair."

"Oh yes, like what?"

"He can feel young again just by doing something childlike. Flying a kite, perhaps."

"How very Mary Poppins of him."

"A good night out then, with stimulating conversation."

"Yes. The meaning of life mixed in with remarks on world politics."

"At least it's an adult thing to do!" I barked.

"Adult? Helping a younger man in the skills of lovemaking is a very adult thing to do. Adam can teach Mannix to talk dirty with better vocabulary. After all, there's nothing more adult than the act of prolonged passion. Two willing bodies licking, tasting, sucking—"

"I get the picture, Fabien. They can lick, taste, and suck all they want, just not with each other!"

"Ipan, one day you're going to become so small-minded your halo will slip down over your head and choke you."

"Hmm," I murmured. "If I had the power to reverse your dangerous spell, I would."

Fabien smirked. His social experiment could not be turned around until he was tired of it, and sadly, there was plenty of mileage in this hex. If Fabien wasn't entertained, the spice rack was full of other condiments.

I shook my head. This wicked spell affected me personally. I understood what it was like to be in love. Fabien couldn't understand a soap opera, let alone real commitment to somebody. I had lost my love. I wasn't ready, but those who guide us assured me it was for her own good. She had to leave the Afterlife and be reborn. There were more life lessons to learn, and she was ready; I wasn't. Every night I lay on my bed alone, wishing she'd return.

"This Adam and Mannix, what are they like?" I asked.

Fabien pulled a metal pail full of water from under the table, scraping the ground with an irritating tone. He crouched beside it, gesturing with an upturned palm for me to sit on the floor while he used a finger on his other hand to gently stir the liquid. The ripples soon made an outline of a man wearing spectacles. The transparent form quickly took on color as his face turned an attractive mid-dark shade. His shaven head became clear, and the shadow of a two-day growth enveloped his chin and cheeks.

"That is Wade, Adam's husband," said the heartless wizard.

"He's quietly confident, it seems."

"You catch on quick, old man."

As Adam arrived home, his face displayed a loving smile at the sight of Wade. His partner returned the look. They embraced and kissed like a pair of lovebirds who'd only just met.

Adam was also shaved bald, light-skinned with a definite goatee. A look that either he hadn't tired of from his younger days, or he discovered too late.

He strolled to the bedroom, kicking off his shoes and changing into an old T-shirt and faded tracksuit pants. Wade waited on the sofa for his partner to ease next to him. His loving fingers keen to rub between Adam's toes. Their cozy lounge pampered them both, sheltering the couple from the cares of the world.

I slowly turned from the scene. I'd have gladly broken every rule of my backward world for one more moment with my true love.

"Rubbing toes! Eek," Fabien said. "That's what I mean. They're boring!"

"It looks like sweet contentment to me."

"Pass me the insulin."

"Fabien, your problem is that you've never been in love."

"I've been in love. You don't know what you're talking about, old man. I've been in love plenty of times."

"That's my point. You've been in love *plenty* of times, but not in love for a *long* time. No real shared history with one lover. Just shared histories with lots of exes." The mischievous warlock snarled. "I don't like what you've done here. Again, you're killing something real."

"I'm adding spice."

"No, you're killing something real! Not just for Adam and Wade, but for Mannix as well."

"Think about it, Ipan. If they go to bed together, there'll be a passing of wisdom."

"Yes, there will. Adam's wisdom will have passed. He'll get weird piercings and go for Botox injections."

"Que sera."

I watched as Wade's dark hands massaged Adam's pale ankles. I used to caress my wife's long red hair whenever she sat reading. My fingers would peek through the strands, as she'd share some of the paragraphs that delighted her. She'd eventually lean into me as I read over her shoulder, surprising her with kisses at stolen moments.

"Do you need a hanky, old man?" asked Fabien.

Tears had rolled down my cheeks. I shut my eyes and wiped the moisture with my arm.

"Damn you, Fabien, Damn you!"

I left the foolish warlock's tent, not stopping to say good-bye.

A discordant recording of an orchestra churned around me, highlighted by angelic vocals of a young man singing opera. The record's dull tone amplified my despair as his voice attempted to give me hope.

I made my way through this district known as the Carnival of Lost Souls. It was a fitting name for this block of the Medieval Sector, here in the Afterlife.

The usual array of exotically clad belly dancers, portrait artists, fortune tellers of varied talent, and the many homespun cooks selling their creations simply traveled past my eyeline. I wanted to be home in peace.

Soon I spied salvation in my path. Sara, my favorite of all these misfits, was brewing her enticing hot dark-chocolate drink. I stopped to greet her, craving her warm infusion.

Drums banged and people chanted as they shouted something about the arrival of the new moon in the Southern Hemisphere back on Earth. The party became infectious to those it passed, while in my mind I stood alone, detached.

As Sara waited for the main ingredient to melt, she watched a juggler in a red-and-white harlequin outfit. His face, tranquil and composed. But his hands jumbled in a chaotic mess as the balls endlessly chased each other round and round.

The mouthwatering chocolate had dissolved and was being stirred into a small portion of creamy hot milk. Its alluring scent was tempting me as I closed my eyes to the world. This was a bad day. Whenever there was revelry, I longed to share it with my lost wife, Rose.

Chapter Four

ADAM

"You seem quite taken by this Mannix guy," said Wade.

He rubbed my toes as we relaxed on the sofa.

"Yeah, strangely so. It was his idea to go for a drink, which was kind of sweet of him."

"Straight guy?"

"I don't think so. Something startled him, and he got all girly. I asked if he had a partner, and he said no. Didn't get to ask his preference."

"Adam, I know your gaydar. It's pretty accurate."

Wade moved my foot from his lap and made a little gesture as if he was daintily drinking a cup of tea. We often communicated in mime.

"Would love one," I replied. "Ginger, please."

Wade stood and made his way to the kitchen as I stretched my legs and rested my feet on the coffee table. I loved these moments at home with him. Here was a balanced universe that entertained only us.

We bought our 1970s apartment fifteen years ago and took pleasure in transforming it into a welcoming environment, for both ourselves and guests. Modern classic furniture, matched with ageless showpieces from too many must-have shopping sprees. The weird thing is, most of these "showpieces" have to do with my obsession: angels.

Yes, I admit it. I went through a tacky stage of renaissance replica prints of cupids, but I've replaced them with all sorts of original artwork of various winged beings. Imaginative charcoal drawings of naked flying men, prints of nineteenth-century nymphs chasing romantic heavenly messengers, and avant-garde oil paintings of airborne spirits watching gospel singers all adorn our walls.

In the glass cabinet in front of me, a petite blue glass cherub hid shyly behind a ceramic angel covering her face with a mask. I'd imagine these two coming to life whenever Wade and I slept. The glass figurine would step forward and ask questions while the other lowered her mask.

But at that moment, I felt the eyes behind that mask inviting me to share my secrets. Soon I was lost in daydreams.

Mannix stands in our kitchen naked, with angel wings and his gorgeous dick limp. For some reason, he's waiting for the kettle to boil. I crawl over like a desperate puppy on my hands and knees, also naked. He peers down at me, licking his lips. His eyes, selfless.

He reaches for my neck, which, strangely, is encircled in a leather collar, and pulls me to his level. And now he's wearing a leather harness, waiting to dominate me in ways only the pure understand.

The kettle whistles. Steam fills the room as he yanks at my collar so my eager cock presses against his.

The kitchen is now a sauna. The sultry mist welcomes us as our bodies sweat into one another. His member rising. His knob pulsating. His mouth, warm and wet as he licks the perspiration from my neck.

"This Mannix guy, can he draw?" asked Wade.

He returned with two boiling cups of tea.

"Oh, he's not a student," I replied.

An unexpected trickle of sweat made its way down my forehead.

"What is he?"

"He was our model."

Wade handed me the cup while raising an eyebrow.

"You went drinking with the nude model." Wade laughed and shook his head. "Typical of my Adam. That's why I love you. Everyone's an instant friend."

"Babe, it was *his* idea to go for the drink. We got to talking about our lives, and I couldn't shut up about you."

"I'm looking forward to meeting this young man. See why you're so taken."

We sipped our tea and chatted before I rinsed the teacups as Wade stood in the kitchen continuing the conversation. Shortly after, we toddled off to bed.

I snuggled up to Wade's back, wrapping my arm around his chest. He was breathing softly, which meant he was almost in slumber. I gradually started kissing his neck. He sighed, fully aware of my intentions. Wade rolled over to face me, then slowly brought his lips to mine. I lurched at his mouth, almost suffocating him, before jumping on top of his body.

Wade was startled by my behavior, but like most men in his situation, he quickly found his rhythm. He clutched onto my back tightly, pressing me against him. His bristly chest hairs massaged my bare chest with the force of a wrestler pinning his opponent to the floor.

Soon his tongue made its way onto mine. They danced, increasing our frenzy. I craved to possess my man wholeheartedly. I gripped his butt cheeks as he kissed harder, groaning at the same time. My hands tugged at his hole as if opening a peach. He mounted himself onto me as we both writhed in blissful desire.

It was an unusually cold night, even for winter. The duck-feather duvet we lay under warmed us slightly, but of course it was our own obsessive lust that kept us well heated. The duvet had only just been bought the weekend before and had never been used until this night. It was a bargain we couldn't resist. Only ninety dollars from a bedding store that just opened in our favorite shopping center. The same day we bought matching sheets and a quilt cover set, all in a burnt-caramel color, even though these accessories weren't discounted.

There was an odor in the room. An aroma exclusive to us and like any couple, it was familiar and comforting to the two involved. The scent left its imprint on the new bed linen. These sheets now christened.

I lazily leaned toward Wade. "Goodnight," I mumbled before kissing him. He rolled over as I caressed the back of his head. Usually he would fall asleep quickly. Not this time.

"Adam, you seem pretty taken by the guy you've just met."

"Who, Mannix? Only as a friend."

"Hmm. I wonder."

"Really, Wade, you're reading too much into it."

"Is that so, Adam? Meeting him seemed to make you pretty horny just now. I've never seen that happen before."

I had no idea what to say. I lay there for a long while and waited for Wade to snore.

Chapter Five

ADAM

"Okay, everyone, you know who you're playing," I said. A team of thespians, holding nineteenth-century clothing, hung on my every word. "We've only got two weeks' rehearsal left so you really need to know all your lines by next week." The actors nodded. "There's already interest from the local paper in reviewing our show, so they're getting front-row seats to our dress rehearsal. So as you can see, we have our work cut out for us."

"Can I just say, Adam, you're going to do an excellent job in guiding us," said Maude. "So it's our job to step up to the mark as quickly as possible."

"Thank you for your encouragement."

Maude was the president of the Petersham Theatre Society, and *Midsummer Mayhem* was her baby. She was playing the lead, Angela, a society woman with a wicked marriage.

Playing her husband, Cecil, was Stephen, one of the oldest members of our group. He loved this type of old-world comedy as much as Maude.

Our youngest players were also our newest members. Mary was starting out in amateur acting circles while taking extras work on the side, waiting to be discovered. She kept reminding us that the difference between amateur and professional theater was that in the latter, you got paid. If this helped her confidence, who was I to argue?

Mary was playing Cecil and Angela's neighbor, who incidentally was also called Mary.

Then there was Shannon. Gays love drama, and this young man was no exception. He was trying to breathe life into the role of Ronny, Mary's husband.

Mary also dug up some long-lost cousin she was trying to bond with for the nonspeaking role of the butler. He only appeared in the first scene, so he gladly volunteered. Maude and I believed that the only reason he was so friendly toward his relative was that he fancied her.

All the actors were busy straightening up bracelets, bowties, and tight-fitting gowns, as this was our first rehearsal in period costume. After fumbling for half an hour, they finally stepped onstage.

The sound of breaking glass was played from a computer by our sound and lighting guy, Gordon. He was a retired old gent who didn't seem to have a social life outside of our theater group. As the audio finished, the stage lights came on. The four main characters sat around a dining table. The butler was cleaning spilled red wine in front of Maude, but for the first time, he had trouble working around her prominent cleavage.

"I like what this corset is doing for my bosom," she said.

"It's funny to watch him clean around you," I replied. "Move around on your seat awkwardly, then flirt with him."

"What should I do?" asked Mary's distant cousin.

"Smile back but look uneasy."

"Okay."

Gordon turned off the lights, and we started again. The audio of the breaking glass played from the flimsy community hall speakers. The lights came back on. Maude looked as if she could devour the butler who was moving faster than a surfer who'd seen a shark's fin.

"What do you mean you're leaving me?" she roared as Angela.

"I'm bored," replies Cecil.

"Who is she?"

"There's no one else."

She turns to their dinner guests.

"What am I going to do for money?"

"Maybe you can marry Tony?" suggests Mary.

"He's poor."

"But he's famous. It's only a matter of time before he makes some money out of it."

"What about Carter?" asks Ronny. "He's loaded!"

"But look at his connections," snipes Cecil. "At least I'm leaving you instead of hiring a hit man to dispose of you."

"This simply will not do," Angela protests. "We can't split up if there's no one else involved. What will the papers say?"

"I know what to do," jokes Mary. "I'll have an affair with your husband."

"Splendid!" exclaims the hostess.

"And so will I," Ronny jests. "You'll get lots of sympathy."

"No, that's way too scandalous. Mary, you have the affair with my husband."

Mary chokes on her wine while clutching Ronny's hand. The butler fetches water.

"But there's still the question of money," Ronny says.

"I shall write a bestselling book," Angela replies.

"What about?" Cecil asks, rolling his eyes.

"About your affair, and my years as a dear faithful wife. So you better have a spicy affair, Mary!"

"Where should they be caught?" asks Ronny. "In bed?"

"Ronny!" his wife shrieks.

"I picture the perfect setting," replies Cecil. "Dutch clogs, a house plant, and five pounds of strawberry ice cream."

"Ah, the memories," says Angela. She smiles wistfully.

"Why would they make love in the kitchen?" asks Ronny.

"Ronny!" his wife shrieks again.

"I wasn't picturing a kitchen," replies Cecil. "I was picturing a barn."

"Fully or partially naked?" Angela asks.

"Definitely fully."

"You realize, Mary, you'll have to stay naked until the reporters arrive."

Cecil winks at her as she turns to her husband in fear.

"Help!" she gasps.

"Thank you, Mary." Angela pats her neighbor's hand. "You're such a dear friend."

Ronny stands and is about to take his wife out of this madhouse.

"April fool!" the hosts sing in unison.

Ronny collapses back in his chair as he and Mary sit with mouths agape. The stage lights go off.

I applauded.

"That's the best I've ever seen you do that first scene," I said. "Congratulations. The pace and timing were perfect."

"I felt good about it," said Shannon.

"And special congratulations to you. That was the first time you didn't stumble over your dialogue."

"There's hope for you yet," added Maude.

Shannon pursed his lips.

"How did it feel in period costume?"

"I felt more like the helpless lass," replied Mary, "rather than a modern woman. It's hard to be dominant in something so flouncy."

"Perfect for your motivation. Are you okay in your dinner jackets, Stephen and Shannon?"

"I feel dapper," our oldest thespian replied.

"Shannon, you're pursing your lips again. What's the matter?"

"My bowtie is pinching me. Can't I just wear a T-shirt under the jacket? People wear T-shirts under jackets all the time."

"Yes, but not in the eighteen hundreds."

"Why is this set in the past? I mean, we were more comfortable in our earlier rehearsals."

"Shannon, darling," said Maude. "It's an old-fashioned comedy of manners. The costumes and our snooty British accents add to the humor."

"But it's just as funny without the outfits. I mean, we had just as much fun in our previous rehearsals."

Maude gave him a deadpan expression, which he didn't notice. From my vantage point, she looked like a serial killer about to strike. Judy Garland's voice sang "Over the Rainbow" from one of the actor's bags in the corner. Our gay thespian ran toward the tune, leaving Maude to grit her teeth.

"Shannon, don't you remember what I said about turning off your phone?" I cried.

"Oh, Adam," he replied. "I only get important phone calls." He reached in and answered it. "Oh, it's Sugar Daddy!"

"Who's Sugar Daddy?"

"My sugar daddy."

"Okay, everyone. Let's have a ten-minute break before we do the next scene. Apparently, Sugar Daddy takes precedence."

"Oh no, Sugar Daddy. It's not a bad time. Yes, I understand the way you're feeling, but Sooty is just a friend."

"Sooty?" Shannon gave me a guilty smile. "Is that a dog or something?"

The actor covered the mouthpiece.

"Sooty sure knows how to doggy," he whispered.

I shook my head as Shannon took his conversation outside. Stephen, Mary, and her distant cousin headed for the tearoom at the back of the hall while our theater president wandered toward me.

"Remind me why he's in our play, Maude."

"Because we're short of young males in our theater group and my character needs a good-looking love interest."

"Couldn't you find both looks and brains?"

"No, Adam. Not in the same person. Besides, he has a sugar daddy. He can't be that dumb."

I bit my lip.

"Okay, I know you're right, but we haven't got time to find a replacement before we perform. And remember how good he was in *Shameless in the Addict*?"

"Maude, he played a camp queen. No acting necessary! And you heard him just now. 'Can't I wear a T-shirt?' Plus it's taken him ages to get his English accent right. Now really, how hard is it to do a toffy royal voice? And be honest, Maude, I know you're also freaking out about Shannon. You looked like you were going to do him in up onstage."

"Shh, Adam. The others are coming back."

"Yeah, and Wonder Slut is still outside convincing Sugar Daddy he's not cheating." Our returning actors laughed. "Oops. I'm a bad director. You weren't supposed to hear that."

"It's okay, Adam," said Stephen. "We were just talking about him. He's not getting as many calls this week."

Shannon skipped in like a five-year-old and sat back onstage, with his phone still in hand.

"You do realize there were no mobile phones in the eighteen hundreds?" I said.

"Really? Couldn't they afford them?"

"How does that question even make sense?" I murmured under my breath. Our theater president looked to the ceiling. "Maude, you're putting on a brave face. I know you too well."

"I have faith in you, director," she replied. The rest of the cast made their way to the set. "That's why I'm the woman of your dreams."

"Hey, hold on," said Mary. "Am I hearing sordid gossip?"

"No," I replied. "It's a private joke."

"Oh, come on. You can't say something like that and expect us not to surmise. We're actors after all!"

"He dreamt about me when he was young," said Maude.

"How young?" asked Stephen.

"About four years young," I replied.

Our president toddled back to the stage, her bosom taking the lead.

"I thought you were gay," said Shannon.

"I am!"

"Then why were you dreaming of old women?"

Maude slapped the back of his head.

"Ouch! That hurt."

"Now that that's over, we'll run through the next scene."

"Adam, we're all curious," said Stephen. "Why were you dreaming about Maude before you even met her?"

"He also has a guardian angel," replied my dream girl.

Stephen, Mary, her cousin, and Shannon all leaned forward.

"Oh, all right. If you really want to know, I had dreams about a woman who looked like Maude, but she was named Maudi. She had a husband, or partner, or lover, or something. And there was an angel in the dream I called Mr. Guy."

"It must have been a vivid dream for you to remember that much," said Mary. "Do you believe in angels?"

"Yeah, I guess I do. But let's talk about this later. We have a play to rehearse."

"My Sugar Daddy's an angel," droned Shannon. "He told me so."

"I think there's an angel looking after me," said Mary. "At really bad times, I pray to him and he comes through."

"Guys, seriously. We're rehearsing a play. Remember?"

"I think my mother came back to see me in her angel form," Stephen alleged. "The light kept coming on in our kitchen."

"Come on, everyone. Let's go from the start of the second act. Only Angela and Mary are onstage."

"And the toast would always burn. I never burnt toast before she died."

"The first line is from you, Mary. You say 'At his vintage, I never believed for a minute Cecil was thinking of leaving you.'"

"Hey, *my* toast burns sometimes," said Shannon. "But what would your mother be visiting me for?"

"And Angela says 'Oh, you're too kind, Mary. But at his vintage, I'm surprised he's still alive.'"

Judy Garland's vocals struck again.

"Hello, Sugar Daddy."

OKAY, SINCE ONE of my oldest friends brought it up, I guess I need to clarify. Maude, or at least a version of her, was in a couple of dreams I had when I was a kid. They were the same dreams that sparked my angel fascination. And although I have trouble remembering my nighttime adventures minutes after waking, these particular dreams have haunted me all my life.

The first began with a lone woman's voice asking a question as if I had no right to be in my own dream.

"Who's the child?"

While still peddling his bike, an angel with soft dove gray wings smiled at me.

"A special friend who's joining us for the day," he replied.

I was riding the red bicycle Santa gave me for Christmas, and had a grin from ear to ear as I thought I was traveling next to a fairy. That very night, my dad read me a story with stepsisters and a glass slipper, where a fairy godmother helps a girl who's down on her luck. I'm not sure what Dad was thinking when he picked such a girly story for an impressionable four-year-old boy, but maybe he'd worked out something about me I was yet to discover.

"Hello, little one," said the voice. "What's your name?"

On the opposite side was an old man and woman, also riding bikes.

"I'm Adam."

"Such an important biblical name for such a young man," she replied. "And where did you live?"

"He still does live," replied the fairy.

"Guy, do you think that's wise?" asked the man.

"Trust me, I know what I'm doing." My fairy god-person winked at me. "Adam's my cheer squad."

The couple shared concerned glances similar to the ones my mum used to share with Tess from next door, when Dad came home late. He'd stumble in before my bedtime, making sure he'd read me a story, while our neighbor drank tea with Mum in our kitchen.

But, let's get back to my dream.

My tires flattened a path in the lush field ahead, spinning water droplets into the air. My socks gradually became more and more damp. But I didn't care. After all, like Cinderella, I had my own magical fairy.

"What do you eat, young man?" the woman asked.

Her loose gown flowed behind her.

"I like chocolate."

"Hmm. I'm not sure I have chocolate in my basket. But how about some boiled lollies?"

"What are they?"

She looked to the fairy.

"What century is this one from? Do they not indulge in the delights of boiled treats in his decade?"

"I'm sure we have something for you, young man," said the grandpa figure.

I shook my head at their silly talk.

"This is a very important day," the woman continued. "We're helping Guy become a strong angel by helping him fly."

"An angel?" I said. "I thought you were a fairy."

"If you want me to be a fairy, then I'm a fairy."

He had a proud grin.

"Why can't you fly?"

"Oh, I can fly, just not very well. I can only do short flights."

"Can you piggyback me while you fly?"

"Um."

"You might fall off his back, Adam," said the man.

"But I think he's a good flyer. You're a good flyer, aren't you, Mr. Guy?"

"I promise I'll piggyback you one day. But today is not the day."

"As long as you promise."

"I promise."

I peddled as hard as I could. The dusty-pink sky highlighted the candy-floss clouds, while the trees opened their branches to welcome us as we passed. The breeze whistled a tune in my ear, tickling my earlobes.

My dreamtime grandparents began singing a strange song about bottles falling off a wall, in perfect harmony with the wind's flutelike voice. I looked to my big brother with wings, and soon, we both sang as well.

When the old people eventually stopped cycling, I helped them unpack their picnic basket, while the angel kept riding his bike in circles.

"Now, dear Adam, my name is Maudi, and my friend here is Frederick."

"They're funny names."

She shook her head before popping a candy in my mouth. Her friend chuckled.

"Little boys shouldn't be judgmental."

Guy rode in a straight line, picking up speed along the way.

"Why is the fairy going so fast?"

"And little boys shouldn't talk with their mouths full."

"Keep watching, Adam," Frederick replied.

Guy's hectic pace made him puff loud enough for us to hear him twenty meters away. Another little boy was watching with his mum, pointing at the frenzied angel. His wings flapped wildly. He let go of the handlebars and flew forward. The bike slowed down of its own accord before its stand flung out, making it rest on the grass.

"Oh my lord," said Maudi. "His confidence is waning."

Guy used his hands for extra thrust, but the awkward flutter of his wings caused him to dart in random directions. The other small boy clutched onto his mother's leg, hiding his face while taking panicked peeks from time to time.

"Come on, Mr. Guy," I yelled. I stood up. "Fairies can fly, and you're a good flyer!"

"Yes, Guy," Frederick called out. "It's important that fairies can fly."

"Precisely," shouted Maudi. Her booming voice startled me. "Adam will be disappointed if you don't!"

Guy's arm movements were now as manic as his wings. He started falling. I raced in his direction. My fantasy grandparents chased after me. Soon I was well ahead of them and closer to my magic fairy.

As he hurtled toward the ground, he forced his hands to sit firmly by his sides. His wings spread out like a martyr's arms on a cross, before they thrust downward, gently rippling like a kite. His descent slowed as he repeated this action over and over.

I stood below him. His arms reached out, and as he hovered near the ground, he picked me up.

"No, Guy!" yelled Frederick.

"What are you thinking?" called Maudi.

But we just hung in the air close to the grass. I wrapped my arms around him. He kissed me on the cheek.

"You're my special friend, Adam."

"You're special too, Mr. Guy."

My whimsical grandparents finally made it to where we defied gravity. Frederick had sweat patches all over his crisp white shirt, while Maudi bent down and flicked blades of grass from her dress.

"Don't even think about it, Guy," she said.

"Don't even think about what?"

"I know what a mischievous angel you can be. The child is not of this world. Don't risk taking him into the skies."

"It did cross my mind, Maudi."

"She's right, Guy," added Frederick. "I've seen how attached you get to some people, but this one is mortal. Put him down."

"He's a fairy," I said. I clutched him tighter. "He can do anything he wants."

My big brother figure casually hovered away from the nagging old folk.

"Don't make us chase you," Frederick called.

"Oh, you're such a stubborn young angel at times!" Maudi hollered.

Guy flew with me, keeping a short distance from the ground. We twirled like waltzing ghosts, gradually making our way to his bike.

"I've missed you, Allan."

"Allan? My name is Adam."

His face turned red.

"Of course it is. I'm a dizzy fairy at times."

I stayed clasped to him, looking over his shoulder as he gently landed on his bicycle and began riding toward the picnic blanket. The old ones began plodding in the same direction.

"Can you come and live with me? I don't have any brothers or sisters."

"What would your mum say?"

"Hmm. You can hide in my cupboard. They don't need to know about you."

"I don't think I ever want to live in a closet, Adam."

"You can hide under my bed."

"I'm not sure that's a good idea either." He looked into my eyes. "I'll make you a promise. Why don't I take care of you from here? I can sneak into your dreams whenever you need me. I'll be your own secret guardian."

"My secret what?"

"Your guardian angel."

"But you're a fairy!"

"Your guardian fairy, then."

"I can't say that word, Mr. Guy. It's too big." I peered over his shoulder again. "Just be my big fairy."

He laughed loudly.

"I think that's a promise I can keep."

Chapter Six

IPAN

I had the perfect vantage point. Anytime I needed to view what was happening back on Earth, I didn't need a magical pail of water. I used my telescope. I've never questioned why I could see anyone I needed to on that lost planet. I simply loved the fact that I could.

The midget with the dark blue beard had given it to me. He dyed his beard, and I really didn't understand why. He lived in my apartment building and knocked on my door one day, then handed it to me. He said he didn't need it anymore. That his work with it was done. But somehow he knew *I* would need it.

This was the second time that my obsessive worrying caused me to spy. My concern was with Wade, the innocent bystander in this scenario, or so I thought. But this tale began reaching out in other directions. It was as if the spell had found tentacles and was sucking everyone into its depraved sport.

Wade sat at his desk while his manager stood beside him, chatting intensely about revenue. I couldn't make head nor tail of what he was babbling about, and by the looks of it, neither could Wade. He was obviously daydreaming, watching this funny little monkey of a man moving his mouth.

Wade gazed at the ceiling above his boss. Someone had knocked a small hole in the paintwork.

"You haven't heard a word I've said. Wade! Hello. Anyone home?"

"Yeah, um, we're running at a loss, Sam. Or was it a profit?"

His boss smiled.

"What's on your mind?"

"Sorry. To be honest, I'm not really sure. You see, Adam met this man the other night."

"Oh, I see. Do you want to come into my office and talk about it?"

Wade pursed his lips.

"No, it's nothing like that. It's a friend. A new colleague he met at art class."

"Right. So why is that playing on your mind?"

"I'm not suspicious."

"Knowing Adam, you've got no reason to be."

"I just have a dying desire to meet this man myself."

Sam pointed to his office, prompting Wade to stand and follow him into the workspace.

Outside his boss' window, glimpses of Sydney Harbor snuck in through the countless office buildings that spread over the landscape. The vibrant blue water urged me to float down to Earth and search for my lost soul. I pictured myself breathing in the salt air, watching the ferries weave through the water in their meditative dance, and finding the peace to dream without tears.

Wade, too, was understandably transfixed by this sight as his supervisor closed the door behind them.

"What's really going on?"

"To be honest, I don't know, Sam. I've been both daydreaming and thinking about this man all day, and I haven't even met him."

"About the same age?"

"No, younger."

His supervisor turned to take in the view. I could hear his thoughts. I found this odd. The last time I used the telescope I could hear most of my subjects' inner dialogue but had only just realized I couldn't hear Wade's. I stopped questioning and paid attention to his feelings.

This boss knew the symptoms. The dread of looking in the mirror for fear of noticing the tummy that, despite the sit-ups and the diet shakes, never seemed to go away. Those hidden silver hairs that presented themselves at inopportune moments as if to say "we're here, and our relatives will be arriving soon!" Worse still were the dark earlobe hairs or the elongated nose hairs that kept growing as if they were trying to set a world record for length. The secret rendezvous with young Rhianna from the cubical next to Wade's was the only thing that put a spring into his step these days. It had happened twelve months ago, but for this mature chap, the scenario kept repeating itself like a pornographic plotline.

"Wade, it's nice to dream about it, but take my advice, don't do it."

"Don't do what?"

"You meet this guy, you like him, and before long you're wearing tight jeans and T-shirts promoting new bands you've never listened to."

"Seriously, Sam, a midlife crisis is not on my agenda. Anyway, I've never met the man. Why would I be thinking of bonking a guy I've never met?"

"But you are, aren't you, Wade?"

He turned his back on the million-dollar view while his subordinate looked back toward the window.

"It's only been today that my mind has been wandering. I keep seeing Mannix—that's his name, Mannix—as the boyish young artist type. I'm taking him by the hand, guiding him to an easel and teaching him to paint. Maybe posing nude for him."

"I didn't know you could paint."

"I can't."

Wade's boss studied the lovelorn man, keeping a deadpan face. This was how his one-night affair with Rhianna had started. A little pay rise. A little promotion. A little afternoon delight when his wife was visiting family.

"Wade, what about Adam?"

"Oh, I've got no intention of leaving Adam. He's my life. I adore that man more than anything else in this world. No, that is what's so weird about this. I feel like I'm in love with two men. One I honestly love, and one I've never met yet. Is that possible?"

"In a word, no."

"What's wrong with me?"

"When was the last time you and Adam had a dirty weekend?"

"My fortieth. We had a room booked in the hotel we had my party in. Very swish."

"Five years ago, eh? Way too long. Wade, I have a holiday house in the mountains. You'll need to take your own sheets, but there are pillows there. Just tell me when you want it, and I'll bring the keys to work."

"Seems a bit drastic."

"Drastic or not, you and Adam are going, but just not the first weekend of next month. My niece has bagged it."

"Let me talk to Adam and give you a date." Wade glanced at the floor before looking straight into his superior's eyes. "Thank you, Sam. I appreciate it, although I'm really not sure what my problem is." His boss mouthed the words "midlife crisis." "No. Like I said, it's not a midlife crisis; otherwise, I'd be bored with Adam."

Wade left the office and sauntered back to his desk. He glanced at his phone, picked it up, and dialed his loving partner. His face beamed. The romantic getaway was starting to make sense. Chilled champagne. Fresh mountain air. Bubble baths. Who wouldn't jump at the chance? His partner answered the phone.

"Adam, I've been thinking. Why don't you invite Mannix for dinner?"

Chapter Seven

MANNIX

I have the best flatmate anyone could ask for. His name is Bruce. We'd met at a party that both of us were trying to avoid, but once we started talking, the conversation never ended. Many pub crawls later, we decided to move in together, and the conversation still hasn't stopped.

All credit went to Nadia, the friend who'd thrown the party. Both Bruce and I had dated her for a nanosecond, so when the invitation came for her thirtieth birthday, we both had the same thought. Why us? We agreed she seemed too flaky to have a serious relationship with, but Bruce accepted the invitation out of fear that she might have been desperate to make up the numbers. I just showed up to fill in time before another party later that night. I still think he liked her more than I ever did.

"You're wearing the burgundy shirt, M," Bruce said.

"And your point is...?"

"That's your *first date* shirt."

"No, it isn't."

"Oh, yes, it is."

Bruce stood behind me as I massaged my scalp with hair gel in front of the bathroom mirror. I was trying to spike the front bit, but it kept wilting like a dead plant. Next I tried to frizzy it up with my hands, but it still didn't look right.

"Why is it my *first date* shirt?"

"Remember Tracey?"

"I didn't wear this shirt when I went out with Tracey."

I noticed a pimple.

"Don't touch that, M. And yes, you did wear that shirt for Tracey."

"I didn't have this shirt when I met Tracey."

"You dated Tracey late last year."

"Was it only last year, Bruce? Are you sure?" The red spot on my forehead was staring back at me, daring me to squeeze it. "No, you're wrong. Tracey was a winter romance."

"Tracey was a summer affair. David was the winter romance, and you bought that shirt for your first date with him." He peered over my shoulder. "And don't even think about attacking that pimple! It'll look worse."

I was now flattening my hair to cover the zit.

"I wonder what happened to David."

"Mannix, I wonder what happened to Tracey, and Murphy, and all the others."

"I'm not that bad."

Bruce didn't answer. He stepped away and left me to deal with the greasy mountain on my face and the catastrophe that was my hair. I stripped off and jumped in the shower, washed away the gel, and scrubbed the life out of my facial intruder. I finally killed it! I dreaded looking back at the mirror and seeing an ugly blotch in its place.

When I looked at my reflection again, I lifted the hair that covered my forehead. Ugh! It looked like an erupted volcano. I dabbed some aftershave on it, and it stung like a bitch slap. I left my hair alone and buttoned my shirt back up. Bruce returned with a glass of beer in hand and a weird expression as if he'd caught me masturbating.

"Putting your lucky shirt back on, M?"

"Will you stop going on about this shirt, Bruce? I don't wear it on all my first dates. And besides, going to dinner at a couple's place does not constitute a date!"

"Okay. So it's *just* a dinner date?"

"Yes, it's just a dinner date."

"A dinner date that you've spent half an hour in the bathroom getting ready for."

He walked back to the lounge room.

"I have not spent half an hour getting ready." He returned with his mobile phone and showed me the time. "I guess I have been in here a long time."

"Now let me get this straight. You've only met one of them, and you've got your *first date* shirt on. You want sex, don't you?"

"Just because I'm wearing this shirt doesn't mean I want sex."

"But putting gel in your hair does."

"Look, Bruce." I pointed at my scalp with both hands. "No gel. See. No gel." He sipped his beer. "All right, there was gel, but there's no gel now. And even if I've worn this shirt before when I'm expecting sex, it's not why I'm wearing it now." He wiped the beer froth from his top lip. "I'm wearing this shirt because I've been invited to dinner by an older couple and I want to make an impression."

"And 'I want sex' is the impression you're going for." He laughed.

"Oh come on now, Adam's already seen me naked. Wearing this shirt isn't going to turn him on. He's already met little Mannix."

"But even you've called it your lucky shirt. You've bragged about its seductive charms."

I looked in the mirror. It *was* a cool shirt. It roped David in on our first date. And maybe Tracey did see me in it.

"Okay, Bruce, you're right. It's my *sure thing* shirt, but it's the best shirt I have. And I've never met Adam's husband, Wade. I'm just trying to make a good impression for Adam's sake. That's all."

He nodded.

"What's Adam like?"

"Dorky but sweet." I stopped facing the mirror and addressed my flatmate. "And he's creative, so that's a plus. He's directing a play."

"Ah, so it's a 'look at me, I'm arty as well' shirt tonight. Not a 'pull me by the collar and drag me off to bed' shirt."

"Enough with this shirt already!"

"And you really expect me to believe you're not interested?"

"Well, maybe some part of me would like there to be a spark, but he's too old for me."

"Sorry, what did you just say?"

"Why?"

"Because it doesn't make sense. You say you'd like a bit of action, but he's too old."

"Yes. At least I'm being honest."

"So which is it, M? You want it, or he's too old for you?"

"Can't it be both?"

"No, it can't." I looked back to my mirror. "M, read between the lines. Your tastes are expanding. He doesn't have to be a Daddy figure. He's just an older man. Something about him has sparked your interest. But remember, he's in a relationship!"

Bruce left me alone while I considered picking another shirt.

Chapter Eight

Ipan

I have a friend. She's charming, witty, and whimsical. She was an important ally when I lost my wife, Rose. She encouraged me to socialize when I felt my world had ended. She forced me out of my home to share red wine, conversation, and scrumptious meals with several women in the Medieval Sector. These encounters felt like chores, so she decided to join us on these dates. She relished playing Cupid.

My friend, Farah, soon realized I was not searching for someone to replace Rose, so she took on the role of social secretary. She had an amazing circle of friends who would pull out musical instruments at whim and convert a relaxed social evening into a night of dance and song.

She is also a white witch. Her richly colored gowns waltz with her movements, no matter how subtle or how bold the tone. Her matching stone jewelry displays pigments as vibrant as her own charismatic nature, and her warmth bathes me in love and support that cannot be matched.

Farah was with me the day I called in on Fabien unannounced. There was something else brewing in this hex that I was unaware of. Something that I suspected involved Wade in this mischievous warlock's wicked plans.

"It's an interesting night, my friends," Fabien announced. We strolled into his marquee. "For some reason, Wade has taken up the initiative and invited Mannix for dinner."

"Who's cooking?" asked Farah. I sighed. "Just making conversation, dear."

"Do you realize what's at stake?"

Farah leaned forward and caressed my arm. I took a breath and let her soothing touch calm me. Besides, if I was to make a difference in any way, it would be without hysterics.

"For the record, it's Wade who's cooking," the warlock replied. "Although Adam prepared the dessert last night. A marbled chocolate and orange cake."

I once again studied the wooden carvings, the main ingredients of the spell. There were still only two mortals, the younger man, and the married man. Both were still topped off with exotic spices, but each had a glass of white wine placed in front of them.

"He's intoxicating them," I quietly said to Farah.

"Maybe it's meant to be a night of passion?"

"If it's *meant* to be, then that silly warlock should leave well enough alone."

My Farah smiled back, a little too devilishly for my liking.

Fabien confidently swaggered over to his laundry where his bucket lay at the foot of the sink. He picked it up, filled it with water, strolled back to us, and set it at our feet. His cocksure manner was distasteful under the circumstances. He blew on the water's surface, making the ripples weave like tiny snakes into the image of the three men.

The oven door was open as Wade carefully scrunched two tea towels and used them as oven mitts.

"Ah, whatever that is, it's making my mouth water," Mannix said.

His hands were nestled on the back of his neck, while he slid down and rested his posterior on the edge of his seat. He stretched out his legs like a contented household cat, waiting to be stroked and pampered. He let out a restless purr, pitched to entice any midlife fool.

It was clear that both Mannix and Adam were tipsy. Adam looked at the young man's inner thigh like his jeans were holding all the riches of the world. He slowly reached toward the treasure as Mannix beamed cheerfully at his lack of etiquette. This unholy connection was about to pass the starting line.

Adam stopped his sly move as Mannix turned his attention to Wade, who was making his way past with the baking tray. The dining table had already been set before his arrival, and even we could smell the enticing aroma of the spinach and mint quiche that was adding to this foreplay.

Wade was another kettle of fish altogether. He kept fussing over Mannix and Adam like they were two schoolkids who couldn't even pack their own lunchboxes. Wade eyed the newcomer as a hungry child would stare at a Sunday roast; an appetite indeed whetted. I begrudgingly watched as the seeds of their discontent were planted.

"You're spoiling me," said Mannix.

He and Adam sat at the table.

"It's what guests are for," replied Wade. He fondly spooned out feta and rocket salad onto their plates.

"All I'm good at is spaghetti bolognese but without the fancy ingredients. Our freezer is full of minced meat and the cupboard is stocked with dried pasta and premade sauces."

"Sounds like you should expand your skills," said Wade. "All men love to cook once they learn how."

"Besides, it's how you keep a husband," interrupted Adam. He chuckled like a mischievous minx. "Keep his stomach full and his balls empty."

Wade shook his head.

"Excuse my husband, Mannix, but it seems he must have started drinking earlier this afternoon."

Adam shrugged while putting down his glass. Fabien tried to share a devious grin with us, but I looked away.

"Adam's okay, Wade. For some reason, I feel pretty lightheaded myself. What is *in* this wine?"

"No idea," Adam replied. "It's just one of a couple of bottles I picked up on the way home. Maybe we're allergic to the preservatives in it or something."

The guest took his first mouthful of quiche, spreading it out over his taste buds by gliding his tongue to the roof of his mouth. The couple watched like aimless puppy dogs, looking at their master for control.

"This food is heaven!" moaned Mannix.

"Just savor that flavor," said Adam.

"I think I'm in love with your quiche."

"I love cooking for new people," replied Wade.

Adam turned to his husband and tried to blow a puff of air into his ear. Sadly only spit was emitted.

"I don't get this," I queried. "Why is Wade mesmerized by Mannix as well? Fabien, what have you done? I demand to know."

"Nothing."

"Fabien!"

"Seriously, nothing. Perhaps that's an honest attraction."

I hadn't noticed I was rubbing the lapels of my burgundy jacket until one of the brass buttons flicked off. It landed at Fabien's feet. He considered it like a man too wealthy to pick up a wayward penny. Farah bent down and gracefully handed it to me.

"Look at the way Mannix is gazing at both his hosts," the warlock said. "He's almost melting at the sight of the couple."

"Ipan, dear, Fabien is right."

My dear Farah reached out for my arm and tried to soothe me again. I studied the younger man's stare. He was taken by these men. Perhaps Fabien was right. His hex might have initially added one complication to their lives, but nature had added another.

"This, my friends, is purely delightful," he concluded. He blew into the pail again.

Mannix lay on the carpet, parallel with the sofa. His hosts were clearing the table until Wade looked over and leisurely wandered to the consenting guest. He positioned himself against the lounge, gently placing the head of their visitor in his lap. Wade ran his fingers through Mannix's thick dark hair with all the care of a lover learning which buttons to press.

As the young man let out a primal moan, Adam placed the used dishes back on the dining table and rushed over to the seduction scene like a virgin scared he'd miss out. He positioned himself at the visitor's feet, then untied his shoelaces with great care. One hand gently pulled at the sneaker, but before Adam could reach for the other shoe, Mannix pushed it off with the heel of his foot.

The drunken host pulled off his guest's well-laundered socks with the grace of a caveman ripping at a piece of meat. His thumb pressed firmly at the base of one foot, before massaging up toward the toes.

Adam and Wade shared a look of sportsmanship. A team that had conquered first base. Mannix extended his arms above his head, stretching his craving body before reaching back to take off his shirt.

I looked away. With the musty scent of the young man's feet was another odor that struck me as odd. At first, I thought it was Wade's aftershave, but there was nothing commercial about the aroma. It was cinnamon. Had this unearthly warlock extended his spell?

I studied Farah and Fabien, noting their expressions as the foreplay continued. I was ready to accuse Fabien of conjuring up this blue movie for his own enjoyment until I realized that Farah seemed equally taken.

This called for drastic measures. I had to intervene. I quietly stepped aside and let the others be engrossed in the scene.

"Who was it?" inquired Adam.

Mannix was sitting on the sofa, staring at his mobile phone in his right palm. The couple were still on the floor.

"My flatmate. Something has happened, but he won't tell me what. He wants to tell me face-to-face."

"Are you okay to drive?" asked Wade.

"Maybe I'd better..."

"Strong coffee?"

"Not a bad idea."

Wade wandered into the kitchen as Adam clumsily slithered onto the settee from the floor. It took him about two attempts to elevate his body and another couple just to sit upright.

"What's your flatmate like?" mumbled the inebriated host.

"A true friend and sounding board. Great when I was trying to find myself."

"You slept with him?"

"No, he's straight. He's cute, but he's a friend. It would be like incest."

"Straight friends are great at making you feel good about yourself when you're gay."

"Bi."

"Huh?"

"Adam, I'm bisexual."

"Not just in a 'still trying to find yourself' sense?"

"No, in a 'certain that I was gay, then found myself obsessing over a female student in art class' sense."

Wade scampered back to the living area.

"That must be fascinating for you."

"It wasn't at first. I'd convinced myself I was gay. Then I had an affair with Lillian for about a month. But I'm still attracted to men as well."

"Lillian wasn't just a phase?" asked Wade.

He kept an ear for the whistle from their designer coffeepot sitting on the stove.

"Oh god no! But coming to terms with a free-spirited sexual preference wasn't easy, as you guys understand."

The couple nodded. Wade went back to the stove as the fragrance of the fresh brew filled the room. He called to Adam to see if he wanted a cup, but his man seemed to be enjoying his inebriated state too much to alter it.

"People are too busy putting labels on everyone. Gay, straight, bi, whatever. I always think of my own sexuality as Adam. Whether that entails going to bed with men or going to bed with a pot plant, my sexuality is just me. I often say it to people who are trying to find themselves."

"I like that. I'm not bisexual; I'm Mannix-sexual."

The young man smiled humbly. Wade placed an arty coffee mug in front of him featuring a flying saucer design in citrus colors, and poured the brew from the pot. He used a gaudy souvenir oven mitten featuring an image of the Big Pineapple in Queensland.

After a little more chat, Mannix finally stood up and kissed his hosts goodnight. They escorted him to the door and dashed to the balcony to wave good-bye. When Mannix's sporty little car was out of sight, the couple cuddled while still gazing down the road.

"Something strange is going on here," alleged Wade.

"I agree," mumbled Adam.

Farah chuckled. Fabien turned to face me, resting his pointer to the left side of his own mouth before pulling downward, giving the illusion that his finger was changing his devious smirk to a frown. I was pleased with myself, but the insensitivity of my dear Farah baffled me.

"You find this amusing?" I questioned. Farah shrugged. "You're up to something, aren't you?"

"Hmm, perhaps."

"Farah, you didn't?"

"Darling, I wasn't going to sit around and hear you talk of a potential illicit affair, so I did what was in my power to soften the blow."

"That explains why I couldn't hear Wade's thoughts through my telescope."

"Huh?" said Fabien.

"I can only hear the thoughts of subjects that have no magic spell cast on them."

"I still don't follow."

"There's another magic charm at work here," I replied.

"Farah, darling, I like the way you think," said Fabien. He wandered over to the wine rack. "Shall we celebrate?"

"Darling, how could you?" I clutched the lapels of my jacket, taking deep breaths.

"Think about it, dear. They may still feel pangs of jealousy, but they're both in the same boat. It's something Adam and Wade will experience together. They'll work through it and strengthen their already tight relationship."

"Irresponsible, that's all I'll say."

"More irresponsible than just letting Mannix and Adam chase each other? Think about it, dear. Really think about it."

I was handed a glass of Shiraz in a fine crystal glass. I clasped it begrudgingly. When Fabien handed Farah her wine, they clinked glasses to honor the change in the social experiment. I glared at them through bitter eyes.

"So Farah, you think Adam and Wade will avoid temptation and work through their shared infatuation together?" I asked.

"Perhaps, my dear. And perhaps the three of them might share something very special. Either way, it's a win-win situation."

"You should marry this woman, Ipan. She has chutzpah!"

She fanned her face with her hand and pretended to blush. Her comic routine quickly subsided.

"In Adam and Wade, I saw the type of love Rose and I once shared. Little glances that relayed dialogue only they can decipher. Small acts of kindness that were not even thought about beforehand, but had become the pattern of their relationship. Quiet loving glances when the other was unaware. This still is a partnership that should not be tampered with."

"Are we talking about Adam and Wade or you and Rose?" Fabien asked.

"Both," replied Farah.

"Oh relax, you 'too serious for your own good' old man. Farah's got the right idea. A ménage à trois." He raised his glass to instigate a toast, but Farah looked to me before deciding not to follow his lead. He gulped down his wine regardless. "Ah, two older men sharing their love with a willing apprentice. What could be sweeter? Very Ancient Greece, don't you think?"

"We should go home," I mumbled.

"Whatever you say, my darling," she replied.

I finished my wine in silence. Farah tried to smile at me, but I felt betrayed. I had been sure she would see it my way. After all, she knew how much Rose had meant to me. She knew how much I believed in true love.

She drank her glass but popped her hand over its rim when Fabien offered to refill it. There were more murmurings from the pail of water, so we watched.

"Seriously, I didn't call," said Bruce. Mannix tapped his phone to bring up the call log. "You're drunk again, aren't you, M?"

"Even if I was drunk, I wouldn't believe I had a conversation that I didn't have." He finally found the list of recent calls. "Look, see..."

They both glanced at the screen, noting there was no listing of Bruce's phone call.

"These guys, they didn't slip something into your drink, did they?"

Mannix thought hard. The smell of takeaway Thai food was wafting from their kitchen, while the thunderous soundtrack of an action movie filled the room from their oversized television. He seemed to think back over the night, then declared that he was certain there was no way his drink was spiked.

The truth was I was responsible for this phantom phone call. Farah waved her hand grandly to suggest I'd cast a spell while Fabien nodded, impressed.

"You're not mistaking my voice with someone else who called you?"

"You're the only one who calls me M."

"What else did I say?"

"That you would tell me what the problem was when I got here. Seriously, Bruce, you did call me, didn't you?"

"M, how did I delete my call from your phone's log?"

Mannix tapped a few more buttons on his mobile, scrutinizing the device intensely. No calls or messages were received that night.

"First I see a ghost at a pub, then I imagine I'm having a phone call with you. Bruce, am I going mad?"

He didn't reply. Mannix headed for the bathroom, visibly shaken. He flicked a sleeping tablet into his mouth and bid his flatmate goodnight.

Chapter Nine

ADAM

"It's about time we threw out that teddy bear," said Wade.

The toy listened to us as it sat on the upholstered chair in our bedroom.

"We can't. It's looked after me since I was a kid."

"I thought you had Mr. Guy looking after you."

"The two go hand in hand."

"You drank too much tonight, Adam. You're not making sense."

"But that's the thing, Wade. I don't feel drunk anymore."

He leaned over and kissed me.

"Should we invite Mannix over this weekend?"

I smirked. "Yeah, let's!"

"Or why don't we take him out, Adam?"

"Where to?"

"A theater event. Or a good film. No, let's stick with the theater, and dinner beforehand."

"What kind of play would he be into?"

"Is there a gay play on?"

I picked up my phone and turned on the Wi-Fi.

"No, not a gay one. But *Wicked* is playing again. It's got camp value."

"Buy tickets for Saturday night."

Wade passed his credit card as I started booking online.

"Hold on."

"What is it, Adam?"

"We don't know if Mannix is free this weekend."

"I'll ring him tomorrow and find out."

"Okay." I turned off the Wi-Fi as Wade switched off his bedside lamp. "Hey, I've got a better idea. Let's go on a picnic. That way we can chat over wine and get to know each other better. He has to be free at some stage over the weekend."

The bedside lamp came on again.

"Yeah, Adam. That's a better idea. Leave it to me. I'll organize it." Off went the light. "Good night."

"Good night, darling."

Twenty minutes later he was snoring, while I lay wide awake. I crept out of bed and made my way to the lounge room, taking my old teddy bear with me. I sat with the stuffed toy in my lap, watching the silhouetted trees dance outside.

It had been years since I clutched onto my bear like this, its dusty fur reminding me that our spring clean was well overdue. But it was hard scrubbing this thing, and it was too big for the washing machine. So it sat gathering dust in our bedroom as a token of my murky childhood.

Why I'd want to remember those early years, especially at this moment, didn't make sense. But our trivial conversation about catching up with Mannix, yet again, was making my mind tick over. Was I getting jealous? Nah. I was just being silly.

I listened for Wade's snore. It comforted me. That old man I'd spent eighteen years with was keeping our bed warm. So why wasn't I asleep with him? We had a great relationship, after all.

The last people to love me as much as my man were my parents, and for some reason, memories of their affection began flooding back.

I loved story time with Dad and shopping for clothes with my mum. And as much as my parents loved me, they didn't share that same respect for each other.

I'd sit on the floor of my bedroom, teddy in my lap, while accusations flew outside. Apparently, Dad was a "no-hoper." Mum was a "floozy." Dad was blamed for gambling away the household budget. Mum was told to get off her lazy ass and get a job. But she'd scream back, saying I needed to be raised.

At times like this, Mr. Guy would visit. I'd have to shut my teary eyes and will myself to sleep before he came, and often, that would take a while. But eventually, I'd be off on some grand adventure with my dreamtime big brother and those old folk who weren't that bad after I got to know them.

My guardian fairy wrapped his protective arms around me as I sat in his lap. We were in a field that never ended. Grass met the sky no matter which way I turned.

Maudi passed a cucumber sandwich with the crusts cut off, which I scrutinized with the same loathing I had for brussels sprouts.

"Adam, you have to get over your fear of different food," she said.

Frederick gave me a cup of homemade lemonade. I drank it and asked for another.

"You should eat the sandwich," said the angel. "You never know, it might help you sprout wings like mine."

I looked at him shrewdly.

"Mr. Guy, I'm never going to have wings. I'm not a fairy."

"How do you know, Adam?" Frederick asked. "You don't know what grand adventures lie before you."

"He's right," Maudi added. "You might be a leader of a country. You may dance with royalty from other lands. But you won't go anywhere, young man, if you don't try new things." She leaned toward me and lowered her voice. "And a cucumber sandwich is a new thing."

"But I still don't think it will make me a fairy."

"Stranger things have been known to happen."

The three adults laughed. I shook my small head.

In the distance, three men dressed in loose robes and black stockings walked purposely toward us. One carried a violin while the others had strange gloves on their hands.

"Good day to you, squire," the violinist called.

"The entertainment is finally here," said Frederick. "You're in for a treat today, Adam."

"Thank you for coming, gentlemen," my angel shouted. "This is the special boy you're performing for."

As they came closer, I noticed that the gloves were actually puppets. Their ceramic faces wore blank expressions, but one was fitted in a sailor's outfit and the other sported a pink bonnet and dress.

"What's going on, Mr. Guy?"

"Just eat your sandwich and watch."

The violin sang its first note as the puppeteers crouched in front of the musician.

"Now this is a tale," said one of the men on his knee.

"A tale that needs telling," said the other.

"Of a mum and a dad."

"Who, too often, are yelling."

They jiggled their dolls.

"But there used to be love."

"Now hidden, we're told."

"I'm sure we can find it."

"And let it loose on the world."

The sky melted like ice cream onto the field. I sank my finger into the ground and made a mark as if the grass was Plasticine. Blue and green blobs swam around me as a sticky paw tapped me on the shoulder.

Behind the angel, a clay version of my teddy bear was gesturing for me to follow.

"What should I do with my sandwich, Mr. Guy?"

"I'll look after it, Adam."

I placed my hand on the angel's shoulder to help me stand. The bear moved steadily backward so I stumbled toward it.

"Look," it said.

I turned. The strange minstrels, the angel, and the old couple were no longer there. But the puppets were life-size with kind expressions where their blank faces once were.

I stepped forward, my foot sinking into soft ground. The sailor stood on one leg and twirled. The other figure took off her bonnet, letting blonde hair stream from her head like fireworks. The seaman grabbed a strand, wrapping himself tight in its silken shine, and then kissed her cheek with his strawberry lips.

"Adam, we're in love, you know," he sang.

"Although it may not always be clear," she grunted.

"But wherever we go as a family."

"Trust me, you'll always be near."

I giggled. The splotchy ground splashed upward, filling the heavens with color. A chorus of hidden violins began to soothe me as my bear danced in front of my puppet parents, singing loudly:

"But when there's no stories from Daddy,

And you hold me to soak up your tears,

Think of Guy and Maudi and Frederick,

Because through me, they'll handle your fears."

Fluorescent pigments darted across the hyperactive sky. The violins were silent, but sparse percussion and heavenly horns took their place. My imaginary parents tap-danced to the jazzy tune. I held my bear's hand, squishing it slightly.

Frantic hues whizzed toward me. They streamed past my vision until their colors blended to black.

I stared at my cucumber sandwich again. My dream world had returned to normal.

"Are you going to eat it, Adam?" my angel asked.

"Should I?"

The performers were walking away in the distance.

"Wouldn't you like to be a leader?" asked Maudi.

"No, not a leader."

"Would you like to waltz with a princess in a foreign land?" Frederick asked.

"No, not really."

"What would you like to do, Adam?" asked my guardian.

"I want to pretend."

"Pretend?" Maudi asked.

"Like the people on television."

"Ah, you want to be an actor, young man."

"Yes. I want people to love me."

But my gloomy early years were well behind me now. I was bathed in love, and there was no way Wade and I would get off track. I mean, as an adult, childhood fantasies just don't cut it. That's why theater takes over, to guard us against real life. Or perhaps I was reading this all wrong.

What if Mannix was the dream maker for us grown-ups? A sensual song that helped us face real life.

I held onto the stuffed toy, determined to find magic again.

Chapter Ten

ADAM

"Three aces or a royal flush?" asked Maude as Angela.

She was sprawled onstage across a couch. Her lavender dress spread against the striped upholstery, showing her bare feet. In hand was a glass of sparkling water, pretending to be gin and tonic.

Shannon stood nearby, in smart trousers and white shirt, rubbing his chin.

"Your line is 'What do you mean by the poker reference...?'" I said.

"Oh yeah," he interrupted. "What do you mean by the poker reference, Maude?"

"No, Shannon, her stage name is Angela." Our theater president bit her bottom lip. "Now let's start again."

"Three aces or a royal flush?" asked Maude.

"What do you mean by the poker reference, Angela?"

"You seem to hold your cards close to your chest."

"How so?"

At this point, Shannon's character Ronny was supposed to stand perfectly still, avoiding eye contact with a woman trying to seduce him. Instead, he stumbled, crashing into the grandfather clock we'd spent half an hour trying to get onstage. Its discordant chimes were as shrill as fingernails on a blackboard. Stephen rushed to it, trying to hold it still.

"Are you drunk, Shannon?" I asked.

"Huh?"

Maude gave him a death glare, as he lay clueless on the floor.

"This is a really important scene to get right. There's no comedy. Just coded words from a bored socialite and her young neighbor. If you can't portray this with just a hint of caution, then what are you doing here?"

"Sorry, Adam. I had a rough night. Sugar Daddy threatened to throw me out."

"So you're either still drunk from last night, or you've had vodka in your Coco Pops."

"When Sugar Daddy's drunk, he's loving. So I poured wine while he told me the reasons I should move out. We kissed and made up, eventually."

"I'm so relieved," mumbled Maude.

"Now, Shannon, do you think you can rehearse?" I asked. He picked himself up and brushed the dirt off his pants. "Good, let's start."

"Three aces or a royal flush?" Maude repeated.

"What do you mean by the poker reference, Angela?"

"You seem to hold your cards close to your chest."

"How so?"

"You hint at a chance to get neighborly, then retract the offer when I'm willing to use the gift voucher."

"We're good neighbors. We have an excellent relationship."

"But you know, and I know, we both want more."

From one of the actor's bags, the Oompa Loompa song rang out. Our young gay artiste rushed to answer, his feet performing an impromptu tap dance as he reached for the zipper.

"What did I say about turning your phone off?" I shouted.

He dismissed me with a flick of his hand. I turned to Maude who ran her finger against her neck as if slicing her throat. I slowly nodded before joining her onstage.

"Oh, you want those blue pills," muttered the useless actor. "I'll try Sooty. Yes, they were good, weren't they? I thought I was Venus. No, I said Venus, the god of love. With a V."

"How much are the blue pills?" Stephen interrupted.

Shannon covered the mouthpiece.

"If I shake my tush right, I get them for half-price. What's that, Sooty?" He stopped covering the phone. "No, my ex gets them for me. Nah, really, that's all I see him for."

"Aren't you too old for blue pills, Stephen?" yelled Maude. He shrugged. "I mean, really, at our age, Mary J is more dignified than staying awake for days grinding our loose teeth away."

"Speak for yourself. I can still cut a rug with the young ones."

Maude turned to me and whispered, "Well, if Sugar Daddy drops Shannon, we've found a new suitor."

"It won't work. I can't see Shannon in Stephen's rundown apartment."

"He could spruce up the place. Movie musical posters on every wall!"

"They can pop blue pills and pretend they're in Oz. Shannon can be Toto, and Stephen can grab a magic wand…"

"Stop, Adam. Once it is imagined, it cannot be unimagined."

"No, no," said the talentless performer. "The pills are fifty, and those little goodie bags are a hundred and fifty."

Stephen toddled back to him.

"Maude, I know someone who can replace him," I said quietly.

"Look, Shannon can act. We've seen it."

"Yes, but Sugar Daddy and fairy pills are his interest now." She looked at his sorry form wavering on the ground. "You know I'm right. And this guy I know is exactly what you're looking for."

"What's he been in?"

"Nothing yet. But he's keen to be onstage." She peered down her nose. "No really, he's dreamy. He's intelligent. He has a great sense of humor. And he's not afraid to be sexy."

"Has Wade met him?"

"Why do you ask?"

"Trust me. I have my reasons."

"Well, as a matter of fact, he has. He loves Mannix just as much as I do." She seemed puzzled.

"But, Adam, he's never acted?"

"But he can get up on this stage and bleed charisma from every pore!"

"Whoever this man is, Adam, you're attracted to him, aren't you?"

I looked to Shannon and Stephen negotiating social enhancements.

"Maude, he is attractive, but…"

"Adam! I know when you're skirting around the truth."

"Okay, he's hot. But I'm not the only one who thinks so. Wade thinks he's hot too!"

"And you both want to sleep with him."

"Maude!"

"I wasn't born yesterday, Adam. And it's not the first time I've seen a long-term couple go through this. What's Wade doing tonight?"

"He's at home. Why?"

"Call him. Let's have drinks at my place."

"But the play? We're really behind schedule. We can work around that silly goose and get the other actors up to speed."

There was a thud. Shannon's rag doll body slumped to the floor. Stephen looked to us like a new father reluctant to change his baby's diaper.

"As theater president, I call tonight's rehearsal off. We can pick up where we left off tomorrow evening when Sugar Daddy spanks some sense into that man-child."

"IT'S LIKE THE Pied Piper, only in reverse," I explained.

Maude sipped her merlot. I thought I was really honest with my metaphor. Instead of a horde of children being captivated by the older piper's musical instrument, it was a case of two men being drawn to a younger performer.

"But the difference is, you want to play *his* flute."

"Touché," I replied.

One phone call was all it took to rescue Wade from mindless channel surfing on the couch, and dive into Maude's wine collection. She put down her glass on the kitchen bench.

I felt judged by our close friend, so to numb my shame, I gently grabbed the half-empty bottle from the worn laminate bench and refilled our glasses. The tired floor creaked as I made my way to each glass, paying attention that each was filled at precisely two-thirds measure. When I returned to my spot in the kitchen, Maude bit her bottom lip and then placed her hand on mine.

"I never imagined you two would fall prey to a midlife crisis," she said.

"I'm not even sure that's what it is," said Wade. "We've seen a few guys go through the dreaded male menopause, and it's nothing like that. I would never leave Adam, and he'd never leave me. We're still very much in love!"

"It's just for some reason, we're drawn to this newcomer," I added.

Maude had known us for about five years now. She knew it wasn't our style to invite supporting cast into our bedroom. She'd seen us weather emotional storms, taking care of each other and those around us. We all knew this juvenile infatuation was out of character.

"What's he like?" she asked.

"Like I said earlier tonight, he's oozing with charisma."

"But I don't think he realizes it," said Wade. "In the time we've known him, we've seen him go out of his way to help his flatmate out."

"Very selfless," I interrupted. I gazed at Wade.

"What does he do for money?"

"He works at a call center and poses for my art class."

Our host remained expressionless. The three of us had talked about others in this situation within amateur theater circles several times before. Couples of all persuasions negotiated new boundaries to their relationships with fly-by-night floozies, often to the detriment of rehearsals. They created more drama offstage than on.

Maude nonchalantly refilled her wine glass. I hated the silence in the room.

"We went on a picnic over the weekend," I said. "Wade was going to organize it, but Mannix insisted that we come empty-handed. He pulled out a chicken quiche he bought from his local bakery that morning, before filling us with champagne."

"We sat around getting to know each other at this lovely seaside spot he knew," added Wade. "He told us he'd always had theatrical aspirations but didn't chase them up. He just writes stories instead."

"I think he needs the artistic outlet. He seems very creative."

Maude clutched her glass with both hands as she stared past us. I thought we were about to hear a disapproving monologue.

"How old is he?"

Again, we glanced at each other to see who would answer. Wade nodded, passing me the task of responding.

"He's thirty-one," I replied.

I giggled like a cougar checking out her son's friends. Maude looked down her nose like a concerned governess. I had seen this stance before. Sugarcoating her thoughts was not an option.

"You guys are fools."

I laughed nervously.

"We know," I replied. "But he's just *so* sweet."

"My darlings, listen to yourselves. You are one of the most 'together' couples I know, gay or straight. But all it takes is this little play-bunny to enter your lives and you both act like Pepé Le Pew pining after what you can't have!"

This was the most stern she had ever been with us. She loved us to death, so I guess we were the last people on earth she wanted to see hoodwinked by some wholesome-acting vixen.

Our friendship with Maude was based on openness from day one. She cast us in a play she was workshopping at the theater group, and we were instantly drawn to her unapologetic spinster status. She took one day at a time, appreciating her posse, never wanting to complicate her life with just one companion. Wade seemed to study her like a poker player weighing up his next move.

"I love you, Maude, but trust us, you've got the situation wrong."

"Have I, Wade? You still know little about him."

"We've met up with him a couple times."

"And tell me, boys, has there been any flirting?" We didn't answer. "I rest my case." She opened the pantry door where she'd stashed more bottles of red. "I think it will take another few glasses for me to talk sense into you."

Before any debate could be entered into, she unscrewed the top and poured. Although Wade expressed concern about driving home inebriated, I welcomed the top-up, even if it was close to midnight with a work day ahead. The crisp raspberry-like scent enticed our palettes.

"Right, my sweethearts, a little perspective. After you met him, Adam, when did you next catch up?"

"We went for a drink that night."

"All three of you?"

"No," replied Wade. "I was at dance class."

"Uh-huh. You chat. You like each other. Then who contacts who?"

"We invite him around for dinner," I answered.

"Quiet night?"

"Pretty quiet," said Wade. "We had dinner, chilled out, then he had to go home to his flatmate as something was wrong."

"Uh-huh. What happened?" Again, we didn't answer. "You actually don't know, do you? You never thought to ask. Are you actually sure this guy has a flatmate, or is it a boyfriend?"

I searched my wine glass for an answer. No mystic visions appeared. Now I knew I was tipsy. Thankfully, Wade was my designated driver.

"And do you get the feeling he might be interested in one of you more than the other?"

"Oh definitely not," Wade said. Like me, he also studied his glass for an answer. "He's taken an interest in both of us, and yes, now that I hear myself say it, it is a bit bizarre, but trust me, Maude, there is no ulterior motive."

"Maude," I added, "I appreciate your concern, but trust us, there's nothing sinister going on here. Just a bit of mutual infatuation, nothing more, nothing less. We're grown men. We're not about to do anything foolish."

"Adam, we've all witnessed too many couples split up when a touch of spice was added, as you know. I'm determined not to see the same thing happen to my closest buddies. Besides, the politics of who to invite to what occasion is something I don't want to go through again."

"Yeah, I know what you mean," I added, "but—"

"Remember when I told you about the time I accompanied Jean and Simon to the circus and witnessed the trapeze artist flirt with Simon. They ended up running away together to live on a farm, while Jean took on the arduous hobby of stalking. First the letters, then the phone calls, followed by those crazy ticking gifts. I don't want to be meat in the sandwich again, and I'm determined not to see *my boys* split up."

"Maude," said Wade, "this friend of ours is guilty before proven innocent."

"Okay, I should really meet this guy before I say anymore."

She seemed to fake a Zen-like smile.

"Shall we organize another picnic?" I asked.

"No, I'd like to have all three of you here, at my place. Dinner next Monday night. Say, seven o'clock?"

"We'll ask him," replied Wade. "I'm sure Mannix will be free."

"Unless he has to go and play his pipe," I joked, sensing my cheeks flush. "Help get those rodents out of town!"

Again, Maude placed her hands on mine.

"As long as *he* doesn't turn out to be the rat!"

Chapter Eleven

ADAM

"What is the story with your wife, Mary?" asked Maude as Angela.

"She's my childhood sweetheart," replied Shannon as Ronny.

Both sat on the couch onstage.

"But childhood things get tiresome as time moves on."

"Oh dear, Angela. I'm not sure I like the way this conversation is going."

"And as a woman of fair comfort, I tend to find people of all levels of character totally enchanting."

"From what Mary and I have seen, you and Cecil work on many levels. Why the interest in me? Is his love for you fading?"

"Oh, Cecil adores me! I mean, he wears my clothes around the house all the time when we're alone. And as they say, 'Imitation is the highest form of flattery.'"

"Do your dresses suit him?"

"Only when he shaves."

"Even with the balding head?"

"Trust me, Ronny, he knows how to sport a bonnet with flair."

"So why are you shopping around if he loves you so much?"

"I'm just saying that, from your point of view, maturity is settling in, and as we get older, we tend to look for something more worldly."

He stood.

"I'm not about to trade Mary in for a new model, like an old hunting dog!"

"Oh, Ronny dear, I didn't mean to offend you."

"Maybe I'm not offended. I expect this is another one of your depraved little jokes. You'll jump into my arms, and Cecil will pop out of the kitchen and challenge me to a duel."

She looked past the fourth wall.

"Now, why didn't I think of that idea, myself?"

Stephen, Mary, her cousin, and I applauded.

"That was quite good," I said. "I'm so pleased you know your lines, Shannon."

"I can be a good actor when I put my mind to it."

Maude gave him a thumbs-up behind his back. I admit I was disappointed that I couldn't offer the role to Mannix, but all day, Shannon had been showing promise. Even his phone was switched off, saving us from Sugar Daddy's haunting presence.

"Can we help you, gentlemen?" said Maude.

I turned. Two police officers strode toward me. One was a blonde Barbie whose hips swayed constantly as she walked. She chewed gum while twirling a set of handcuffs around her finger. The other was a rough dude, whose chest bulged so much his buttons clutched for their lives, trying to keep his shirt from popping open.

"Did someone call the strippers?" Shannon asked.

"Which one of you is Sugar Cheeks?" asked the male cop.

Maude stepped offstage while her theatrical love interest fainted onto the couch.

"I think that answers your question," I replied.

"What's he done?" asked Mary.

"We suspect he's a drug dealer," answered the bombshell.

"No!" said Stephen. "Sweet little Shannon? Why, butter wouldn't melt in his mouth."

"No, it would sizzle," I muttered under my breath.

"Shall I revive him?" Maude asked.

"Nah," replied Mary. "This big bloke can carry him over his shoulder. Shannon will get a kick out of that." The officer gave her a stern look. "Just saying."

"I'll go and get Sugar Cheeks some water," said Maude.

She headed for the dressing room.

"Are you sure he's dealing drugs?" I asked. "I mean, we play in front of an audience next week, and we really need him onstage."

"The law is the law!" said the male cop.

"Well, thank you, officer, for your succinct response. I'm so glad you've answered my question."

"Glad to be of service to the community."

I rolled my eyes. Maude dripped water from a glass onto Shannon's face. He woke. The policewoman whirled the handcuffs above her bleached hair and headed for the stage.

"Aren't you only supposed to use handcuffs for dangerous criminals or if someone is resisting arrest?"

"Yeah," said the male cop. "But Sharon has been at me all day to use them." He winked. "You know how it is. I have to keep the girl happy."

"I'd rather be cuffed by the stud in uniform," our naïve thespian called.

"You know what they say," I added. "You have to keep the boy happy."

"Oh, but you promised," said Sharon.

"Officer, it's all part of your diversity training."

"Hulky Baby, please. I want to feel like Wonder Woman."

"Why don't you go up there and help her. She might chip a nail, and if she does, she won't be happy."

He nodded and followed.

"No, you can't take him away," cried Stephen. "We can look over this misdemeanor, can't we?"

"Why does he care?" I whispered to Mary.

"He's already paid for his pills."

"I mean, it's probably his first offense," the aged actor continued. "Look at that innocent face, Officer. That's not the face of a lowlife scum feeding from the personal tragedies of those less fortunate." All eyes were on Stephen. "Well, I'm just saying, he's an angel in disguise."

"Yes, we can all see that," I said quietly. "He's so flighty his feet never touch the ground."

"Can we get him out on bail?" Maude asked.

"Yes, Sugar Daddy will pay whatever it takes!"

"I'm not sure, ma'am," said the policeman.

"What?" our theater president shrieked. "You're an officer arresting this actor, and you don't know the law?"

"Don't we just give him one phone call and put him in the cell overnight?" Sharon asked.

"I don't know," the muscular cop replied. "This is my first drug bust."

"Drug bust?" questioned Maude. "Pardon my semantics, but for a drug bust, doesn't there need to be drugs?"

"We have evidence."

"They must have," said Shannon. "They knew my dealer code name, Sugar Cheeks."

Maude's palm landed flat on her forehead.

"Well, I guess it's no use arguing now, is it, Shannon?"

The himbo actor was cuffed and marched off the stage toward the front entrance.

"Can I order takeaway in jail? I mean, I've seen those prison movies, and I don't think the food agrees with my diet."

"Which station are you taking him to, Officer?" Maude asked.

"In case she bakes a cake with a nail file in it," I mumbled.

"Ashfield," the policewoman replied. "Don't worry, there's lots of good takeaway there. Pizza. Kebab. He can take his pick."

"Does the kebab store give good hummus?" Shannon asked.

"It's passable. But their falafel is to die for!"

The three stooges exited.

"Well, what are we going to do now?" Stephen asked.

"Find another dealer," I replied.

"It may look like I have no choice," said Maude.

I tried to stop myself from smiling, but the corners of my lips spread like wildfire across my face.

"What are you grinning about?" asked Mary.

My old actress friend applauded me.

"Congratulations, Adam. Your prayers have just been answered!"

Chapter Twelve

Mannix

"I'm in?" I turned to Bruce with my phone to my face. "I'm in!" My flatmate shrugged. "I'm in Adam's play." He nodded. "Who's Maude? Oh, Maude, the president. Dinner? Yeah, I get it. She has to meet me. So I'm in? Yes! Adam, thank you so much. I'll cut back on work. No, I can afford it." Bruce stared at me. "Yep, private rehearsal. Got it! Bye, Adam, and thank you again."

"Private rehearsal?"

"With Maude, the woman who wrote the piece and who tries to seduce me."

His head tilted. "M, we have to talk."

"Why?"

He sat on the floor next to our coffee table and poured me a beer.

"Just looking after your interests." He topped up his half-filled glass.

"Okay, what are you worried about, Bruce?"

"These friends who I've never met."

He was right. I talked about my new mates ad nauseam but hadn't invited them over. He handed me my beer, while nodding and pursing his lips. I sipped the foam from the top of my glass, before sitting on the carpet opposite Bruce.

"Trust me, you'll meet them."

"M, they seem to have captured your heart, so to speak."

"Bruce, I don't know what you mean."

"To put it bluntly, you're obsessed."

I idiotically chuckled. "Bruce, to be honest, yes I'm a bit obsessed, but I don't have a clue why."

"I thought so. Which one are you captivated by, Adam or Wade?"

"They're both interesting in different ways."

"That's not what I asked. Which one?"

"Both."

"So you want a threesome?"

"Yes, I guess. I'm not sure."

"I see."

"Bruce, this is the first time I haven't really understood how I felt."

"Are you in love, M?"

"Definitely not in love."

"You're in lust, then."

I smirked. As a straight man, Bruce liked analyzing me. I think it gave him a fresh insight into the male psyche. He questioned my bi life, establishing that certain behavior was common to both of us just in the simple fact we were both men.

"When I first met Adam, I thought he was a sweet guy who I had a connection with, so I invited him out for a drink. On the way home, I started fantasizing about him, so I realized there was an attraction. That's where I was going to leave it."

"Until?"

"Until he rang me about coming to their place for dinner. I honestly thought the next time I'd see him would be in drawing class, at a safe distance."

"You dream of running away with him, don't you, M?"

"No! Not at all. Like I said, he rang me, and I almost jumped out of my skin. And now he's cast me in the play he's directing, although, really, he's not my type. But I know I'm drawn to him somehow."

"You're in love with him, Mannix."

"No I'm not, seriously. In lust, yes. In love, no. I have the same feelings for his partner."

"Mate, I've seen you go out for casual sex before, but this is the first time I've seen you beat yourself up about it. Do they play around?"

"No. But around me they're showing interest."

"Ah. I get it. You're caught between coming between them and wanting to share cum between them."

"Yep."

Bruce topped up our glasses. He admitted he was enjoying this exchange more than he thought he would. He never knew anyone in this dilemma before, and in this world of male-to-male sexual politics, he was intrigued.

"Like you said, they're both showing interest, but not as a team."

"I wish they'd just invite me to their bedroom and get on with it, instead of double-checking each other's mood all the time."

"They're newbies at this."

"So am I."

Bruce began counting on his fingers.

"One, inexperienced at threesomes on all sides," he said. "Two, weird lustful thoughts. Three, not wanting to jeopardize a part in a play. Four, definitely not wanting to be the one to break up a successful marriage. Have I forgotten anything, M?"

"No. They're definitely the main points."

We sipped our beers and sat quietly.

"The internet," said Bruce, suddenly breaking the silence.

"The internet?"

"The internet."

"Why the internet? They don't do social media."

"M, there are tips on everything from objects in the home that can double up as sex toys to how to bonsai your dog so it stays puppy size. There has to be advice somewhere on the net on how to instigate a ménage à trois. What cocktails to mix. What to wear. What to do to keep the couple equally involved."

Before I could reply, Bruce darted to his bedroom to grab his laptop. While he plugged into the World Wide Web, I finished my beer before finding myself in daydream mode.

Wade knocked the last peg into the ground. The tent was now sturdy. He dropped the mallet onto the grass and examined the sweat stains on his ripped khaki shirt. His macho odor drew me in.

He pulled at his collar and popped open a few buttons, letting the cool air breathe onto his chest.

Adam appeared from behind the tent, dressed as a Boy Scout with an equally sweaty shirt and shorts so tight his cock fought against the buttoned fly. His legs were also soaked with sweat. I clutched his ankles and began licking toward his...

"Jelly wrestling!" shrieked Bruce. I stared in his direction. "Sorry, M, I knew you were miles away. Those fantasies are taking over again, aren't they? Were you in X-rated bliss?"

"No. More like bad seventies porn. I'm curious on how it turns out."

"Well, one suggestion on 'Thirteen ways to instigate a threesome' says to try jelly wrestling."

"Where? In their bathtub?"

"Does jelly set at room temperature, M?"

"No idea, Bruce. Does it give hints on what flavor the jelly should be?"

"Maybe raspberry would be the sexiest flavor."

"Why raspberry?"

"Give everyone a healthy glow. Lime would only make everyone look gaunt, like zombies."

"Is there a better suggestion on the list?" I asked. I tapped my empty glass.

"Yes, friends on vacation."

"On vacation. Where would we go?"

"Paris, the home of the ménage à trois," Bruce joked. "Or Amsterdam. The home of letting yourself loose."

"Or camping, in the hope that we take the word literally."

Bruce headed to the fridge to fetch more beer.

"You know, M," he called out from the kitchen, "that has a certain 'men getting back to their roots' quality about it, so to speak."

"Getting down and dirty in the dirt?"

"Yeah. Just refine it with a few bottles of red wine, and the rest will play out perfectly."

"Bruce, what if one of them gets jealous?"

"More wine, M. Fill up the green-eyed partner with more wine."

I gave my flatmate a deadpan expression.

"Okay. Maybe you just need to make sure neither of them feels left out. Work out what makes each one tick and apply your charm."

I let the words sink in. I realized I had to keep an eye on my own desires and not let them take over. My strategy would be to work on both Wade and Adam as individuals, keeping careful watch over their attitude toward each other. If only they had an open marriage! If only they weren't together so I'd have two new friends with benefits. But they were together, very much together. Bruce was right. I didn't want to come between them, but I desperately wanted to share in their love for each other.

Chapter Thirteen

ADAM

"What lovely cutlery," commented Mannix. He was examining his fork. "Did you bring it out especially for this evening?"

"No, darling," replied Maude. "I don't believe in special-occasion dinnerware. I'm a woman who likes to spoil myself and my friends, every day. Life's too short not to use the good stuff."

"Hear! Hear!" cheered Wade. "Good wine, good friends, good conversation. That's our motto."

"And good cutlery," added Mannix.

We were seated at Maude's rustic dinner table. Two long benches instead of dining chairs made this setting cry out for a banquet of oversized roasted turkey with lashings of crispy vegetables and homemade gravy to drown our plates while a tired old butler played the harpsichord, adding gothic flavor to our sumptuous feast.

But this wasn't Maude. Instead, she had complemented the benches with homemade cushions. One long cushion for each that featured the antique pattern of light blue wrens on a darker background.

The furniture came from a deceased estate, and she'd snapped it up at auction for a song. None of the other bidders could see its aged clumpy appeal. The cutlery, though, was a gift from a short-lived affair with a wealthy dentist. He was hardly exciting, but at least Maude got her teeth whitened.

While Wade carefully poured some pinot noir into Mannix's wine glass, I noted the chemistry between them. A young man feigning innocence, lapping up the attention that his older yearning friend was bestowing on him. The polite thank-you from Mannix, delivered with a Cheshire grin, seemed to make Wade weak at the knees.

Even while watching this, I took delight in the attraction between my partner and our new acquaintance, mixed with an undertone of longing for the same reaction from Mannix, someway, somehow.

"Do you like the wine?" I asked.

I was premature. Our favorite new companion hadn't even tasted it.

"It smells okay, I think," replied Mannix. "How are you supposed to smell wine?"

Both Wade and I were about to answer in unison. As our first syllables slipped out, Maude intervened.

"Swirl it first, darling," she said. He did. "Now what do you smell?"

"Am I supposed to sense the odor of cauliflower and freshly cut lawn?"

"Don't analyze it. Just be honest with yourself. Do you like the scent or not?"

Wade and I leaned toward him. We must have looked like bookends facing Maude and Mannix on the opposite side. She looked at us, pokerfaced, while we waited for what seemed like God to speak. It was bad romantic comedy.

"Yeah, it's kinda soothing," replied Mannix.

His nose was buried in his wine glass.

"Interesting analogy," she noted. "Basically, if you like the smell, you'll like the vino. Simple as that."

He took his first sip as we followed suit. Maude was still studying us, before tasting the wine herself.

"Not bad," she said, "considering it was on special as a 'buy one, get one free' deal at the shopping center."

She served up supermarket fresh fettuccini with fragrant homemade pesto blended finely in her sturdy food processor. It was a top-brand German appliance. Another gift from her former dentist lover. We twirled the food around our forks, before skillfully placing the vivid green slop into our mouths.

"Do you like camping?" asked Mannix.

"I don't mind it," I replied.

Maude knew I was lying. About six months ago, Wade, Maude, and I were taken to the bush by a mutual acquaintance from the theater company. Everything was fine up until bedtime. Conversing around the campfire was fun. Admiring the star-filled night sky was fascinating. Even using a small spade as a toilet utensil was novel. But why do bush mosquitoes ignore the simple urban etiquette of keeping away from people drenched in insect repellent?

I returned from our one night of camping looking like a tasting plate from a vampire's banquet. Wade and Maude remembered how I doused myself in vinegar, smelling like a side salad. I rubbed myself against the carpet to soothe the itching like a mangy flea-ridden mutt.

They were the words I would use whenever I recalled our encounter with nature, but somehow the usual inclination to tell this story after Mannix had brought up the subject of camping had gone. It had vanished like a politician's credibility.

"Camping? We both love it!" announced Wade.

"We should go," I replied.

"Good. I know a spot," said Mannix.

"When?" asked Wade.

"Friday evening?" suggested Mannix.

"Perfect," I said. "It's a date!"

The three of us raised our glasses and toasted our future social engagement. Maude was no longer pokerfaced. She eyed me like I was a double agent about to be exposed, but I ignored her expression.

"Of course, you can come too, Maude," said Mannix.

"Um. No, darling. Whenever I go bush, I get eaten by mosquitoes! Besides, if I remember correctly, we're rehearsing a play over the weekend."

Wade and I both sniggered nervously.

"Oh, sorry," I said. "I got carried away in the moment."

"I can see that." She shook her head. "Now, Mannix, I heard you've had no acting experience."

"Zilch. I'm interested in theater and scripts and all that stuff. This play is sort of a starting point for me."

"You've got to admit, he has charm," I said.

"Charisma to burn," Wade added.

"Have you read it yet?" she asked.

"Yes, he has," I butted in, blatantly lying. "I took it over last night, and we read it together."

This was quarter true. I'd dropped it over during my lunch break that day. The young man told me he'd have no time to read it before the dinner party. He sat silent and sipped his wine.

"So, Mannix, what's your favorite line in the script?"

She had a wicked smirk.

"That one about 'playing with fire.' You know, when Ronny has that monologue about not wanting to lead Angela on, but his dad is encouraging him to add a sophisticated notch on his bedpost."

"I'm impressed."

I tried hard not to audibly breathe a sigh of relief.

"So what are you hoping to achieve from your introduction into acting?"

"I want to write."

"Write scripts?"

"Maybe. I've written short stories, but I've had some characters in my head for as long as I can remember. They'd be perfect for a play."

I was pleasantly surprised. What other hidden talents might this boy have?

"Fascinating," replied Maude. "Do tell."

"They're characters that have been with me since as long as I can remember. Two warlocks and a witch." Mannix paused. He seemed unnerved.

"Are you okay?" asked Wade.

"Sorry, just distracted. Um, I'm not sure what the warlocks and the witch get up to, but I seem to know them well. They've been with me since childhood."

"Just like my guardian angel, Mr. Guy."

"Oh, not him again," said Maude. "Seriously, you must hold some sort of record for the number of times you've told me about those dreams. Now, Mannix, tell us more about your childhood characters. Were they imaginary play friends?"

"Nothing like that. I've just always had a strong sense of who they are. One is mischievous and selfish. Another is kindhearted but cautious. And the woman is more of a free spirit. Like you, Maude."

"You have Maude in your childhood dreams too?" I asked. "Wow, she gets around!"

"Yes, but your version of me sounds like an old spinster, even if she is with that man she hangs around. I'm sure they're not actually *doing it*. Now let's get back to Mannix's imaginary creatures."

"But you have to admit, it is pretty freaky!"

"Yes, Adam, but not everything is about you." She sighed. "Our dear newest cast member, can you see yourself writing about these mystical folk one day?"

"I think after this play, I will."

"Now, I'm about to be your cougar in our play. Is that close enough to a casting couch for you?"

"Maude, if I ever get around to writing my thoughts down, you'll be the first actress cast."

"Sounds like the characters in a morality play," I said.

"Yeah, I guess they are." He nodded gently. "Never thought about them like that before. That's why I'm looking forward to rehearsal. It will spark my creativity."

I got the feeling that Maude had become as charmed by our new friend as we were. Who wouldn't have been? Smart. Cute. Sexy. Someone you just wanted to whisk away to a penthouse apartment with a harbor view and a lavish bedroom sporting a king-sized bed fitted with a thousand-count white Egyptian cotton sheets. But I digress.

"Wow. What type of pie is this?" asked Mannix.

The scent of the baked delight found its way to the dining room. Maude carefully carried out the hot dessert on a large wooden chopping block and placed it in the center of the dining table.

"You've made our favorite, haven't you?" said Wade.

"Rhubarb and custard crumble," I added.

"Would I let my boys down?" said our host.

"Ah. Just in time. I feel like tasting something hot and sticky," teased Mannix.

"That's later. When we give you a lift home," replied Wade.

"Hmm. The after-dinner mints," said Mannix. "Sweet and refreshing."

"Oh please," Maude interrupted. "I've got a bedroom with a mirrored wardrobe if you want to get over this phase as quickly as possible. I can play early Donna Summer with tacky suggestive lyrics. I'll roll you a joint if you want."

Usually this type of sarcasm would have made anyone in our situation stop. Not us. Perhaps we were too drunk. We savored the crumble with several more blatant innuendos and a shoulder rub from Mannix to Wade. Maude didn't comment. At the end of dinner, we gave our host a group hug, almost squashing her.

"Drunk men don't know their own strength," she said.

While still embraced, we all took turns at giving Maude a peck on the cheek, then turned to each other to share kisses. Wade gave Mannix a prolonged kiss, before Mannix grabbed me by the collar and pulled me toward his lips. Another lingering kiss was shared. Why we did this right under Maude's nose was anyone's guess. It was only later that Wade and I realized we forgot to kiss each other.

Maude opened the front door, so we stepped into the foyer of her apartment building.

"Wade, Adam, *and* Mannix, you are all sweet guys. Just keep an eye on who's in control here. The baton keeps being passed around."

She quietly shut the door, leaving us to ponder.

Chapter Fourteen

ADAM

"Are we losing the plot?" I asked Wade.

"In a word, yes!" he replied.

As he steered his car from the quiet streets of Maude's neighborhood, I welcomed the chance to think. Think about my love for Wade. Think about my love for Mannix. Think about the possibility that this was all getting out of hand. Think about the possibility that if it got out of hand, a lot of fun would come of it. I also welcomed Wade's response to my question. Up until that point, we seemed to play along with our obsession, but not chat about it.

"What are we going to do about it?" I asked.

"Wait for the car crash."

"Babe, you don't think we're headed for disaster?"

"Adam, I have no idea. We're sane enough not to let this get to us, or at least we used to be."

Wade turned down a beautiful leafy avenue, pulled over, and parked his relatively new car in front of a sweet little brick house. The discussion had started. No use putting it on hold until we got home. The shadowy trees listened to our confessions in this street of slumber.

"I'm not in love with him, Wade."

"Me neither. But we're acting like two eager kids going through puppy love."

"So what are your fantasies?"

He leaned forward and rested his arms on the steering wheel.

"Fantasies, eh? Adam, they're always with the three of us."

"Agreed. There are various situations I could see us all in."

"Like?"

"Mannix has crept up behind me as I stir something on the stove. He reaches around and covers my eyes, and I reach down..." My partner moved away from the steering wheel and sunk back into his leather seat. "I reach down and feel for his uh, um, but he tactfully moves aside and all I feel is his other hand. His other hand has your hand in it. Mannix has quietly snuck up to me with you in tow." Wade closed his eyes and sighed. "Then he presses himself against me, while he pulls at your hand so you surge forward to warm his back. You and I make a little Mannix sandwich." My partner giggled. "I realize that he's somehow exposed himself, and his hot shaft is cleverly sliding itself under my T-shirt, whetting my appetite."

"How did his dick get out of his pants, Adam?"

"That's not the point."

"Did I unzip it with my other hand?"

"If it makes sense to you, Wade, then yes!"

"No, that doesn't make sense." He opened his eyes. "My hand would still be on his cock, and you'd feel it under your T-shirt."

"Maybe you let go of it just in time?"

"What, just before we sandwiched him?"

"I don't know! Ask Mannix. It's his dick!"

We laughed uncontrollably. We were the spark in this quiet universe of silhouetted trees and lonely houses. As our mirth slowly faded, my ageless partner leaned over and kissed me.

"Wade, I love you."

"I love you too, babe."

"Is this what a midlife crisis feels like?"

"I don't think so, Adam."

"Why do you say that?"

"We still love each other."

"So?"

"Think about it, Adam."

I observed the appealing brick house we parked in front of. Someone had spent their hard-earned cash to buy it, and maybe someone had spent more money renovating it. Perhaps in old-world elegance or as an understated minimalist designer statement. They would have argued under its roof. Possibly committed illegal acts in the shed. Made love with the curtains open. Either way, someone had built up a past in this house, just as we had in *our* home. There was no chance in hell I would give it all up.

"You're right, we're still madly in love," I said. "Neither of us is stupid enough to believe that we've fallen for Mannix. We're just going through a phase."

"True, Adam. Let's not forget Simon and Jean. Now that's a midlife crisis!"

"Oh god, yes! I can see why a trapeze artist would be a good catch to a man with an uptight wife, but at least he could have stopped to think about what he was getting himself into beforehand."

"Two bratty kids to a second marriage when he should've been thinking about retirement."

"That Oscar and his little peeing problem. A six-year-old shouldn't still be wearing nappies when they visit friends."

Wade started the engine.

"They claim it's a medical condition, Adam."

"Medical condition, my ass! He wants attention, and Simon is past the parenting age. As for that trapeze artist, well, there's a circus short of a clown."

The car made its way down the street with ease. I loved this luxury vehicle better than the secondhand one I drove. Wade fussed over it, washing it so often it was a wonder that its deep red paint hadn't worn off. Still, I got to drive it on the weekend, cruising along like a corporate player with a cocaine habit.

"What are we going to do?" my husband asked.

"Seduce him."

"Are you serious?"

"Wade, look at how he plays with us. That brief neck massage he quickly gave Maude to break down her defenses, before extending the favor to you for at least ten minutes."

"I'm not sure it was ten minutes."

"Close enough."

"But look at the way he flirts with you, Adam. That line about 'looking after his assets, up close and personal.' I don't even know how that line came about, but it was clearly directed at you."

"Wade, we were talking about what jewelry we wore. My gold ring, the ring you wear on your pinkie, and that necklace with the blue gemstone that Maude wears. Mannix wore a bracelet tonight and talked about how he only wore it for special occasions."

"So how did we get onto his 'assets'?"

"He joked about having a Prince Albert and said something about me giving his jewelry a spit polish."

Wade grinned. "I think we're onto something," he said. "It's the way he flirts with us. He's verbal with you but tactile with me."

"Are you sure?"

"Tonight *I* got the shoulder rub, although we both shared the innuendos."

"Yes, there's less of a tendency to feel me up, so to speak."

"Remember that picnic, Adam. For some reason, you pulled away when he first put his hand on your shoulder to coerce your head into his lap."

"We were in public. A suburban setting is not the place for me to lie back in the lap of a younger man."

"I didn't mind. After your reaction, I let him lie back in my lap. You shouldn't be so uptight."

"Sorry, but this situation is confronting me. Turning me on and confronting me at the same time. It's just too bizarre. There's no logic in it."

"Then go with it."

"Wade, I know it's doing your head in as well."

"Yeah, true. Maybe we should take control."

"I think we tried to at our place."

"And it almost worked, Adam, if it wasn't for that phone call." I pressed the remote for the roller door as we pulled into our garage. "But what I'm getting at is that we need to take control of this situation ourselves. We're older than he is. Let's not get carried away in our own fantasies." Wade turned off the engine as I let my seat belt slide back. "Let's make sure Mannix has the time of his life if we ever find ourselves in bed together. We'll check for clues on what he's into and provide service with a smile."

I turned away from my other half. He made a lot of sense. It was like enrolling Mannix into the School of Desire. First lesson, simple caressing. Second lesson, swapping kisses. Play-lunch, cheese platter, and champagne. Third lesson, finding ways to make all his Christmases come at once!

Chapter Fifteen

ADAM

And yet again, I couldn't sleep. This time I left the teddy bear in our bedroom, sat on the lounge, and thought about the night Dad left.

It was only a week before my fifth birthday. He woke me holding a small bag and said good-bye.

"Will you be gone long?" I asked.

"Adam, you're going to meet someone special one day, who'll take my place. He'll love you and comfort you with all the affection you deserve."

"But will he read me stories?"

"You'll write those stories together."

"All right. I love you, Daddy."

"And I'll always love you, Adam, no matter where I am."

He kissed me and tiptoed out. As the moments passed, I realized that he was gone for good. He'd never walk me to school anymore. I'd never indulge in the lush chocolate frogs he'd buy for me when Mum wasn't looking. And stories of witches, warlocks, and fantasy lands would be heard no more.

Eventually, I cried myself to sleep.

"What are you doing here?" Mr. Guy asked.

"I need to see you," I replied.

"But I didn't send for you. How did you get here?"

"I don't know."

Frederick looked to my fairy and then back to the ground, appearing as sad as Dad had been only moments ago.

The endless field we stood on was flourishing with daisies, yet they looked ill in color. A doctor would have ordered them to lie down and rest. The murky skies ignored us like an audience losing interest in a play.

"Where's Maudi," I asked.

Frederick wiped his eyes with a light blue handkerchief as Mr. Guy walked me away from him.

"Maudi has moved on to *your* world, Adam."

"I don't get it."

"My friend, there's this world and your world, and people like you move back and forth."

"Oh. Like the way I come here at night."

"Not quite. You usually come here because I'm looking for you. Remember, I'm your guardian fairy." He glanced at Frederick for a second and then scratched his head. "But why are you here now?"

"Because Daddy has left."

He crouched and held me tight, his wings surrounding me like a shield, keeping his love trapped in. My tears dampened his shoulder.

"Adam, don't think about the love you've lost. Think about how happy you made your dad while he was around."

"It doesn't help, Mr. Guy."

He kissed my wet cheek. "Well, what if I tell you I'll never leave you. Will that help?"

"But you're here. You're not in *my* world. You only make me happy when I sleep." I pulled away from his hug. "Why don't you come back with me?"

"Adam, I can't. I belong in this world. I'm not allowed to visit your world."

"But I come to your world all the time. And Maudi has gone to mine. Why can't you come to mine?"

He stood, lifting me and meeting my eyes.

"I've got a secret. You're not supposed to be here—well, not yet, anyway. But I brought you here because you're special to me."

"Oh, Mr. Guy, are you in trouble?"

"Well, I might be."

"But Maudi is in *your* world and *my* world?"

"Yes, you're right. She's gone back to your world so you can meet her again one day."

"Mr. Guy, you're not making sense."

"Maybe you should give it a rest," Frederick said. He had wandered over. "It's too much for this little one to understand."

"Just remember, Adam, that I'm looking out for you, and I will always be near. I'm your guardian angel."

"No. You're my guardian fairy."

"No. I'm your guardian angel because I chose to be. And I'll always be there for you."

But that was the last of my childhood dreams with Mr. Guy.

Wade snored lightly while I sat alone on this wintery night. A few lone cars lit up our lounge room like the beam of a lighthouse warning a captain. The charcoal drawing of angels tangoed for a moment in the spotlight. The blue cherub eyed me from behind the masked ornament as the glow in the room vanished.

The room was darker than before, until a smoky neon light cast an aura around a humanlike form.

"Mr. Guy!"

"Adam, you're much too old to call me Mister anything. Just Guy will do."

We were sitting at a booth in some kind of nightclub. He tasted his champagne cocktail.

"I didn't think angels drank alcohol."

I looked at my hand. It held the same drink.

"I only party with good friends." He raised his glass to toast, but I didn't follow his lead. "What's the matter?"

"I never saw you again when my dad left."

"You never saw your dad again, but you're seeing me now."

I drank, slowly. Behind me, an exotic voice was at odds with the country ballad it was singing. A dark statuesque woman, in a striped shirt and pale blue cowboy hat, snapped her fingers in time with a song about a sheriff who'd found a unique bond with his horse. An older gent with missing teeth enthusiastically accompanied her on a ukulele.

A few other booths were situated near us with other punters, while the rest of the layout consisted of mismatched tables and chairs. Framed portraits lavished the back wall, with many faces staring with self-doubt and seduction in equal measure.

"Where am I? A thespian drinking hall?"

"You got it in one," Guy replied. He beamed. "Do you remember this place? It's called the Pedestal."

"No. Should I remember? Most of the time we were in that never-ending grass field."

"Well, I guess all memories aren't forever. But, as you love the theater, isn't it the perfect place for creatives to share a drink, revise lines, and study the characters around them?"

I looked about. He was right. There were two gay guys and a female friend with scripts in hand at one of the tables, passionately discussing the play rather than going over lines. An established female couple sipped white wine while eyeing the stage, as their pagan god kept them in a trance with her song. A drunken punk rocker sat subdued, almost falling onto his martini and battling his eyelids not to pull down their shutters.

"Guy, why am I here?"

"To share your problems over a drink with an old friend."

"But I've got Maude. She's my oldest friend."

"Adam, don't resent me. I've been keeping an eye on you, trust me."

"Then why didn't you show yourself?"

"I didn't need to. You met your soul mate, Wade. He's been looking after you. Just as you've been looking after him."

"But there's a long gap between being four and being in my forties!"

His wings fluttered. I sighed.

"I stayed away because I had to watch from afar. That's what guardian angels do. That's what they should always do."

"So why are you with me now?"

He shook his head.

"Because something's going on with you and Wade and Mannix, and I need to get to the bottom of it."

He tilted his head. I let the bubbles in my beverage refresh me. The mood had changed in the bar. The vocalist had slowed her ballad with a tender tone.

"Guy, have you ever been in love?"

"I'm in a relationship."

He had that "new love" smile.

"Dreamy?"

"Yeah, Adam. I can't stop thinking about him."

"What's his name?"

"Joshua."

A second wistful grin painted his face.

"Tell me about him."

"Adam, I'm here to listen to you."

"I just need to hear you talk about him. Trust me, Guy, I know what I'm doing."

For a moment, he didn't say anything. He took a sip and paused thoughtfully.

"Joshua was a teenage friend who tried to teach me to fly. I had a crush on him back then, but lost contact. He found me again, recently. Shortly after, we moved away from here."

"Moved away?"

"Sorry, Adam. Um, I used to live here among the theater folk. I moved away for a bit of perspective. Glad I did."

"You said he taught you to fly."

"Tried to. Another special friend helped me on the right path much later on."

He winked at me. I had no idea why.

"Tell me about Joshua."

"Soothing. Kind. A voice that would melt butter. Someone who's my kindred spirit..."

"Yep," I interrupted. "You've got it bad."

"I'm sure you know what I'm talking about, Adam."

The bartender brought two more champagne cocktails. His dark buttoned vest hugged his white T-shirt, making me dream of running my tongue down his toned chest. His faded ripped jeans and a chunky belt buckle looked as if they'd spent last night feverishly dancing in a crowded warehouse, echoing with house music.

Guy snapped his fingers to get my attention.

"Sorry, it's just that his dress sense reminds me of my courting days with Wade."

"So, talk about it."

"But if you've been watching from afar, you already know about it."

"It doesn't matter. I want to hear your memories of those early days."

"Laser lights. Large dance floors. They're the backdrop of our courting. His gentle face looking at me as if there is no other, and me, drenching myself in his calm." I looked to the singer. "I think the world stops for couples. They're protected by a shield of their own well-kept secrets and passions, and that's where the source of their strength lies." I turned to Guy. "I look at his balding form today and still see that young man I fell for with rich curly hair and burning ambition, replaced with composure and tranquility."

"You've been smitten for a long time."

The angel rested his hands at the base of his champagne glass.

"There'll never be a time when I won't be. We have so much history—parties, real estate, holidays, friends. We've weathered dramas, and friends with dramas. And through all that, we're still very much smitten."

"Are you smitten with Mannix?"

"God no! Attracted, yes, but not smitten. I love that young man, but I'm *in* love with my old man."

"You're answering your own dilemma, Adam."

This angel was right. If we weren't still smitten, we'd be planning separate rendezvous with our new friend.

"Guy, why are we attracted to Mannix?"

"I don't know, Adam. I don't know. Damn curious, though."

"It's doing our heads in."

"I know, Adam. That's why I'm here to talk. What is it about Mannix you like?"

"His carefree attitude. His confidence. The fact that he's happy to go nude in front of art class. And he's friendly."

"Sexy?"

"Sexually confident. I love his bisexuality. It means he's comfortable with himself, and yes, I guess I find that sexy."

"And Wade? Why do you think Wade's attracted?"

I was about to answer that his reasons were the same as mine. The fact was, I wasn't sure.

"I think Wade sees something else in him. Maybe elements of himself when he was younger?"

"Or is he having a midlife crisis, Adam?"

"Of course not. Wade just sees a young guy finding his feet, yet with a can-do attitude. After all, Wade approached me when we first met. He knew when to make his move. Not unlike Mannix insisting on a drink after our initial meeting."

"I get it," Guy replied. "This guy's won you over. In fact, he's won you both over. And there's an attraction there. You don't know why, but you're sorting it out."

"God, I wish we could sort it out." I lifted my glass and swigged half the cocktail. "It's doing our heads in on all levels. One minute, we think we're in control, and the next thing I know, I'm jealous. Then I think I'm an absolute hypocrite for feeling like that!"

"Hmm."

"What?"

"I'm stumped. I think next time we go for a drink I might warrant a second opinion."

"Who? The Almighty?"

Guy chuckled.

"Someone more subdued than that. I think we have to nut this out with my Joshua. He's had a few lovers so he knows a bit about the subject."

"He's experienced. You're a lucky man both physically and emotionally."

"Emotionally, yes, but as yet, physically, no."

"What's wrong?"

"Oh nothing's wrong. He says he wants to wait. He has something special in mind."

We sat silent. I took a sip, and Guy followed my lead. The sultry singer was breathlessly interpreting "I Will Always Love You" by Dolly Parton while the lesbian couple slowly danced in front of the stage.

"This Joshua guy, he's an angel too?" I stopped watching the lovebirds. "I mean, he has to be. He was teaching you to fly once upon a time."

"Oh yes. He has the perfect wings and face and—"

"You've got it bad. So how come your parents didn't teach you to fly? My mum taught me to drive. Isn't it in the same ballpark?"

"We'll go into that the next time we have a drink together. For the time being, look after Wade and yourself. And Mannix of course. Everyone you meet is there for a reason."

"Like Maude, I guess. She is Maudi, isn't she?"

He winked.

"But don't tell her. She'll just think you're loony."

"I have and she already does." He shrugged. "Guy, it's really good to see you again. I've missed you."

"I've never been far away. All your angel paraphernalia can attest to that."

I grinned like someone truly loved. The singer's husky vocals continued a little longer before the bar, my guardian, and everyone around me faded to black.

I SKETCHED MANNIX'S head as carefully as I could. I didn't want to spend the class focusing on our object of desire's lower half, so I meticulously worked on what wasn't considered my strong point: faces. I began with the eyes. Those deep green eyes. Such a rare color on such a rare person.

I lightly slapped myself on the cheek. I was off in fairyland again and had to focus back on the task at hand. Ah yes, at hand. My fingers could explore that silky tuft of hair on Mannix's chest. Then my hand could cradle his neck as my tongue could take over massaging his chest.

"I'd double-check the shape of the eyes, Adam," my tutor said while wandering past.

How dare the teacher bring me back to earth? Now where was I? Ah yes, the eyes. Those stunning green eyes. Um, err, yes, the eyes. They were the wrong shape. I used an eraser and blended some of the lines with my finger. I looked up at Mannix who fixed his gaze back at me.

Ah yes, Mannix's eyes. His square jaw. His neck in a white collar. Mannix in uniform. A horseman. Gallantly storming into my native village on his stallion. I, naked, watched in eagerness. He wasn't not overly masculine, but he knew himself. He was confident. He saw me and pulled the reins. The horse slowed down and headed in my direction.

There were a few other naked men sitting on their porches watching the newcomer, but it was my turn to be treated by this stud. The others realized that today was not their day in the lottery of lust. My mysterious man in uniform was about to take his prize for the day. He was about to treat me to the secrets and the treasures that were waiting back at his manor.

"You want more than this, don't you?" he said. He was still mounted on his beast. "You want a new direction. A new thrill in life."

I nodded awkwardly. Mannix jumped off his steed, grabbed me under the arms, and threw me on the saddle. He leaped onto the horse with me and kissed me on the back of the neck. He dug in his spurs as the beast charged through the forest.

I had a date with destiny. A solid rocking on a horse if I could reach down...

Mannix didn't notice the mood change in the classroom. There were a few gasps and several friendly sniggers as the teacher headed toward him. But I was there first with my unfinished artwork in hand, covering the model's rather delighted member. I guess his fantasies were as raunchy as mine.

"Impressive," I whispered, and I wasn't merely being polite. Long, slender with a few faint purple veins to accent shape. Its head was a succulent rosy helmet.

Mannix went beetroot red, but I couldn't stop staring. Now everyone was dead silent to try to minimize the model's discomfiture. I wanted to applaud his party trick. He reached for his jeans and clumsily tried to put them on.

"Are you okay?"

He nodded, but as reality sunk in, he shook his head. I helped him with his jeans and T-shirt and escorted him out of the class. The lecturer called out something about it happening before once with a different model, but neither of us turned to listen. We went into the hallway. Soon the tutor joined us. He mentioned that it was best to "get back on the horse straight away"; otherwise, Mannix would fret about taking his clothes off next time. I smirked at the equine analogy.

"I promise I'll be fine next time," he replied.

"You can go back in and model with your clothes on if you like, or just topless," the teacher said.

"Is it okay if I go home? No need to pay me for this class."

"What will they sketch?"

"I reckon you could get Ian to take off his clothes," I suggested.

"I'm not sure if the class is ready for that. They need form, not fat."

I looked at the lecturer as if I had a wounded animal that needed nursing. He nodded.

"Well, I guess it's going to be me with my gear off. I've done it before in the name of art, though not in front of my own students. I guess it's a night of firsts."

We all smiled. Shortly after, I took Mannix back to my place.

Chapter Sixteen

IPAN

"How do you know they won't share their own special memories?" Farah asked.

I couldn't answer. She sat contentedly on my bed. I looked toward Earth through my telescope. I prized that telescope. It helped my mind either focus or wander as I needed. It took up most of my studio apartment, squeezing my single brass bed against one wall. It had been a long time since I slept in a bed made for two. In fact, it had been ages since I lived in accommodation built for two. I had walked out of our love nest with just a few clothes, the moment Rose moved on.

I was led to this place by my hot chocolate specialist, Sara. She took my hand one day as I numbed my sorrow with absentmindedness. My mumbling and half sentences streamed from me as my savior slowly walked with me through the Carnival of Lost Souls. She reached into her pocket and jiggled some keys before escorting me into the dusty hovel.

As I sat at an antique desk, I thumbed my way through two dusty piles of handwritten spells. Sara changed the sheets on the single bed. When I sat up to help, she laid her hands on my shoulders and gradually pushed me back onto the chair. I watched her polish obsessively, giving new life to the vintage furniture. I got up and stumbled around the room, trying to assist but not really knowing what to do. She ignored me. After a while, she left. I lay in bed, silent.

The next day I studied the various magic charms, carefully avoiding any hint of a love spell, and as the day wore on, I took in the fresh scent of gardenias from outside the one solitary window. I discovered weird little knickknacks on the shelves that matched the ingredients used in the various potions. Soon I appreciated the high timber ceiling that gave this limited space a sense of grandeur. I grew to like the neutral elegance of the white walls. I began to keep the one single blind open all the time to feel connected with the outside world.

Later in that week, the golden telescope was given as a gift from a blue-bearded neighbor. It takes pride of place in my abode. Everything else has been pushed against the walls to give *it* room.

"You haven't heard a word I've said, have you, dear?" Farah asked.

"Dear, I understand why you extended the spell to include Wade. In many ways, I feel that it was a good idea. It helps the couple work through this horrible dilemma together." I moved away from the eyepiece. "But who's there for Mannix?"

"Bruce, of course." Her kind tone did nothing to appease me. "And there's Adam and Wade. They're not a selfish couple. They're open."

"Well, they're learning to be more open than they've ever been before."

"And that's a bad thing because...?"

I joined Farah on the bed.

"And that's a bad thing because it may not work out for them."

"Darling, Adam and Wade are not silly young fools. They've been around the block, and considering their age, they've been around the park, the city center, and the outskirts as well. Neither of them is in love with Mannix. In fact, all of them are just experiencing a little sexual infatuation."

"Farah, are you considering that old devil called jealousy?"

"That's exactly what I considered when I cast my spell on Wade. To leave the spell as Fabien had left it would be irresponsible."

I felt the urge to argue my point further, but no words came to mind. She calmly gazed in my direction. I wandered back to the telescope and studied the mortal world once again.

Adam had brought Mannix home to the eager delight of his partner, and after the visitor took off his jacket, Wade hung it on their old-fashioned coat stand. He took Mannix by the hand and led him to the couch as Adam looked on, smiling fondly.

"I'm not sure I'm totally comfortable with what I'm seeing," I announced. But like a voyeur, I was glued to the eyepiece. "However, I do see your point. It's not the way I'd like things to be, but it's a fair point, nevertheless."

"Sweetheart, move away from the curiosities of earthly beings and come and sit next to me again. It's hard to reason with you when you're tied up in other people's affairs."

"They're pouring wine, Farah."

"So let them, in peace."

I looked away. This beautiful woman patted the bedspread next to her.

"What if it all falls apart? I have to keep watching."

"Trust me, it won't fall apart."

"How can you be sure?"

"Like I said, Mannix is in good hands. He's surrounded by two men who genuinely love each other. Nothing is going to tear them apart, not even a curious thirty-one-year-old."

She patted the bed once more. I clumsily parked myself next to her. She moved her hand tenderly toward mine, cupping my clenched fingers, which pushed on the quilt, supporting my posture.

"Now, my dear Ipan, what about us?" she whispered.

I didn't speak. I felt shame as the woman who nurtured me in recent times leaned forward with her eyes closed. A hazardous act. My body yearned for that kiss, and for a millisecond, I so desperately wanted to lose myself in her essence. My solemn lips met hers, but soon that millisecond stretched to an eternity. She puckered her lips, but mine never kissed back.

I cried. At first, it was just a whimper, but it gave way to an intense sob. Farah embraced me as my tears dribbled onto her shoulder. She held me tighter. I drifted into my own private world as evening fell on this district of lost souls.

Chapter Seventeen

MANNIX

An hour after I "rose to the occasion," I was chilled out on Wade and Adam's couch sipping Shiraz. Wade sat next to me, while Adam stretched on the floor like a cat waiting to be spoiled.

I wanted "little Mannix" to give an encore performance. I wanted Wade to place his hand on it while I kept eye contact with Adam, both of us entertaining him with a double act.

"You seem over your dilemma," said Adam.

"I think I can face the class again for my next shift."

"What happened?" asked Wade.

"I had a little incident during my modeling stint tonight."

"I'd say more than just a *little* incident," Adam teased. "You gave the class something interesting to draw."

"Ah," Wade replied. "Compass pointing north, was it?"

"North will never be the same in my books," said Adam. "One look at that compass and any sailor would be distracted."

"Okay, guys, you're making it harder for me to forget about it."

"So what was on your mind tonight?" asked Wade. "Or more to the point, who was on your mind?"

I couldn't answer. I lifted my glass and took a swig. How could I tell Wade that the reason I extended myself in class was because of a silly fantasy about his husband? Adam took the wine bottle from the table and topped up our glasses. I closed my eyes.

But there he was, latex mask and long black cape. Me, rubbery red top and nothing else. Batman and Robin. I tugged at the soft black leathery shorts that engulfed his perfectly shaped ass, as he helped me untie the laces in front. I looked at his thighs, wanting to cover them with my own juices, but not quite yet. As I pulled his shorts down, I stopped at the base of his cock and buried my face into the lustrous hairy patch that was there to entice me to seek the rewards down south.

"You have a right to avoid the question," said Adam.
He placed the wine bottle down.
"I think I've forgotten the question," I said.
"Who were you thinking about when you reached your full potential?"
"A gentleman never tells."
"Unless he has something to hide," said Wade.
"Like you said, Adam, I have the right to avoid the question."

The time passed. As we drank, flirtation became our social pastime. At certain stages, for the most insignificant reasons, Wade or Adam would steal a kiss from me, and of course, I thrived on the attention. Once, as Wade reached across to fill my glass, he supported himself with his hand on my knee. I returned the gesture by placing my own hand on Wade's. I stared at Adam and reached out with my other arm. Adam raised himself from the floor and cruised toward us.

He grasped my hand and reached for Wade's, and soon he gently guided us back to the floor. We sat in a circle. Our intoxication was at its peak.

First, the couple kissed. Mouth open but subtle. Loving. Their bodies instinctively moved with each other. An action carried out hundreds, maybe thousands of times before, yet each touch seemed new and fresh.

Adam nodded to his partner. Wade leaned over and reached around the back of my neck with both hands. He pulled me toward him. We kissed. I was a panting puppy in need of doggy action. A sniff here and there was what I needed, but Wade pulled away, leaving me wanting more.

Adam now leaned over, and I couldn't wait to continue. His lips wet mine with their tender touch. This was cloud nine. Blissful. Sexy. Cheeky. I breathed him in as my tongue entered his mouth with a will of its own. He tasted oh so good. I wanted to linger here in his spirit, taking more and more of him as every conceivable sexual position entered my mind. He pulled away.

Again, Wade and Adam turned to each other and kissed. Their passions heightened as their display got me hotter. They lost themselves as I caressed their backs. I didn't want to miss out. I massaged their shoulders and worked up to their necks. I watched them up close. I needed them. I placed my hands firmly on their chins and turned them toward me for a three-way kiss.

Our tongues danced as I took in their individual flavors. Adam tasted of spice. Exotic and delicious. Wade was stronger; more masculine. A sampler of flavors to come. He reached for my lower back, tracing his finger under my shirt. Leisurely, it moved just above my crack. Wade rubbed in small circles, teasing me while I let out a hungry purr while still engaging with Adam's luscious mouth.

Then I moved away.

"Guys, I have to go."

Before my hosts said a word, I stood up, forcing Wade to retract his hand. I rushed for the front door. The couple stumbled to their feet, looking awkward and confused.

"We can stop," said Adam.

He probably felt like he'd been practicing the rhythm method, stopping at the point of no return.

"It's not you guys. You haven't done anything wrong. I mean, I helped instigate this. No, it's okay. Can we talk about this later?"

"Can we talk about this now?" asked Wade.

I didn't answer. I stood near the door, distressed, waiting politely for my hosts to see me out. I had just switched from adoring minx to ice maiden. If I couldn't grasp my Jekyll and Hyde reactions, how could they?

"It's okay, Mannix," Adam said. "Whatever happened, we're sorry."

"No, I'm sorry. I'm so sorry. I led you guys on."

"Darl, we can talk?" asked Wade. "We don't have to go into territory that you're not comfortable with."

"Can we talk next time? Seriously, guys, I love you both, but I just would like to go."

"That's fine, darling. Are you still free for rehearsal at my place with Maude?"

"Of course. Wouldn't miss that for the world. I just need my space."

They opened the door, and both gave me an affectionate peck on the cheek. I got into my car but didn't turn on the engine. I questioned why I'd just walked out on the very thing I was after. I somehow got scared when Pandora's box was finally opened. What was happening to me? Sexually confident male turns to water during hot threesome action. This can't be right. Should I go back and try again?

They were still at the door watching me in my car. I had let them down. I had let myself down. What were they thinking? I must have been the class moron in their eyes. Or the class tease.

I looked back and nervously waved. They waved back. I started the engine and honked before driving away.

"I DIDN'T EXPECT you home," Bruce said.

He watched me throw myself on the lounge. I didn't reply. I glanced at him, turned away, and began rubbing my chin. I looked at him again.

He was reading the motorcycle magazine, *Wild Women on Wheels*. Well, he was admiring the pictures, anyway.

I liked our uncomplicated bachelor home life. I just wished my sex life was as uncomplicated.

"What's up?" he asked.

"Not sure."

"Have you seen another ghost, M?"

"May as well have."

"I'm taking a wild guess here, but I take it Adam was in class tonight."

"Uh-huh."

"And you fantasized about him again."

"Uh-huh."

"Mate, if I'm prying, I'll shut up and go back to my mag."

Bruce unfolded the centerfold. For the second time in months, he hit the jackpot. The model was nude!

"What am I doing, Bruce?"

He stared at Miss July. Thirty seconds past. Nothing was said. The model had a sleek black motorbike perched between her legs, with only a pair of glossy red stilettos to keep her warm. She fondled her peroxide hair while her mouth drew in a breath like she'd kicked the habit of smoking but still needed something poised on her lips.

"Bruce, really, what am I doing?"

"Not making much sense at the moment, M. That's what you're doing."

"Uh-huh."

"M, are you in love?"

"I'm in something, but it's not love."

"Lust?"

"No. If it was lust, then tonight wouldn't have been a problem." I stared into space. "Bruce, I think I've just got a dose of infatuation."

"Rewind. What happened tonight, M?"

"We all kissed."

"Here I am fantasizing about a woman in a magazine I'm never going to meet, while you've hit first base with two guys you're dying to bonk! What's the problem?"

"I'm not sure. They're a couple, and they're in love. But when I'm around, they're like two kids who are trying to impress the teen next door. They fuss, they study each other for reactions, they compete a bit when it comes to seduction..."

"M, they're two gay guys. I think they know what bits go in where."

"Yeah, with each other. What if I break them up?"

"Was there jealousy tonight?"

"No."

"So what went wrong?"

"I went wrong."

Bruce flung his magazine on the coffee table and sat next to me on the couch.

"You chickened out, M."

I stared into space again. After ten seconds, I nodded.

"I never thought I'd see the day when Romeo lost his mojo," said Bruce. I looked at him. "Actually, mate, I take that back. You haven't lost your mojo. Otherwise, these guys would have lost interest. You're just in uncharted waters."

"In what way?"

"I've seen you long for guys and girls like I long for that nude chick in my magazine. Other times, you're careful, like me when I meet girls like the one in my magazine. But at this point, you're uncertain, like I feel when I've laid my best line on *that* type of girl and she looks at me like I'm a try-hard."

"I know what to do in a threesome."

"In theory, not in practice."

I got up and headed for the kitchen sink. I filled a glass with water and sat against the cabinet. Bruce joined me in the kitchen. I drank my water.

"M, you're teasing them."

"No, I'm not!"

"Mate, you're giving the signals, but you're not delivering."

"Maybe I'm not ready."

"Then don't act like you are!"

I filled my glass a second time.

"They're just as much to blame, Bruce."

"How, M? Did they lead you into their playpen, then lock up all the toys?"

"Yes, they led me into their playpen."

"And *you* ran off with the toys."

I grunted. I couldn't argue so I grunted. Bruce was no fool. Girls he longed for treated him the same way. They promised a garden of earthly delights, then locked the gate. For me, it was different. Girls and boys liked me. If one potential one-nighter didn't come through, there'd be easy pickings within my own sex. Couldn't Adam and Wade find another plaything if they were desperate to experiment?

"Maybe I shouldn't see them, Bruce."

"But you're in Adam's play."

"Oh, yeah."

I sipped more water.

"M, make up your mind. Either throw caution to the wind and bonk these guys or stop leading them on. But if I were you, mate, I'd stop fart-assing around and just do it. You're trying to be the stud, but tonight it backfired on you—yet it's every male's fantasy to go three-way. And yes, I know I'm not bi or gay, but seriously, I'd lay bets on the fact that a threesome, a foursome, and perhaps even a tensome is definitely a fantasy among guys who like guys." I sniggered guiltily. "You know I'm right. Even if you need more to drink, just go there. Otherwise, stop making these guys feel they're in with a chance."

"Maybe I have a fear of success. If I go through with it, what is there to long for?"

"Go through with it, M, and the fear will be gone. It's like those characters you keep going on about. Sometimes you're the hedonistic dude out for a good time, like Fabien. Then you're the loving, caring, sharing one, like Farah. And then you go all frigid like Ipan. For god's sake, you're not an old man yet. Stop being a prick tease!"

Chapter Eighteen

ADAM

He had the perfect V-shaped torso. The kind that would turn on a dozen potential lovers if he wandered into a gay bar. And while his faultless crew cut was artificially red, his other natural features were as intense as James Dean's. I could go riding in his sports car, feeling the breeze as we headed to Lover's Lane. He'd admire me with his penetrating eyes before undressing me for a lovemaking session so powerful not even a night with a handpicked selection of porn stars would compare.

But unlike anyone I'd ever met, he was blessed with soft charcoal-colored wings. This was Guy's boyfriend, Joshua. I was back at that thespian drinking haven, the Pedestal, at some stage between going to bed and waking up the next morning.

I tried not to drool at this bad boy, while picturing myself taking off his well-fitted leather jacket, slowly. I wanted to let out an orgasmic moan, before any foreplay had begun.

"I think you need to sleep with Mannix," he said.

He sipped on a Bloody Mary.

"Joshua!" his loving partner reprimanded.

"Joshua, we tried," I said.

"And what happened, sweetheart?"

"He freaked out. He gives us all the signals and then runs off in terror."

"Tsk, tsk. Now why would he do that? You're not exactly on the ugly scale."

"Thanks," I replied. "I think."

"Joshua, that's not the issue here," Guy said. "I've been watching over them, and they're getting obsessed with Mannix. And just as odd, Mannix is obsessed with them. It doesn't make sense."

"What's there to make sense of, Petal? They're grown men looking for a bit of spice. This Mannix dude is the spice. Supply and demand. No problem."

"But Guy has a point," I said. "This is doing my head in. One minute, Wade and I are respectable grown men, the next we're one step away from toupees and face-lifts."

"And is this causing you two to argue? Fight? Split up?"

"Strangely, no."

I picked up my cocktail, resting the top of the glass on my lower lip before sipping slowly.

"Joshua, it's still causing drama," continued Guy. "Adam and Wade have their heads in no-man's-land, and Mannix is just as bemused."

"Oh my darlings, they're men. Adult men. Every one of them. That which doesn't kill them will make them stronger. Or separated but I can't see any hint of that. Can you, Adam?" I nodded tensely. "There, you see, Guy? It might be causing a bit of grief, but in the end, they're men. Once they stop questioning it with their emotions, they'll solve it physically and wonder why they didn't get down and dirty sooner."

I sat with the two angels, none the wiser. That dark-skinned woman was back onstage. Sultry jazz was her genre of choice today, and her small ensemble cruised into mellow tones that could set you adrift on a small boat. As she crooned the first lines of "Someone to Watch Over Me," Guy sang the words with her under his breath.

Around me, the mismatched furniture complemented the mismatched cast. A lone African woman, wearing more colors than a peacock's tail, stood transfixed as if the singer was secretly robbing her soul. Her fingers tapped on an imaginary piano, and her wide-eyed stare gave me goose bumps.

An old lady, dressed in clothes her own granddaughter would wear, clutched her wine glass like it was a precious jewel. At the same time, she gazed into the eyes of a mature athletic man who looked like he once had a passion for ballet dancing. Their loving gaze reminded me of the way Wade sometimes looked at me.

"So, Joshua, you think we're making too much of a big deal about this?"

He rubbed the tip of his sculptured jawline as Guy casually leaned toward him.

"Adam, darling, there are men who put themselves through hell and back trying to do the right thing. They won't act until they work out all the final consequences. And let's face it, as much pontificating as humanly possible is not ever going to let you know the final outcome, really! And there are men who are a lot more spirited and take life as a challenge. Go forth and take the risk and see where it leads you."

"Joshua, Adam understands that," Guy said. "But there's Wade to consider. What if their marriage falls apart?"

"Darling, seriously. From what you've told me, they're not going to fall apart. It's all just a bit of fun. Mannix is a new appliance, like a fridge or a vibrator. Something that has a use. And think, Adam. Think of the uses you can come up with, for your new appliance."

"Joshua, this is no laughing matter. I asked you here for a second opinion. Let's face it, you've had more sordid relationships than a priest, so I thought you could shed some light on this."

"I thought I was."

"Well, I don't see your point."

I watched these two argue. It reminded me of the early days when Wade and I were first sussing each other out. We'd see what we could say or do to test each other's boundaries. Boundaries we both knew we would eventually push. In time, these angels would get to know each other better, though at this stage I wasn't quite sure *I* was *getting* Joshua.

"Guy," he said, "think about yourself when we first met as teenagers. You were like Adam back then. You had no one to teach you how to fly, and I tried to lend a helping hand. In the end, I gave up. Not because I didn't believe in you. It's because you didn't believe in yourself."

"You don't think I believe in myself?" I asked.

"Adam, I'm saying that *both* you and Wade don't believe in yourselves. Mannix as well. You think you're on shaky ground, but you're not. You're men. Trust me, you won't fail if you all take a stand and decide to do it. No ifs. No buts. No maybes."

The old couple started to rhumba as if they'd learned their steps from a bad 1980s dance film. Onstage, our statuesque entertainer gave us a breathy rendition of "Sexual Healing."

I shook my head while admiring my drinking buddies' striking wings. I was sitting here with real angels. Wow! And one of them almost never took flight. That was like a Mormon not preaching.

"So, Guy, how come your parents never taught you to fly?"

Guy looked to Joshua who shrugged.

"You may as well tell him," he said. "It's not like he's going think less of you."

I sat up with interest. Guy had an uncertain smile.

"I never knew my parents."

"What? You were an orphan?" I asked. "No, wait, you couldn't be. Angels don't die. At least I think they don't. You're heavenly creatures."

There was silence.

"Adam, they were banished," replied Joshua. "He was brought up by a family friend."

"Why were they banished?"

"I wish I knew," Guy replied.

This fragile angel eased against his boyfriend, who in turn wrapped an arm around him. I had spoken out of turn. It was the last thing I wanted to do as I loved my guardian angel, even if I didn't know what to make of Joshua.

I grinned at my celestial companions as the scene faded to black.

Chapter Nineteen

FABIEN

Let's get real here. There were more sides to this story than a day in divorce court. And even then, this scenario couldn't have been more tedious. First, there was Ipan and Farah, obviously in love but too dim-witted to see it. If I had to deal with that stupid moralizing old fart again, I swore I'd cast an impotence spell on him!

Plus, there were the three grown horny men not getting it on with each other. Please! What alternate universe was this? I had to up the ante on what had become a placid magic charm.

I headed for my pantry for spices that could heat up these men's waning passions. I took out a container of ground fennel seeds and gave it a sniff. The smell was almost aniseed, like various liquors frequently favored by teenagers. The preferred "rite of passage" in discovering alcohol. Maybe a sprinkle over my models of Adam and Mannix might take them back to a time when sexual discovery was the other "rite of passage." I realized quickly that this connection was way too obscure. What if it just made them crave licorice? Or better still, made them alcoholics?

Then there was the ground allspice. This was a very masculine odor, reminiscent of sandalwood. But these men were already attracted to the scent of men. How could allspice add to their appeal? I put it aside and continued searching.

I found dried thyme leaves and garlic granules. Flavors one adds to a Sunday roast. Succulent aromas would be brought to mind. Adam could relish the taste against Mannix's skin, while memories of weekend pleasures would infiltrate his senses. But these luscious flavors might simply stir hunger pains.

Adding ingredients was not the answer. There was already cayenne pepper and ground chili powder for passion, and other sweet spices for attraction. The answer lay in lust.

I closed the pantry door and made my way to the bookcase. There weren't many books, just three traditional leather-bound editions on magic spells and a journal with scribbled notes written in pencil. I reached for the journal, then sat at my desk to skim its pages.

It was a log of love spells, which had once belonged to Rose. It was the one item I'd asked Ipan for once she left the Afterlife. Rose was very much into the ways of love, even though she was committed to Ipan. Both would take pleasure in sweet spells that created love in a troubled world. I wasn't sure if I could expect to find a stronger charm for attraction within its pages, so I read the index.

The gentle persuasion spell. The nymph's desire spell. Cupid's love spell. Pan's playing for pleasure spell. The seven-year itch spell. The snake in Eden spell.

At first glance, I considered Pan's pleasure spell and the snake in Eden. The nymph's spell was very similar to what I already used on the two unsuspecting men, which only made them long for each other with no end result. I read the snake spell. That seemed to be the one. Adam's midlife crisis would be more tragic than an aging movie star still playing action heroes.

But there was a problem. It made no sense to put them both under this spell. If Adam got hornier, Wade would yield the benefits. But if Mannix was the sole receiver of this magic charm, on top of the desire spell already in place, his increased libido would cause all sorts of delicious dramas. Adam was in for one hell of a seduction.

The snake in Eden spell needed a snake, to point out the bleeding obvious, and a quick visit to the markets near Ipan would help me in my quest. Patrick's stall was the perfect place for odd ingredients. He carried a few snakes in specially designed glass jars with air holes. Although several seemed the perfect size, if you were implying snakes were a phallic symbol, it was a small lime-colored reptile that caught my attention. He was the perfect green-eyed monster. I brought him home and in no time was bringing the other ingredients together.

In a pot of boiling water, I added ground turmeric, cumin, and a teaspoon of ground vanilla. Next was the snake. It quivered in delicious fear as I held it over the boiling pot. I let it go. Its body melted, infusing with the other elements. I stirred before adding the last ingredient, a splash of aftershave lotion. The spell called for the fragrance that depended on the sex you are trying to court. As Mannix was bisexual, I wanted to make sure it was Adam he would conquer, and not one of Bruce's rejects.

A spine-chilling holler came from the pot. It looked back at me with eyes as evil as a murderer's. An ear-piercing roar followed as I was thrown back against the wall, not from the sound, but from breath so lethal it could've euthanized a small nation.

"Who has summoned me?" the monster shrieked.

His newfound pudgy legs reached over the cooking vessel and placed themselves on the ground.

"Fabien, warlock extraordinaire, begging for your service, sir."

"Warlock extraordinaire? You look like a scared child to me!"

"You startled me, oh great one. Mere fright, I assure you."

"Whatever." This loathsome reptile dismissed me with one gesture of its tail. "Now judging from the crap in this pot, you need to drench someone in unearthly desire."

"I need to strengthen a spell I've cast."

"And who's about to bite the apple?"

"A young man who needs closure. His name is Mannix."

I gestured to my models of the two men suffering unrequited desire.

"Do you understand the consequences of what you are doing, Fabien?"

"Do you think I don't know what I'm doing?"

"Don't answer a question with a question, Fabien. I'm here because you feel you need me. I can always refuse your request."

At this point, I wanted to tear this reptilian bore apart. But I resisted and thought of the lustful infamy Mannix could achieve.

"Dear snake, the man is in love but ever so shy. He needs to express his wishes on the man he desires."

The creature nodded again, before waving his small limbs around in the air like a frantic conductor. Neon-blue bolts zapped from his fingers to add drama to his already pompous theatrical dialogue. He faced the heavens with his eyes closed.

"All the mysterious shadows who pull the strings of your earthly marionettes, help Mannix find his true nature. Let him dance in desire and frolic with those frisky. Let him overcome his fears and understand the true nature of passion."

One more loud bolt echoed through my tent as I crashed to the floor like a majestic tree fallen victim to a woodcutter's axe. As the vibrations passed, my scared little snake wriggled around in a puddle of water. I tried to reach for it, but it jolted toward my bed. I grasped it below its head and returned this once dominating creature back to its jar.

I sat, smirking proudly to myself. I had just upped the ante on a lame spell. No wishy-washy outcomes. No polite gentlemen worried over broken hearts. Just pure lust with Mannix as my messenger.

Chapter Twenty

ADAM

"So what is going on, Wade?"

I tried to read a book in bed, but I couldn't concentrate.

"You could only be talking about one thing, Adam. If we could harness the energy we spend thinking about Mannix, we could power our apartment for a year."

"Is it us? Are we looking for new adventures?"

My partner raised his head from his pillow. "Of course not. If we were, we would have gone looking for action long before we met Mannix."

"Yeah, that's the way I see it. Then was he looking for us? A couple to start exploring with?"

"Perhaps? But then why did he run away the other night?"

"Maybe he wants one of us more than he wants the other?"

Wade sat up. He observed the stars outside our window for a while before turning to me.

"Nah, Adam. We'd pick up on that. Mannix is making advances to both of us. We saw that the other night. And don't forget that toiletry bag he left in the bathroom earlier that same evening. We both saw it, unzipped with a packet of condoms sitting on top. Ribbed ones too. It's something he wanted both of us to see."

"Perhaps he's just a tease?"

"Maybe? I hope not."

"Or perhaps he's too scared to have a threesome? Maybe we think he's a stud muffin, but he's just a frustrated donut."

"Now I know you're overanalyzing, Adam."

"Okay, not a donut. A frustrated..."

"A frustrated young man, exploring the world on his terms. And we have to do our best not to get too caught up in his actions."

I leaned over and fondly kissed my husband.

"Wade, when did we become those older gay guys we used to look up to when we were young?"

"Sometime between dance clubs and real estate."

We chuckled. I kissed him as his cheerful expression gave me the confidence to mention something I'd been putting off.

"Guy has been in my dreams again, twice."

"Isn't it Mr. Guy?"

"He told me I was too old to call him Mister."

"And you've dreamed of him twice?"

"Yes. I didn't want to tell you because it sounded loony."

"Adam, I live with dozens of angels in our apartment. I already know you're loony."

"Thanks!"

"You know I'm joking."

"I even met his boyfriend."

"A gay angel. How convenient. What's his boyfriend like?"

"The verdict's still out on that one."

"Well, Adam, all I'll say is that he's obviously here for a reason. Not everyone knows an angel."

I smiled, admiring my loving husband. My reading lamp cast a shadow behind him, projecting a silent guardian who watched over me, making sure I would come to no harm. I kissed him. His nose brushed against mine as those lips I had tasted a thousand times reminded me that whatever the dilemma, the end tale was about Adam and Wade.

THE NEXT NIGHT I caught up with our object of desire and decided not to ask what went wrong. I had a few scenes to rehearse at home with just him and Maude; an obsession to explore with their fictional characters, rather than in our personal lives.

"Three aces or a royal flush?" said Maude as Angela.

She sprawled on our couch with her shoes off and a gin and tonic in hand. Mannix stood in front of her. Neither were in their period costume.

"What do you mean by the poker reference, Angela?"

"You seem to hold your cards close to your chest."

"How so?"

They didn't move. Ronny was in his comfort zone, not making direct eye contact with her. Angela sipped her drink, weighing up the best way to express herself.

"You hint at a chance to get neighborly, then retract the offer when I'm willing to use the gift voucher."

"We're good neighbors. We have an excellent relationship."

"But you know and I know, we both want more."

"In what regard?" replied Ronny, acting dumb.

Angela undid the top two buttons of her blouse.

"Good tension," I said.

"How should Ronny react to Angela undoing her buttons?" asked Mannix.

"What's your own gut instinct as Ronny?"

"I think Ronny is scared."

"Of what?"

"Of putting his foot in it."

"So what is Ronny's worst-case scenario?" I asked.

"That..." Mannix paused. "That there are repercussions if the husband finds out."

"What might happen if he finds out?"

"He'd be responsible for breaking up a marriage. Plus, Ronny is not the type of guy who deals with confrontation. Chances are the husband would punch him out."

"And what would Mannix do in this situation?" was the question on the tip of my tongue. I glanced at Maude. She glanced back, subtly winking so that only I would see.

"Are you interested in Angela?" I asked.

"God yes!" the young actor blurted with more eagerness than Donald Trump in a wig shop.

"How do you feel about her?" Maude asked.

"She's a mystery that Ronny wants to explore. No. She's more than that. She's experience. She's experience that Ronny desperately feels he should explore, but he doesn't want her to know he's inexperienced."

"Why is that an issue?" I asked.

"It's an issue because..." Mannix paused again.

"Don't you think Angela would consider his inexperience? After all, she'd be expecting it."

"I think it's something Ronny doesn't want to admit to himself. He wants sex with Angela, but maybe he wants it to happen just like in his fantasies? He's in control. There's no fallout. They live happily ever after. But in life, I mean, in this scenario with Angela, there are too many uncertainties."

"Nothing ventured, nothing gained," I said.

Maude looked down her nose at me.

"So, Adam, should I play Ronny as eager? Out to recklessly give into Angela's seductive ways?"

"You're just as seductive, my dear fellow," noted Maude.

"Yes, you are," I confirmed. "But in this scene, I want you to play all of that ambivalence we just talked about. Let it all go through your head as you say the lines."

Maude buttoned up her blouse as I refilled her pretend gin and tonic with soda water and ice. Mannix placed his finger gently on his bottom lip before slipping into character.

"Three aces or a royal flush?" Maude said as Angela.

She was more direct this time.

"What do you mean by the poker reference?" Ronny replied. He lowered his gaze.

"You seem to hold your cards close to your chest."

She stared seductively at the bubbles in her cocktail.

"How so?"

This time, Angela kept her eyes on her drink.

"You hint at a chance to get neighborly." She met his eyes. "Then you retract the offer when I'm willing to cash in my gift voucher."

Ronny paused. "We're good neighbors. We have an excellent relationship."

"But you know and I know, we both want more."

"In what regard?" replied Ronny. He let out a silent breath.

Angela casually put down her drink, before releasing the top two buttons of her blouse, slower than in the last rehearsal.

I nodded.

"That was so much better," I said.

Several more scenes were rehearsed that day but nothing too raunchy. We had open discussions on motivation, playing with Angela's slow-paced seduction and Ronny's gradual release from inner fear.

Eventually Maude bid farewell for the day while Mannix stayed behind to help me tidy up. We both picked up several bottles and glasses that had been used as props and strolled into the kitchen.

As I emptied ice cubes into the sink, Mannix clutched my shoulders with both hands and yanked me toward his lips. He kissed me like a lover going away on a business trip. I made a sound like a wounded ox, so he pulled away.

"That's the most brazen you've been at coming forward while we've both been sober. Was something said today that turned you on?"

"Adam, I'm just seizing the moment."

"Bad moment, Mannix. Wade's not home."

"Maybe it's the perfect moment?"

"Mannix, Wade's not home."

He let go of my shoulders.

"I'm sorry. I should have known better."

"Mannix, I'm flattered, but I'm not going to play behind—"

The aspiring actor lurched at me once again, this time with mouth open while pulling me toward him with my collar. My pained expressions turned to groans. I opened my mouth and let in the young man's delicious tongue. I tasted him, drinking in his scent. The beautiful male I had longed for was now right here for the taking, without Wade's feelings to consider.

Mannix reached for the bottom of my shirt without intruding on our feverish kiss. I moved my mouth to savor his neck, before licking my way down to his divine chest. He now pulled at the shirt harder, forcing it up over my head. I grabbed his hand just as he was about to drop it to the floor.

"Mannix, we can't."

"Yes, we can, Adam."

"The hell we can!"

"Adam, come on. Let's just do it."

"Mannix, what's come over you?"

"You, hopefully."

"Mannix!"

I grabbed my shirt from him and quickly put it back on. Mannix's head drooped.

"It's okay, Mannix. Well, it's not okay, but it's okay now."

"I'm so sorry, Adam."

"No, seriously, Mannix, it's okay."

"No, it isn't, Adam. I am truly sorry. Forgive me."

"I have."

"Not yet, you haven't."

The young man took a breath before heading out of the kitchen and toward the front door.

"Mannix, don't just leave again!"

"I shouldn't be here, Adam."

"Oh for goodness sake, Mannix, it's okay. You know I want it as well, but just not without my Wade."

But the front door slammed halfway through my sentence. I was going to run after my confused friend, but I just stayed in the kitchen, letting out an audible gulp. A minute passed before I collected ice from the freezer and plonked the cubes into a short glass. I liberally poured vodka before topping the drink off with a dash of cranberry juice.

As I sipped, I considered what I was going to tell Wade. How could I phrase this in a way that wouldn't alter our friendship with Mannix? Would Wade feel left out, or would he see this as a positive step into getting our young friend to bed? Perhaps some things were better left unsaid until the time was right.

I looked at the wall clock and realized that Wade would be home from work in half an hour. I didn't want this to play on my mind all night, but at this stage, I didn't want to talk it over with Maude either. It could change the subtext between the fictional characters my two friends were playing.

I decided to keep it to myself until I saw Mannix at rehearsal the next night, if he showed up. It was something we had to sort out between ourselves.

Chapter Twenty-One

IPAN

The man in the mirror stared back at me. His weary eyes were stretched in all directions by his bony fingers, trying to smooth out his melancholy wrinkles. What a sad old sod he'd become, trying to live in the past. His hands moved away from his face as he searched for meaning in that wretched body.

A living corpse, with joints as rigid as a tree whose only use was to be turned into matchsticks. I looked into my palm. Roadmaps to nowhere spread without purpose. I couldn't run from my reflection.

Someone knocked with a polite tone on my door.

"Who is it?" I called.

"Someone who cares for you," Farah replied.

I opened the door. There she was. My closest friend in a simple lilac dress. How uncomplicated she was. Not an ounce of pretense on her kind face, and not a brush of makeup to mask its beauty.

She breezed in like she'd come home. Her long red locks bounced on her back, inviting me to hide in their strands and seek refuge like a miniature doll veiled from a world that made no sense. I'd stay until her motherly charm helped me find the adult I once was. The adult who could steer my course bravely and not hide in the dwelling of a broken soul.

"What are the boys up to?" she asked. I was puzzled. "The boys. Mannix, Adam, and Wade."

"I've stopped spying."

Farah studied my face.

"But you were obsessed. Did they finally make love?"

"I don't know."

She took my hand and carefully led me to the single bed. As we sat, she let go and steadily rubbed her palm against my forearm.

"What's the matter, Ipan?"

"I had to get away for a while. Sort myself out."

"Oh, I see. I called in a few times to check on you but thought I just missed you. I wandered through the neighborhood for an hour once, thinking you'd return."

"I'm sorry, Farah. After your last visit, I was immensely confused, so I drifted. Just drifted. No destination. No plans."

"You didn't pack?"

"I didn't know I'd be gone for that long."

"Who is she?" Farah stopped rubbing my arm and clutched it firmly instead.

"No. No. No. There's no one."

My kind friend closed her eyes and smiled.

"Where did you go, my love?"

"The Limelight Quarter. The Ancient Sector. I just kept wandering."

"Looking for Rose?"

"I know she's been reborn back into the world, but it doesn't stop me searching."

Farah leaned against me, resting her head on my shoulder. Her hair had a vanilla scent. I yearned to be younger, rolling in a poppy field naked with her. A guitar would strum, enchanting a trio of mischievous pixies to twirl and sway for the cosmic gods.

"Did you meet anyone interesting on your travels?" she asked.

"An angel with whom I shared a drink."

"You were blessed to share such company, Ipan."

"He seemed to know who I was and that I was missing someone. We sat in the most eccentric bar."

"Eccentric?"

"Full of dramatic types. They even called the bar the Pedestal."

"In the theater district, no doubt."

"Yes. The good old Limelight Quarter. He was tall with beautiful dove-gray wings, which reached taller than himself. After he let me talk about Rose, he told me how important *I* was. That people like me help other lost souls find their path. I thought it was all a little obscure. I mean, I'm the lost soul here. Who can I help?"

"What else did he say?"

"That some of us are created for this world to nurture others. To speak on their behalf. Help them move on. I suppose I was here to help Rose find her path back to Earth."

"Are you sure that's what he meant?" Farah asked. She sat up.

"Darling, he's an angel. When does anyone fully understand what angels are talking about? Same old riddles, leaving us to figure it out."

She kissed me on the cheek. I treasured her warm lips. "Maybe *I'm* in need of getting onto the right path, Ipan?"

"No. I think that's your job for the moment. To get me back on the right path."

Her fingers glided over the coarse surface of my red jacket. She pulled me closer to her lips. We briefly kissed.

"Your charming old-world wisdom needs to be set free from its solitude." she said.

"There's too much pain to wipe away."

"Baby steps."

I hugged her like Adam, too scared to make a move. She pressed her supple cheek against mine. I wrapped my arms around her to cocoon us from this dark world.

My protective desire to keep an eye on earthly beings had vanished. We had our own lives to lead and our own longed-for passions to explore.

Chapter Twenty-Two

MANNIX

"I've made a fool of myself," I said.

We strolled to a spare table in our favorite pub.

"I know where this is heading, M," Bruce replied. "Let me buy the first round."

I was still shaken from my failed seduction attempt on Adam several hours earlier. I tapped my fingers on the table before realizing that I was annoying the other drinkers.

Had those other drinkers ever felt like I felt? Of course not. This was a man's pub. No pretense, no makeovers. Just sticky carpet and furniture that was cheap and comfortable. None of these jokers would be drawn to a male couple.

A father and son, both in blue overalls, bonded over a beer at the bar. Imagine the son turning to his dad and saying that he wanted to bonk two of his mates. Any dreams of becoming a grandfather would be just that, a dream.

And there was that old codger counting out his meager pension. If he ever was attracted to his own sex, he would have experimented long before his addiction to loneliness.

Loud talk about girlfriends came from two half-tanked pals drinking scotch on the rocks. The blond was mouthing off about a head job he once had while his dark-haired mate sat motionless like a glazed ham. Nope, they definitely weren't going to hit up any gay guys soon.

Bruce proudly returned with two icy beers.

"You didn't run from Adam and Wade again, did you?"

"Not quite. In some way, I led a full-scale attack," I replied.

"What? They didn't reciprocate?"

"I sort of did a one on one."

"Adam or Wade?"

"Well..."

"You know I'm against you trying a one on one. Don't be the guy that splits them up." Bruce took a sip and then wiped the froth from his upper lip. "Besides, every gay couple must fantasize about a threesome at least once in their lives. God, most straight men do. This can't be a big deal if you play your cards right."

"If I play my cards right?"

"Just watch them both carefully for hints of jealousy. If one of them feels left out, plant a lingering kiss on the one missing out. I've never done this, but I'm sure common sense comes into play."

We stopped talking. I felt like I was being watched. The two guys drinking scotch were looking in our direction.

"I've done this. I can give you some pointers," the blond called out.

I invited him over with a hand gesture. My new adviser grabbed his drink, took a few steps, and stood behind Bruce, gripping the back of his chair.

"I'm making an assumption, but is this a bisexual thing? Like, is it a girl and guy who want to sleep with you?"

"No. Two guys."

"A long-term couple or a new fling?"

"Long-term."

"I see. Is it both their idea or just one?"

"Both."

The guy sat himself at our table. Bruce rolled his eyes so that only I could see. The dark-haired one got up, wandered over, and stood behind me.

"You haven't slept with one of them already?" the blond one asked.

I didn't answer. I cowardly picked up my glass and drank half my beer.

"M, which one?" Bruce asked coldly.

I still found it hard to reply.

"My guess is it's the one you're more sexually attracted to, rather than emotionally attracted to," alleged our standing ally.

"It's Wade, isn't it?" my flatmate asked.

My lips tightened.

"M, it's the way you talk about them individually. Together they're their own entity. Separately, Wade is the one you lust over and Adam is the one you want to make love to." Bruce gave me two playful slaps on the cheek before addressing the brown-haired expert. "But that doesn't make sense. Wouldn't Adam, who M dreams to have a romantic night with, be the first cab off the rank?"

"It's all about the quickie," our consultant replied. "It's a lot easier to give into mutual sexual attraction than mutual emotional attraction. The latter has too many variables in the mix, while the former is a sure thing."

"I just tried to fix things," I said.

"You didn't tell Adam, did you, M?"

"No. I sprung myself on him instead."

"And it backfired?"

"Uh-huh."

The brunette pulled up a chair as Bruce and our new acquaintances prepared themselves for all the sordid details.

TWO DAYS BEFORE, I called in to see Adam and rehearse my scenes. Maude couldn't make it there that day, although I can't remember why, so it was just going to be us two and possibly Wade.

For some reason, I wanted to look my best. I even gelled my hair, but when one strand refused to stay down, I took a pair of scissors and cut it off. I didn't normally care that much about the way I looked, but it was like I was going on the most important date I've ever been on.

I knocked on their door, eager to pick up acting tips while dying to play out my fantasies through my fictional character. For several days, my daydreams had become more severe. In fact, they were hallucinogenic.

In the first one, I was dressed in a white shirt and red tie, with jeans and thin-rimmed glasses. The newspaper had sent me to the jungle to find the man who had been raised by apes. From below, I watched Adam in his tan loincloth, swinging between trees on a vine. His cock looked down at me from under the fabric.

Then he scooped me up without warning—his knob moist. It stained my jeans, but I didn't care. The wet patch got warmer as my denim rubbed him to attention.

We landed in his tree house. He offered me some coconuts and a banana. My hunger needed to be rewarded.

Wade answered the door and apologized to me for Adam's absence. He was still caught up at art class and was going to be home in about half an hour.

"Red wine," Wade asked. "I've just opened a bottle."

"As long as it doesn't impair my acting skills."

"One glass should be okay. Just sip it slowly."

I hung my jacket on their antique coat hanger near the front door. I could smell something tasty roasting in the oven. I let my last ounce of testosterone slip away by prancing through their lounge room, following Wade into the kitchen.

"You've got a spring in your step. Did you just get laid?"

"I wish. No, I'm not sure what the reason is. Just looking forward to rehearsing, I guess."

I must have sounded like a real loser.

Wade grabbed a glass and poured the merlot. As I reached for the wine, I became fixated with his hand passing me the glass. A strong hand. One that could grip firmly where it counted. One that could tug on anyone, making them groan, as he looked you in the eye and demanded action.

See! Even now just talking about it, I'm getting worked up on the most trivial things. A hand, for goodness sake!

"Why is Adam held up at art class?" I asked. "Did another model get an erection?"

"I'm not sure. He rang before and said he was held up. Something about staying back to master outlining necks. He was complaining his looked more like tree trunks."

"He could give his models wooden expressions."

"Maybe even birds-nest hairdos."

Wade gestured toward the lounge so we drifted in that direction. I sat down and let out a relieved sigh. Just out of the blue. It was as if I'd stimulated all my G-spots at the same time. Wade was turned on by my moan and with his masculine hand reached out for mine, nestling it between his palms.

"What was that groan all about, Mannix?"

"Frustration."

"About the play?"

"No. I've been weirdly turned on by everything. No matter how trivial."

"Like what?"

"Hand towels. The rolling pin. Household taps. Umbrellas. Even my collectible *Star Wars* figurines!"

"Are you thinking of getting it on with Han Solo?"

"Trust me, my hands *have* been working solo a lot lately. No, it's Artoo-Detoo. That little toy is just the right size to get up to all sorts of mischief."

"Just don't end up in the emergency ward with your X-rays posted on the internet."

I laughed before groaning again, making Wade strengthen the grip on my hand.

"Wade, even you holding my palm is turning me on."

I planted a kiss on this hot unsuspecting man. Wade seemed to hold back. I'm sure he felt guilty, so I went in for the kill. I slowly stood up, encouraging Wade to follow. My tongue pushed against his lips so Wade opened his hungry mouth.

It was better than I imagined. I was even hoping that Adam would come home, disrupting us like a teacher finding some naughty school kids, adding to the heat. He'd wander in and forget about discipline.

"Mannix."

"Call me Frank."

"Frank?"

"It's my first name. Mannix is my middle name."

We kissed a little more.

"But why...?"

"I like Mannix more than Frank. But when I'm about to lose myself, I'm Frank."

"Am I about to explore your alter ego?"

"If you stop talking long enough, you will."

I let out another breathless sigh and beat my chest Tarzan style. Wade slowly drew me onto the floor and lay on top of me, kissing me passionately while running his fingers through my hair. I kept moaning, even with Wade's probing tongue in my mouth.

"Did Adam catch you?" Bruce asked.

"Of course not. I left before he got home."

"But what about the rehearsal?"

"I've been avoiding his calls."

Our two new drinking buddies gave me a congratulatory pat on the back. Bruce's eyes widened.

"Man, from what I gather, this dude ain't gonna tell his partner," said the blond one. "Just don't go there again."

"But what if Adam says something to Wade about me cracking onto him?"

"There's no guarantee Wade will tell Adam about your Technicolor raunch session," said Bruce. "Guilt is a powerful emotion."

"Even so, mate, don't see them again," advised the brown-haired one.

"I'm a nude model in Adam's art class. That's how we met. We're going to see each other again at some stage, anyhow. Maybe I should be the one to tell Adam?"

"No," the others shrieked in unison.

"M, as much as you were the catalyst for jumping Wade's bones, this is not about you anymore." Bruce sipped his beer before sitting silent. I waited on the edge of my seat for his voice of reason. "Mate, this is all about Adam and Wade. Adam may never find out. Wade might take this to his grave. But if he doesn't, keep out of the firing line."

"Bruce, my nude modeling, remember? Adam is still a student, and I need the cash. I'll be right up there in that firing line!"

"Oh yes, M. It is still about you. Did Adam nearly give in when you tried it with him?"

"A little."

"I like your approach, man," the blond butted in. "Do the do with the other one. They can both have their dirty little secrets."

"He's right, M. If Adam and Wade were both unfaithful, you'd never be accused of being a home-wrecker. If they keep their secrets, you'll be safe from blame. Although it's morally bankrupt, it places all of you on a level playing field." My friend paused. "I don't think it's the best idea, but it might be your only option, M. If you go through with it, take Adam back to our place. Text me on your way home, and I'll make myself scarce. I'll even roll a joint for you."

"Ooh. Let's get this party started right," sang the blond. "I know a good dealer if you want something stronger that's sure to do the trick."

I considered the offer for a moment.

"Not for the seduction, but maybe for a party."

Bruce agreed.

"I have to have sex with Adam. If I don't, then I'll be walking on eggshells every time I see either of them."

"M, what about finally going through with the threesome? Then you're all there together. You'll help dissolve Wade's guilt, and your previous rendezvous can stay a dirty little secret just between you two. But at least

Adam gets a piece of the pie as well, without going behind Wade's back. It's not a great solution. There's still a sordid secret. But there's less chance of Adam finding out or even caring if he does find out." He tapped his beer glass. "I hope I'm right."

The two scotch drinkers nodded. I thought it through. I knew that the next day I'd have to play it cool for another rehearsal, but I could suggest a quiet dinner later in the week so I could finish what I started.

"Bruce, I'm too nervous to see either of them for the moment, but I guess you're right. I have to man up. I have to take these bulls by their horns and get on top of the situation!"

Our drinking mates raised their glasses to our schemes. Bruce reluctantly joined their toast.

Chapter Twenty-Three

Mannix

I buzzed the front door intercom. I held a bottle of Shiraz in one hand and practiced my best innocent-but-sultry expression. I was keen to catch up with my favorite couple and even keener to put things right after rehearsal. In my pocket was a joint, which Bruce had rolled to get us in the mood.

I stood for what seemed to be two minutes before I buzzed again. I ran my hand over the pocket of my jeans to feel the outline of the marijuana cigarette. It was my security blanket. With it, my fears would fade and I'd find the balls to just let the vibe take us. Or at least I hoped.

It was quiet. There was still no answer. For the first time, I noticed that the street lights were down the opposite side of the road to their apartment block. There wasn't one directly behind me, but the others cast a dim glow on the couple's balcony. I hummed to myself before questioning if they were home. Perhaps they were out buying wine? I looked at the new moon before closing my eyes and humming once more.

I saw myself on a deserted island in a hut that I and some other castaways had built. I locked myself away, trying to make two coconut shells and an existing transistor radio into some sort of mobile phone device. It was a desperate attempt to help me and my friends talk to someone who could rescue us off the island. My concentration was interrupted by a knock on my grassy bamboo door.

"Professor, are you okay in there?" called a familiar voice from outside.

"I'm perfectly okay, Gilligan. Come in."

Two muscular guys wandered in. One was Adam, wearing a checkered red shirt, ripped blue jeans, and a white cowboy hat. The other was Wade in a white sailor's outfit.

"We just came to check up on you," said the sailor. "We haven't seen you all week."

"Skipper, I think I'm close to finding a way off the island."

"That's fine, Professor," said the cowboy. "But you missed the Howell's golf tournament a couple of days ago and Ginger's one-woman show last night. Actually, that may be your good fortune. Her rendition of Broadway songs started wearing thin. 'Don't Cry for Me Argentina' just doesn't cut it when a Marilyn Monroe wannabe is singing it."

"But you know what they say," the sailor interrupted. "All work and no play makes a very boring scientist."

"But I've almost invented a wireless phone."

"That's nice, Professor, but the Skipper and I have been picking mushrooms and I've made a very special soup. You won't need a phone. You'll be convinced you're talking to the universe after a bowl of my special recipe."

"Yes, Professor. You know how Gilligan's cooking always puts you in an accommodating state of mind. We could play games. You could be the wild adventurer, and we could be the tribal headhunters, hunting for head."

I was buzzed into the apartment block. At their front door, Adam welcomed me with a forced grin. He looked as if he'd won the lottery but lost the ticket. In fact, as I wandered in, that strange smile never left his face.

"Let me take that Shiraz," he said. "I don't mind Shiraz sometimes. Perfect for a pasta sauce if it's not too tart."

I looked around for Wade. Both his and Maude's absence made me a feel uneasy.

"I've brought a joint for us as well."

"Oh you did, did you? How sweet. Perfect to whet our appetites."

"Where's Maude and Wade?"

"I told Maude not to come, but Wade's getting dressed, I think." Adam turned toward their bedroom. "Wade, are you still getting dressed? Come out naked if you want. Mannix won't mind. I'm sure he's seen it all before!"

My heart sank faster than a mobster in cement shoes. Wade toddled sheepishly from the bedroom in jeans and a half-buttoned shirt. Adam gritted his teeth. This cat had his mouse.

"Mannix, you know my partner Wade. Cheaper than a small-town hooker. Wade, meet Mannix, toy-boy extraordinaire."

"Adam, be nice. He's our guest."

"Darling. Sweetheart. The night is still young. There's plenty of time for niceties."

"Adam, I'm sorry," I said. He snatched the wine from my hand. "It just happened. We didn't plan it. I'd do anything to take it all back."

"What was that, Mannix? You want to take Wade from the back? Again? My, my, we are randy, aren't we?"

Adam marched to the front door, giving me a brief sense of relief. I was sure I was going to be asked to leave. But instead of opening the door to set my guilt-ridden body free, Adam locked it and placed the keys in the pocket of his jeans. He then reached over to the hat stand where Wade's set of keys were, took them off the hook, and placed them in his other pocket.

"Adam," cried Wade.

"Hush," Adam replied with his finger to his lips.

"Should I check on dinner?" asked his intimidated partner.

"Leave it to me, dear. I still have to grate the razor blades for the soup."

Adam strutted toward the kitchen. I started looking for an open window to jump out of.

"When did he find out?" I whispered.

"Only an hour ago. But he's been suspicious for a while."

"How?"

"We slipped. We should have got our stories straight. I said you never showed up for rehearsal. You said you called by but had to go suddenly. Something about catching up with Bruce? You should have let me know what you said. I think Adam even asked you if you had a glass of wine with me. You said yes."

"That's right, boys," yelled Adam from the kitchen. "Wade forgot to wash the wine glasses. It seemed odd to me that there were two dirty glasses at the time, but I thought nothing of it. Maybe he tipped out a glass of stale wine and opened another bottle. Didn't want the wines to mix."

"So we shared some wine, that doesn't mean that..." I stopped midsentence. I looked up at Adam like the driver of a broken down car stuck on railway tracks. "I guess it does mean something when our stories are different."

"It didn't faze me at first," said Adam. He swanned back to the lounge room with a cocktail in hand, but no drinks for us. "I thought that my two favorite men were up to something. A surprise perhaps. Something that would make me love them both even more. I was like Cleopatra."

"What?" I asked warily. "You were the Queen of the Nile?"

"Yes, Frank. I was the queen of denial!"

Wade rolled his eyes at Adam, who was laying on the theatrics thicker than Elvis Presley's waistline.

"Okay, confession time," I said. "You know I've wanted both of you."

"Oh really, Frank. Wade, did you know that? You didn't know it the other night. Did you know that to begin with?"

"Adam, stop. Let Mannix speak."

"Oh, Frank, you have more to say, have you?" Adam had a cold stare. Half zombie, half drag queen. "Well go on, dear. The court's in session."

"I'm not sure what came over me."

"My husband did, from what I gather."

"I mean, it just happened."

"These things usually do, sweetheart."

"I was hoping you'd be home before we got too far."

"What? So you could rub it in my face?"

"No, Adam, that's not what I meant. What about the three of us? Why don't we...?"

Wade blurted a syllable but stopped. Maybe he'd seen Adam like this before? Best to stay quiet and avoid the daggers. I was hoping the bitter homo would run out of steam. My prayers were answered. Wade's decision not to speak somehow calmed things down, shutting Adam up. He stood like an actor who'd got a bad review before taking himself and his drink to their bedroom.

"What do we do now?" I whispered.

"Go home, Mannix. Leave this to me."

"How? Adam has all the keys."

"Not *all*."

Wade tiptoed to the kitchen where he fetched a pair of spare keys from a teapot. Calmly he opened the lock to the front door, kissed me on the cheek, and let me escape the wrath of his partner.

"What will you do?" I asked, standing outside their door.

"This is not going to end for a while. But I don't blame you, Mannix. I need a stiff scotch, a little cry, and a few nights of sleeping pills to keep me from having restless nights in the guest bedroom."

It was my turn to kiss him on the cheek before he quietly closed the door.

Chapter Twenty-Four

FABIEN

While the world was crumbling below, Farah and Ipan's affair began to bloom. Thankfully, this kept them uninterested in my social experiment.

These were just mere mortals, after all. Too routine. Too dull. Too much planning. Relationships. Babies. Family and friends.

As long as everything went to plan, these living souls didn't *seek* variety. No room to just go with what alternate routes came their way.

So it *wasn't* Adam who slept with Mannix. So what? Surely Wade could run off with the toy-boy. Buy a gleaming black sports car and pierce a nipple. Mannix could be a kept man in a seaside apartment, keeping the place clean between martinis. Once Ipan got back to spying through his telescope, it could give him something worthwhile to watch.

As for Adam, he could find a new life online. Sex parties for the reborn single. Wall-to-wall lubricant and social additives! The end of this relationship could've been the start of an unchained life.

What was wrong with these mortal types? What was this obsession with morality?

I sat staring at the snake in the glass jar when a visitor came to my door.

"Fabien, that spell you showed me the other day…"

"The one you weren't really interested in."

"Well, it was a sex spell on gay guys. Come on, now. It's hardly going to change the course of history on Earth."

He strolled in like a rock star visiting briefly before catching up with a groupie. And how I wished I was that groupie. His demon wings were enough to make me quiver for a taste of his depraved soul.

"These are my playthings." I gestured to the figurines. "I've meddled a little more since I began this hex." He didn't say a word. He studied the carvings like an archaeologist making sense of his find, before staring at me through empty eyes. "I take it you're still not impressed."

"I really don't understand what you've done, Fabien."

"Simple. Old boring gay man yearning for a younger bedmate. And younger bedmate keen as mustard."

"And I suspect that's not the whole story."

"Old boring man is with another old boring man."

"How deliciously delightful."

"I knew you'd be impressed once you knew what I was doing."

"It's not the most original spell, but sometimes men have to learn to grow old disgracefully." He made his way to the sink. His form striding with uber-confidence as he helped himself to a glass of water. "And tell me, Fabien, who else knows of your fiendish little curse?"

"Ipan and Farah. In fact, Farah has upped the ante. She's added her own spell, making the older man's husband yearn for the younger man as well."

"I see."

My Underworld guest leaned back against the sink, letting his perfect chest swell under his tight-fitting T-shirt. I wanted to take him then and there. I wanted to worship every inch he had to offer. But sex was out of the question as I knew he didn't want me. But it didn't stop him teasing my imagination into overdrive.

"What are you thinking about?" I asked.

"My thoughts aren't that deep. I was just trying to remember if I knew Ipan. Farah, I know. She's the whimsical lass with more free-flowing gowns than Stevie Nicks."

"True, that's her. And Ipan is the type of man accountants make jokes about."

"That boring, eh?"

"Oh, don't start me on that meddling windbag."

"I think my boyfriend ran into him the other day. He tried to cheer him up." He leaned forward. "It's only later he considered Ipan might be involved in your experiment, as I'd mentioned it days before."

"Like I said, he's a meddling windbag."

"But knowing you, Fabien, you probably invited him to see your magic spell. You needed his opposing view."

I looked away.

"Is this the reason you came to visit? You wanted to judge me?"

"I'm sorry." He put down his glass. "I'm genuinely sorry. That was not my intention at all." He plodded toward me like a man in ill-fitted shoes. "There are murmurings of this spell on the grapevine. And it seems you've gone too far with this one."

"How so? You seemed impressed at first, and now you're telling me I've got it all wrong! Now listen here. Adam was more routine than a laundry wash cycle. For goodness sake, I've spiced up his life. And Mannix—well, he had to expand his life view. I think I did a good job. It's what I'm here to do!"

"That which doesn't kill them makes them stronger. Is that it, Fabien?"

"Exactly!"

"There's a rumor that you made yourself known to the younger man. Mannix, you said his name was?"

"Yes, that's his name. Okay, I got carried away and went down to see what was happening for myself."

"Scared the shit out of him, I heard."

"Yes, yes, it wasn't my finest moment, I confess."

"And it's set the cat among the pigeons. Yours is not the only visitation your circus has started."

"So there's nothing gained in chastising me."

"Fabien, the other visitations have been repair jobs. Guy has had to mop up the spillage."

"He's made himself known?"

"He had no choice. You've tampered with the laws of this world and your mortals. Until they die, you have no reason to meddle."

"The grapevine also says that Guy has visited Adam before."

"Sometimes these calls are better made by an angel."

"And you care what this angel thinks? You're not exactly pure as snow."

"Now wait here..."

"No, you listen. You're the one leading a double life. At least I'm being true to my nature." He looked at the ground. "I never want to see you here in my home again until I get an apology for the way you've just acted. You do not hold all the cards here, do you understand? So I've played with the rules and fashioned them to my own design. At least I know who and what I am."

The coward never met my gaze. He silently stepped outside.

ADAM

"Adam, are you awake?"

"Yes, Guy, I'm awake."

The tireless alarm clock lit my friend's magnificent wings with a haunting glow as I turned to see the time. It was only one fifty-nine in the morning.

"Kicking Wade out of the house was a bit overdramatic," he said.

"It's the middle of the night. Can't you lecture me at a normal hour?"

"I'm not here to lecture. I'm here to talk. What happened for you to kick him out?"

"Guy, you're an angel. I'm sure you already know."

"I do. But I want to hear your version of events."

"Why?"

"Because at the moment, you need a friend, and the only other person you can talk to has had to take your husband in."

I sat up as he reached over and fluffed the pillow behind me.

"I admit it. I'm being as overdramatic as a silent movie."

"None of us are perfect. Not even us angels."

"But after that minx left, Wade came to our bedroom, and I was so angry I threw his keys at his feet!"

I clenched my fists and slowed my breathing.

"Anger is healthy, Adam. I've heard that if it's repressed, it leads to physical problems."

"Then my poor Wade drove off. I became frantic."

"Frantic?"

"Yes, Guy, frantic along with a whole lot of other mixed emotions. It was only later when Maude rang that I knew where he was."

"And you were relieved?"

His gentle smile was a bit much to take in.

"Yes. No. Kind of. At first, I just hated Wade, and then felt betrayed, and then I hated him again. I know there's an irony about how I feel toward Wade. He only did what I wanted to do so often. But the difference was that my slimeball husband actually tasted the forbidden fruit!"

"Go on, Adam."

"And Mannix or Frank or whatever his bloody name is, it's his fault! That dirty little temptress was swanning around, teasing but never going there, until he was alone with my man. Was the reality of testing the waters with both of us a little too much for poor little Frankie? Poor filthy, little Frankie!"

I choked on my last word. Guy extended his arms so I welcomed the comfort. It was only a few seconds later I realized I was naked. As I tried to move away, he held me tighter.

"My friend, speak to me."

"I'm being spiteful and hateful."

"You're being human, and trust me, I've seen worse."

I looked up at my savior and lowered my voice. His kind eyes had taken in my words.

"Wade and Mannix can run off together if they want. The forty-something and his apprentice, tiring Wade out on the dance floor as he tries to recapture his youth. Bloody stupid Wade. Mannix will eventually run off with the first young thing that takes a shine to him. He will fall in love, rather than sniff around *my* tired old man."

"Adam, this isn't healthy."

"Guy, you're the one who's telling me to get my anger out."

"Well, okay, I did say that, but..."

"I wonder if Mannix has ever been in love. He should have realized he was playing with fire. Poor little Mannix. Poor dumb little Frankie or Mannix or what's-his-name." I laughed like a maniac. "If only things worked out the way they should have. If only Mannix had shared his body and soul with both of us. In some ways, maybe we all bared our souls? Maybe Wade and I have not bared our souls enough?"

"Oh trust me, Adam, you and Wade have done a lot of soul baring over the years. You know each other inside and out."

"Then what went wrong?"

"Well, for a start, you're overanalyzing."

I broke away from his arms.

"Oh come on, Guy. What else do I have at the moment? We've never had an open relationship, and we weren't in the market for one when Mannix turned up. And my husband took the bait!"

"But *you* wanted to take that bait as well."

"But when push came to shove, I didn't!" His kind eyes went blank. "Sorry, Guy, I didn't mean to shout. It's just that I can't make any sense of this. I feel lonelier than I have for two decades."

A tear ran down my cheek. My angel companion opened his arms again. I hugged him like a child's soft toy. He kissed me tenderly on the forehead as I wiped my eyes.

"Adam, I think you need to look at this a different way."

"What do you mean?"

"You, and I for that matter, have to get to the bottom of what happened."

"Is Wade more mixed up than me? Maybe Wade was scared of seeing me return sexual favors with that trampy young thing? So he went it alone. We should have talked more."

"Adam, most men wouldn't cut themselves up this much in the same situation, but then again..."

"But then again what?" He didn't answer. "Guy, you can't just leave me hanging half-sentence. But then again what?"

He gently moved me away from his embrace and pointed to my wardrobe.

"It's time for us to go for a drink."

"At this hour on a school night? How will I explain your wings?"

"No, Adam, it's time to visit my world again. So pack an overnighter."

Chapter Twenty-Five

Fabien

How dare that trumped-up demon preach to me! The superior edge is my domain, and I wear it well. There were no prizes for being second best in my book.

And then there was that tedious train wreck back in "mortal land." Guys avoiding a threesome. What was their problem? While I was being judged for trying to help these wilted souls find a life, Guy was nosing around putting the puzzle together.

All this, while the unfaithful husband was seeking solace from Maude. They sat in her living room drinking gin and tonic.

"I'm sorry, Maude. There's no way Mannix will face Adam at rehearsal now!"

"Wade, that's the last thing on my mind. My boys are in pain, and their wise friend is here to the rescue."

"But the play?"

"Stop worrying about that damn play. We can close for a season."

He sighed.

"But Adam told me Mannix was good in the role."

"You know, I wasn't sure he could act at first, because all I saw were you two swanning around him as if he was a Playboy Bunny. And *he* was just as bad, dying to move into the main bedroom of the Playboy Mansion."

"And that's when your alarm bells rang?"

"At first, I thought it would end in tears," she said. "But then I started believing that it might turn out okay."

"What made you change your mind?"

Wade was observing his glass as if a mosquito just drowned in it.

"Mannix is a good kid. And you all wanted to sleep together. That was obvious. So I just assumed all apprehensions would get washed away."

"It's just that I caved into temptation prematurely."

"And that's the issue, isn't it. I mean, if I had an affair with a younger man, then you two would pat me on the back and congratulate me. Even an older gay couple with a younger lover seems passable these days. But someone giving into temptation behind their partner's back? Why, that's considered the ultimate betrayal! And that's where you went wrong."

"I should have known better."

"Yes, my dear, you should've known better." Maude paused. She theatrically peered out the glass doors to her balcony as if she was about to utter something important. "But it was uncharted waters."

"The threesome thing?"

"Yes, you guys don't fool around. It caught you off guard."

"Yet Adam and I are the adults here. Mannix was the kid. We're the ones with life experience. We could've worked it out."

"My dear, experience is what you get when you don't get what you want in life."

Wade peered onto the balcony.

Oh please! What was wrong with these people? With a little help from Farah, we rocked their world, and instead of taking the bait, they crumbled like poor excuses for gay men.

The seduction should be easy. A joint and a dose of bad TV followed by the porn disc that just happened to be in the DVD player when they were about to load *Torch Song Trilogy*. This all could have worked out so well, as long as it wasn't that home movie Adam and Wade made when they were drunk that time. But then again? On second thought, no. It was shot before the diet.

"You know," said Wade trying to sound smart, "as the elders, we did try to take charge, but Mannix ran home when confronted."

"That's why I like him. I still do, even though you both should have known better."

"I guess he was just too scared to cause ripples between us."

"Ironically, as the costar in your midlife crisis, he has."

"But he made me feel young."

"I don't think Adam ever made you feel old."

"He didn't. But Mannix had a smile that made me melt."

"Oh please, darling, don't justify yourself. Men justifying their carnal desires are as tired as reruns of sixties sitcoms."

"But Adam was taken by his charisma as well!"

"And I'm sure Adam got more than he bargained for from your moment of weakness." The old queen began to wail. "Sorry, dear. That was mean of me."

"Yes, it was, Maude! Adam was in the same boat!"

He whimpered like a wounded dog. I, on the other hand, was trying to think up a way to get this dreary drama back on track. Resolution was not in my vocabulary.

"Sweetheart, look at it this way. Mannix was a muse sent to you to discover something about your relationship. But be wary of muses. They can get out of hand. They'll take over a sonnet, take charge of a play, or redirect a good story."

She passed Wade a hanky.

"Maude, I've just wiped away the last two decades with our muse."

"Oh, don't be so dramatic, sweetheart."

This was the smartest thing she'd said all night.

Wade choked on his drink. Maude thumped him several times on the back. He cleared his throat.

"Water?" she offered.

"No. Gin," he replied. Good call on his part. She handed the drink to him. "So much for not being dramatic."

"Wade, I know Adam. You haven't wiped away two decades."

"That's the problem, Maude. I don't think you're right."

It was at this point I realized these mortals were as interesting as wet dishcloths. Fortunately, visitors saved me. Farah swanned in, nearly tripping over the pail of water.

"You've been keeping up with the action on Earth," she declared.

"What's been happening?" asked Ipan.

They looked sickly sweet huddled together.

"What's been happening, you ask," I replied. "Let's just say, kiddies, there's more action in your lives at the moment than with our gay playthings."

"So the dust has settled?" Ipan asked.

"Settled? My horny friend, it's more like the *proverbial* has hit the fan!"

"Oh dear," said Farah. "Did we go too far?"

"Not far enough. Only one of the men has helped Mannix with his homework. The other is getting a visitation."

"A visitation? That's serious." Ipan liked to claim the obvious. "I should have kept an eye on them."

"And did what, old man? For once, you have a *life,* and you're worried about people you've never even met."

Ipan was about to reply, but Farah held up her hand like a traffic cop.

"Who is visiting? Is Wade okay?"

"Oh, Wade is fine, my wispy friend. He's been treated like a queen by his prince. Adam is the one licking his wounds."

"Oh dear."

"I told you both not to—"

Farah reinstated her hand signal.

"Fabien, who is doing the visitation?"

"Guy."

"Who's Guy?"

"Adam's guardian angel."

"Oh, I've heard of him. Isn't he Joshua's boyfriend?"

"That's the one."

Farah pressed her finger to her lips as she stepped away from her dreary lover.

"Now will you let me speak?" he said.

"Sorry, darling, I'm trying to think of a way to put this right."

"It's pretty much derailed by the sounds of it."

"Yes, sweetheart, but I refuse to leave it like this. There has to be a way for a happy ending."

"Why bother?" I said.

They both stared through my dark core.

"It's time to take a leaf from our host's book," said Ipan. "As sinister as he is, his actions may be our starting block."

"I'm intrigued," she replied.

"I'm intrigued as well," I said. "Do I smell a compliment in the air, old man?"

"Your visitation was ill-timed," he replied. "But maybe if we think this through, we can intervene through our own visitation."

Farah made her way back to Ipan, holding out her hand. I cringed.

"My darling, it's not like you to want to break the rules, but in this case, we don't have a choice. We're getting out of hand."

Chapter Twenty-Six

ADAM

"So this is your place," I said.

We walked up a sparkling footpath to a charming building of four flats. Besides a few folk breathing life to the main street, the only other human form was clumping around in a suit of armor on one of the balconies. His helm was resting on a garden chair nearby, while he shielded his eyes from the radiant sun to see who we were.

"Hello, Guy," he yelled.

"Hi, Tyson. How did you get into that outfit? It looks like it's weighing you down."

"Patricia helped me. She's just gone to the markets to get lunch, so I'm stuck in it until she gets back."

"Guy, why is that man dressed like a knight?" I whispered.

"Tyson loves to dress up," my angel replied. His wings quickly fluttered before looking back to the balcony. "We'll come and help you get out of that thing."

"No, no. It's okay. I'm feeling empowered. When Patricia returns, she can be my damsel in distress."

"It looks like you're the one in distress."

The hapless adventurer smiled.

"All is fine, Guy. I will escort my fair maiden to my bed chamber after she returns with a feast of roasted pheasant."

I rolled my eyes.

"Is she protected by a chastity belt?" Guy asked.

"Nay, my godly messenger." Tyson made some heroic arm motion that looked like he was addressing his loyal subjects. "And who is that walking beside my favorite angel?"

"Oh sorry, Tyson. This is my friend, Adam."

"Nice to meet you, Tyson," I yelled.

"You're in good hands, Adam. Guy is the best friend anyone can have."

"Yes, I'm realizing that I'm blessed."

"Bye, Tyson," said Guy. He shuffled me toward the front door as I waved good-bye to the misguided knight. "So, Adam, welcome to the Carnival of Lost Souls."

"You're right about lost souls," I quietly replied.

"No, Adam. You're visiting my home in the Carnival of Lost Souls. It's a district of the Afterlife."

"Aptly named by the looks of it."

As we stepped through the door, I was blinded by the bright staircase. It shimmered the same way as the footpath.

"You'll get used to it shortly, Adam."

"What's with the glowing surfaces? Have your angel footprints left their mark?" I giggled, but Guy gazed at me blankly. "I'm right, aren't I? You're leaving fairy dust where you walk."

"Well, we don't need to turn the lights on in the entrance at night anymore, but I'm not sure if it's my doing."

We stepped up as the glow warmed the soles of my shoes. A sense of love and protection weaved up my body like a swarming vine as the angel led the way. Soon we were at the top of the stairs, entering the apartment next to Tyson's.

Inside, the walls and furnishings shrieked of the 1960s, but in pastel tones. A boxlike cabinet proudly displayed a faded pink candelabra with half-melted candles. It shared a wall with a painting I couldn't call art. White square lounges, luxurious enough to make love on, faced each other socially around a kidney-shaped table.

Guy strolled to an automatic record player. Beside it stood stereo speakers covered in checked fabric.

"Adam, it's time to funk."

He pulled out an album with a trippy cover by a band called the Undisputed Truth, and carefully placed it on the spindle. I wandered to the bar and ran my hand over its cream leather surface. Its cold texture displayed circular patterns of sticky residue from spilled drinks. As a tribal beat burst from the sound system, my friend swayed on the carpet, peering up at me with his wing tips pointing at the cabinet.

"You want me to go through your belongings?"

"I'll get us a cocktail while you tend to the goodies hidden away in the top drawer."

Male vocals sang in pre-disco fashion as I made my way to the mystery reward. I could smell the dope before I could see it. A timber box with a sliding lid, not unlike one made by a high school student in a woodwork class, sat next to an ashtray with small squares of gold paper.

"Guy, you want me to roll a joint?"

"Uh-huh."

He didn't look up to answer me. In front of him were two camp-looking drinks with tiny umbrellas.

"I'm not going to burn in hell for this, am I? I mean, I'm getting stoned with an angel. That can't be good."

"Adam, stop analyzing and start rolling. You, my friend, need to chill out."

"All right."

I took the implements to the coffee table as Guy sat next to me on the sofa. Soon we shared our first puff, and mixed with the blue curacao concoction, my body felt lighter than air. My angel friend stared vaguely at the spinning record.

"So tell me, what's this Mannix infatuation all about?" I asked.

"That, Earth Boy, is what I *don't* understand. You and Wade are destiny."

"We're destiny?"

"If you say it slower, it will make sense."

"Wade—and—I—are—destiny." Guy nodded continuously. "I still don't get it." His nod turned to a shake of the head. "Do you want to explain it to me?"

He pointed to the hallway. My feet grooved in that direction.

A corkboard displaying pencil-sketched portraits took me by surprise. I didn't know what I was expecting, but homemade art wasn't it. There was Maudi from my dreams as a child. Her regal quality shone through as, for some reason, she wore an eighteenth-century dress with a parasol. She looked so much like Maude in our play. Not in appearance but in spirit.

I was impressed at how disciplined these drawings were. Ten more years of art class would never put me in this league. Two other images caught my attention.

The first was of a young guy in a tacky 1970s tracksuit. Its colors reminded me of licorice allsorts but nowhere near as inviting. He had a retro hairstyle and a knowing smile. It was the type of smile I often saw on Mannix. The orange outline of a typewriter was prominent in the background. It sat on a bound manuscript. At the bottom of the sketch in purple pencil was the name Francis followed by "aka Gloria's Son."

Poems written on lined paper were pinned next to some of the pictures. These notes had been ripped from a spiral pad. Their jagged edges were at odds with the neat penmanship. Next to Francis' image was this strange verse:

We stared at each other
You wouldn't give up the gaze.
I looked away, humiliated.

Dying on the battlefield
I was filthy and wet.
The heavy armor too much to bear.

The bleeding kept me warm,
As I overlooked the pain
My cowardly crying choked me.

Then you were my child,
We stared at each other.
This time, I kept my gaze.

Was Francis overcoming a bad authority figure? Perhaps his dad? Nah! That was the dope playing with my mind.

The other illustration that drew me was of a younger gay couple in their twenties. Their skin tones were different, just like Wade and I. The one with the goatee was pale, while the handsome one was a latte color. The latter was snuggling against his mate, but the former looked to the floor as if he was preoccupied with something as trivial as trying to remember where he'd left his keys.

Handwritten again in purple were the names Allan and Warwick. I shivered as I read those names. I looked back at the one named Allan and felt his ghostly presence trying to connect with my soul. I looked away, but I still felt his calling so I closed my eyes and breathed deeply. But I wanted to read the poem next to their picture.

My eyelids slowly opened like curtains on a stage, as I avoided eye contact with Allan's image. As I read, the portrait of the couple came to life like an animated film.

Allan was a female with eyes as dark as ravens, shivering against a run-down farm building and holding lifeless Warwick in his arms.

In another life, we were paupers
I fell ill
You held me tight
I died too soon

The colored graphite swirled around the paper until the form of Warwick as a woman stared aimlessly into a field from her castle. Allan was walking away.

In another life, we were lovers
You yearned for respect
You yearned for affection
I seldom listened

The pencil colors formed a rainbow, breaking off into rich purple hues that created the next intricate picture. It was the couple, naked, holding each other tenderly under the sheets of an enormous bed in a house-sized room. Again, Warwick was the woman.

In another life, we were royalty
Our world was our own
I held you tight
We kissed, we slept

Next, a child ran through the image from right to left, as seaside waves made an appearance. Allan was the female this time as they both sported swimwear that covered them from neck to knees.

In another life, we had a child
Sandcastle building
Insect collecting
We had a child

Allan's long hair shortened as both were now men. Warwick was driving, eyes firmly on the road. Allan sat in the passenger seat, gazing at his partner like a loyal pet.

In another life, we missed the boat
We shared our lives
Held back on love
But finally, we sailed

And now Allan and Warwick were a young Adam and Wade, holding hands with their backs to me. Laser lights shot out of a huge building ahead, reminding me of our courting days, dancing the night away.

In this life, we'll know it all
Tales of triumph
Wisdom collated
Journey completed

"Guy, I'm spooked!"
"What's the matter, Petal? Too much to take in?"
I crept back toward him. His wings were drooping, and his cocktail glass was almost empty. He held the joint toward me, offering it into the distance like a shortsighted man.
"I need that puff." I ambled to the couch and sank as low into its reassuring cushions as I could. "I never considered reincarnation, but it looks like Wade and I are on a treadmill going round and round and..."
"Think of it as the School of Life, Adam."
"Brilliant! Suddenly, I'm this empty canvas with someone else writing my story."
"Not quite, my pet project. You are still you. The script is half-written. What happens depends on how you react to the main scenes."
His wisdom wafted over in muted waves, enough to tip my head against his shoulder. I looked up into his glazed eyes.
"How can I not feel like the outsider after Wade slept with that slutty tart?"
Guy's loving fingers danced on my forehead before gently shutting my eyelids. The funk-disco fusion faded as a rabble of well-spoken voices became the new soundtrack. I opened my eyes.

In front of me was a magazine called *The Stage Door,* which someone had left in the booth I was seated at. Inside was gossip, articles on up-and-coming writers and directors, and reviews on various theater productions currently showing. One of my favorite Alan Ayckbourn plays, *Joking Apart*, was being performed by a visiting acting troop. But the show was receiving some harsh criticism by some writer named Wilma who seemed to have missed the fact that she was watching a comedy.

I could hear k.d. lang's hit "Constant Craving" being sung Shirley Bassey style. I looked up from the journal to view that statuesque singer in a dress that sparkled so much, it lit the room like a disco ball.

I was back at the Pedestal, and on the other side of my table was Guy. The whites of his eyes were clear of any red road maps, and my mood was equally focused. That thing he called a boyfriend was heading toward us with three glasses of champagne.

"Ah, the jilted one," said Joshua.

"I wouldn't say I'm jilted," I replied. "Just pissed off."

"And you've been brooding over this for a while now."

"I just have to let my feelings out."

"Spoken like a true drama queen, Adam. Scream. Shout. Feel every moment. Keep it in your memory in case you have to play it onstage."

"I'm not that dramatic."

"Oh please, you're like a has-been followed by paparazzi."

"Guy, why do you go out with him?"

The angel had a charmed expression.

"Look at me," Joshua replied. "I'm sex on two legs. Who wouldn't go out with me?"

I reluctantly grinned. "I'm getting advice left, right, and center."

"Adam, I've got a bit more perspective on your life since the last time we spoke. Now it's time to talk some sense into you."

"Could you please be gentler with my emotions, Joshua?"

"Tough love, sweetie, tough love."

I nervously sipped my bubbly. Guy seemed deep in thought at a time I wanted him to come to my rescue. His cocksure partner flicked the stem of his glass, making it chime. As if this was his cue, my guardian angel cleared his throat and looked at me like a business partner wanting me out of the company.

"Adam, I've been watching you for a long time, and I've discovered that out of all your friends, you're the drama queen."

Joshua nodded ardently.

"I'm not that bad, am I?"

"Not usually. You often have a good handle on life. But Mannix has thrown your world out of kilter, and under normal circumstances, he shouldn't have."

"After all, Mannix is the innocent bystander in all of this," Joshua added.

"No he's not! He bonked my husband!"

"But you wanted to make love to him as well. Give us a break, Adam. Your intentions were crystal clear!"

"Well..." In unison, they peered down their noses. "Okay, yes. I also wanted a bit of Mannix action."

"Are you more upset that Wade cheated on you, or that Mannix slept with Wade instead of you?" Joshua asked.

"I'm upset that it wasn't a three-way."

"That wasn't the question."

He held his glass against his cheek, giving me a catwalk model stare.

"No, it should have been the three of us."

"But if you had secretly slept with Mannix, would you have told Wade?"

"We have a great relationship—"

"Again, not the question."

"Guy, save me from your boyfriend's bad-cop routine."

"Adam, this time we're getting to the bottom of your drama," he replied. The edge of his lip turned up. "And Joshua is better at this type of thing than I am."

He sipped his drink while looking at his partner with eyes of desire. The interrogating angel sighed, losing his stern face.

"Adam, let me ask you again," Joshua said. "Would you have told Wade if the shoe was on the other foot?"

"I wouldn't know how to tell him."

"Maybe Wade didn't know how to tell you," Guy reasoned. "Maybe Mannix didn't know either. They know they did the wrong thing, but you can't punish them forever."

"I can try."

"Oh, drop the tantrum, darling," said Joshua.

"No, Adam, you can't punish them forever," added Guy. "Someone as opened-minded as you? It's not your nature."

He gestured to the other patrons in the bar. A shirtless guy in smart pants danced with an imaginary being, looking as stoned as I felt before. He wore no shoes either, his socks dusting the path clean for his private tango.

A woman dressed in a classy black coat laughed so hard over dinner with a man I thought her teeth would fly out. He bashfully looked at his plate, waiting for her to run out of steam. Then unexpectedly, he blew her a kiss.

In the opposite corner, two beautiful twenty-something men were paying a fifty-something Korean woman too much attention. One caressed her shoulder while the other lifted a cocktail to her mouth, spilling some of it down her chin as she giggled.

"They're your crowd, Adam," Guy said. "Bohemians. Artists. Trying their best to stay carefree."

"I'm not sure I see your point."

"They're all seeking a little attention," declared Joshua. "Just like Wade did. Just like Mannix did. But it could have been you instead."

"It's hard because it wasn't."

"And Wade is just like you: artistic," Guy continued. "It was him instead. He's not only your partner, he's your best friend. Be happy for him. He got a bit. I'm sure after eighteen years, this is not the end of your relationship. It's just something he tried without you. It was between him and Mannix. This encounter had nothing to do with you."

"That's a little harsh. You can't dismiss the way I feel about this."

"No, we can't," said Joshua. "But use it in your directing, your acting, and your scriptwriting. In short, get it out of your system and move on. Stop, breathe, and reassess. You'll find Wade and Mannix broke the ice, making you a step closer to what you really want." He gave me a devilish wink. "And let's face it, Adam, they're both feeling guilty as sin. They'll want to make it up to you."

I smirked.

"If I'm not careful, Joshua, I'll actually start thinking like you."

"Hallelujah!"

We raised our glasses to toast, but as the wicked angel brought his champagne toward mine, I caught a glimpse of his distorted image through his glass. He quickly slammed down his drink. I rubbed my eyes, but the strange vision wouldn't leave my memory.

"I must be under some sort of spell," I murmured.

"That's why we're here, Adam," he replied, "Because you are under a spell."

"No, Joshua, cut the bullshit. What exactly are you?"

Chapter Twenty-Seven

ADAM

"Won't you lose your angel status or something?"

"I know what I'm doing, Adam."

I helped mix another four blue cocktails at his bar. I didn't feel stoned or tipsy, but I did notice three more joints waiting to be lit on his coffee table.

"How did we get back here?"

"My favorite human friend, I didn't want you to make a scene at the Pedestal."

"I know this should be doing my head in, but it's not. How can it? I was stoned, and then I wasn't. I was at home, then here, then there, and now I'm back here. That psychedelic music is still on the turntable, right here, right now. Although it looks like it's on side two. An image of Wade and my former selves turns into a cartoon. And I meet two angels, and one of them has hidden devil's horns and bat wings when you see his reflection. Hell, what would I know? Maybe that's the latest bad-boy angel look this season? Bugger this! I need another joint."

I headed to the coffee table and picked up one of the spliffs.

"Can you help me with two of these drinks, Adam?"

"Why did you mix four drinks?"

"One for me, one for you, one for Joshua, and one for our mystery guest."

I scanned the room like a surveillance camera.

"Joshua's not here."

"He's getting changed in my bedroom." I crashed onto the sofa. "That's fine, Adam. I'll bring over these drinks to the table myself."

"What is he, the devil?"

"No. Of course not."

"Well, he's not an angel."

Guy looked to the ceiling before meeting my eyes.

"He's a demon," he whispered.

"A what?" I screamed. My angel friend shrugged. "Why are you going out with a demon?"

"He knows where my parents are."

At that moment, there was a knock on the door. I heard Joshua greet the guest.

"Oh no," I grunted.

"Adam, light that joint."

"I want to have my wits about me when he comes into this room."

"What about the talk we just had at the Pedestal?"

"Talking is one thing. How I feel is another."

The visitor waltzed into the lounge room with his trademark smile, viewing me with a serenity I wasn't expecting. He was sporting a pair of black jeans to die for. I sat staring with my mouth agape.

"Did he have a puff?" Joshua asked Guy.

The demon stood behind the guest in his angel form.

"No, but I wish he would."

"Que será, será." Joshua turned to address me. "Adam, drink up instead. It won't add clarity, but it will make this afternoon a hell of a lot more interesting."

Guy's wings fluttered. The guest strolled to me with his arms outstretched. I stood up and hesitantly hugged him.

"Mannix, what are you doing here?" I asked.

"It's a long story, Adam."

I broke away as anger steamed up my body like boiling water in a kettle. Guy shuffled for one of the joints, lit it, and held it to my face. Joshua sniggered mischievously as I ignored my guardian angel's offer.

I closed my eyes and breathed deeply. Guy took a puff and blew the smoke casually toward my face.

"Adam, say what you need to say to me and let's get it over and done with," Mannix replied. "I can take it."

Another waft of marijuana made it to my nostrils as I calmly opened my eyes, reached for one of the cocktails, and steadily lifted the glass to my lips.

"I don't think I should have puffed that joint so soon," Guy said. "It's starting to hit me."

"Pass it here, lover," Joshua replied. "He's gonna slap that bitch into next week, and I love being stoned for a floor show."

"You clearly aren't a match made in heaven," I replied. I took a sip. "And I'm not going to slap anyone. I am calm and collected and..."

"And what, Adam?" the home-wrecker asked. "You can confide in me."

"Can I, Mannix? Can I? I wouldn't confide in you if you were the last person on earth! Or in the Afterlife, for that matter. Wherever we are!" He stood as Zen as a monk, infuriating me more. "If it wasn't for you, my husband would still be at home. Some friend you turned out to be."

"Nuclear fallout," Joshua proclaimed. "Drink some more, Adam."

If looks could kill, Guy's stare at his boyfriend would have knocked him out cold.

"Adam, in many ways, I was in the same boat as you," my nemesis replied.

"How, Mannix? How were you in the same boat? Let's work this out, shall we? Were you in a relationship of your own? No, you weren't. Were you in a relationship in which, oh I don't know, someone came along and put a wedge between you and your loved one? The answer? A big fat no!"

"I've never noticed how ugly the carpet is in this apartment," Guy slurred. "I wouldn't have moved in if I'd noticed."

Joshua sniggered again before putting the joint in his mouth.

"Look, Adam," said Mannix, "It's not really my fault."

"Really? Oh I see. It's my fault. My fault for being so stupid I let this charismatic stranger into my home to wreak havoc on my life. When I had a life! Mannix, you have no idea how I'm feeling. You're the bi-hussy who's not too fussy. Now please, get off my case."

My last line came with a sweeping arm gesture that made the drink leap out of my glass and onto the coffee table.

"I see you set aside this special time to humiliate yourself among friends," uttered Joshua.

"Oh, I get it. Like humor, but different."

Female vocals funked in the background, soon joined by a soulful male. In this playful atmosphere, I was the only one feeling awkward, like I was at knifepoint surrounded by kids with plastic swords. I searched for calm in the disco groove.

Guy started coughing.

"I think I swallowed a clown," he said.

Joshua handed the angel his cocktail so he could soothe his throat. But as he clumsily placed the blue concoction back on the table, he wet his sleeve on my spilled drink.

"Adam, you've never told me how you and Wade met," said Mannix.

I ignored his white flag. I headed for the kitchen and reached for a cloth, before halting as if Medusa had turned me to stone.

"Mannix, what are you doing here?" I asked.

"The lovebirds invited me."

"No. I mean here, in the Afterlife. Did Guy come and take you from your bed?"

He looked to the angel and shrugged.

"You know what?" said Guy. His words chugged along in first gear. "If we were mortal, imagine the fun a family next door would have with us queers as neighbors. We'd be stoned on the back porch, putting on a show better than cable."

"That one actually made sense," Mannix remarked. "Is he sobering up?"

"It will pass," Joshua replied. "Surrealism is sure to recommence."

"How come you're not stoned?"

"Dear, I'm from the Underworld. I grew up on vice."

"Is it 'Teensy Weensy Spider' that climbs up the water spout?" asked our stoned angel. His wings spread on the couch like a throwover. "Or is it 'Itsy Bitsy'?"

I tried not to laugh, but Mannix's cheeky smirk made me lose my composure.

"My favorite stoned angel, it can't be 'Itsy Bitsy,'" I replied. "'Itsy Bitsy' is a little yellow polka-dot bikini."

"I always thought it was 'Eensy Weensy,'" said Joshua. The demon flounced around as if his limbs were made of rubber.

"I thought you didn't get stoned," stated Mannix.

Joshua grinned.

"Mannix, why are you here?" I asked.

Mannix poured some of his cocktail in my empty glass, clutched my arm, and gently eased me to the floor. We sat cross-legged facing each other.

"Car crash."

"What?"

"I was in a car crash, and Guy pulled me out in time."

"How? Why?"

"I got in my car after leaving your place the other night. At some stage, I realized I was on some lonely road out of the city. Solitary petrol stations whisked past. I considered food, but as a fried chicken joint came into view, I lost my appetite. Perhaps I should have stopped. Ordering food would have given me something to break my guilty train of thought. But I didn't stop. I just stayed on my escape route."

"Mannix, that's all a bit dramatic. My wrath isn't that bad."

Joshua lit up a new joint and handed it to the young man.

"Something ran onto the road. A small white animal. It hit the car. I hit the brakes. The sound of the screeching beast is replaced by the sound of screeching tires. I skidded, manically clutching the shaking steering wheel. The car slid to one side as I lost sight of the road. Grass. That's all I'll see. Wild grass whipped past my windshield. Then a big inflatable bag burst from the steering wheel, and..." He pointed to Guy. "I met your guardian angel." I hugged Mannix tightly. "Don't fret, Adam. I'm okay now."

"I think he'll make a good actor," said the demon. "That story held me captive."

"They're getting along so well now," Guy added.

"Well, they are both Australian. Where people are friendly and Kylie Minogue is Prime Minister."

"That's so true, my darling. And Dame Edna is the first lady."

Both Mannix and I studied the stoner pair. Their gestures would've made Perez Hilton seem butch.

"They're the perfect duo," I said.

"Like Kiki Dee and Elton John," Mannix replied.

"Like Donny and Marie Osmond."

"Like Peaches and Herb."

"Like Barbra Streisand and Kris Kristofferson."

"Adam, we should be as stoned as they are. Why aren't we?"

"Mannix, take another puff of that joint."

Guy snuggled into Joshua's chest as if he'd found the perfect pillow. The demon tenderly rubbed his boyfriend's angelic cheek.

"So, Adam, I still don't know how you and Wade met."

"We met at a park." My audience all raised their eyebrows. "No, not that sort of park. We were both on separate picnics. Our group was throwing around a Frisbee, and Wade and a friend came to join us."

"What?" asked Joshua. "Wade gate-crashed your party?"

"No, it wasn't like that."

"I thought dancing to ABBA was the gay mating ritual," said Guy.

"I noticed him with his frizzy cropped hair and his upbeat expression, outgoing but gentle. Someone I wanted to get to know. At that stage, I just thought I'd chat to him at the picnic and become friends."

"When did it become about the sex?" Mannix asked.

He handed me the joint.

"It was never about the sex. It was about being friends. Our group ended up at a bar after the picnic, and he joined us. I think the others knew they were watching the start of a relationship while I just saw him as a friend. The others turned out to be right."

"Falling in love is like being gay," Guy declared. "Everyone around you realizes before you do."

"Good point. You're making sense again." I took a puff. "So Wade and I exchanged phone numbers and went our separate ways. A few days later, we got together for dinner, which sort of turned into a date." I took another puff.

"Don't stop there, Adam," said Mannix. "When did you start getting serious?"

"After too much wine. We sat, genuinely interested in each other. We talked about our work life, our past boyfriends, and shared flatmate horror stories. And then over dessert and coffee, he kissed me. I took a chance and kissed back. Time paused for that kiss. Eighteen years later, time still pauses when we kiss, but the mystery is replaced with a sense of true belonging."

I handed the joint back to Mannix, but he passed it on to Joshua. The demon had a smoke before passing it to Guy, who waved it away. It came back to me.

"I'm truly sorry, Adam," the young man said. His eyes lowered. "I've had some reflection time, and I'm sorry about the way I made you feel."

"The problem is, friends..." Guy paused as he sat up, bringing his wings close to his body and flapping twice. As he did, he almost knocked Joshua's drink from his hand. "Friends, Mannix is the sort of guy that both Adam and Wade would cheat with, if they had the inclination to cheat on each other."

"He's still making sense," said Mannix.

"Yes," I replied. "Brutally honest sense."

"Oh wake up, girlfriend," said Joshua. His head tilted. "Your magic universe of two became a one-man show for a brief moment. Wade's one-man show. You felt like the costar while Mannix was elevated to the main cast. It wasn't like they were having a private joke behind your back."

"Do I really need to hear this?"

"Listen, honey. Whether you are demoted at work, a friend starts snubbing you, or your father walks out on you when you're a child, the emotion is the same. But in this case, you were never yesterday's news!"

"I thought you were stoned."

He shrugged.

Chapter Twenty-Eight

Adam

"Guy, it still hurts," I said.

"That's why we're here."

We were walking off yesterday's stoned state of mind. It was just the two of us. My angel friend insisted that thing with attitude he called a boyfriend and that thing I used to call a home-wrecker stay home. We were at the local markets.

My face nearly fried as a fire-breather greeted us at the first stall. He was still dexterous enough to whirl a baton with his left hand at the same time. A man of talent and charm rolled into one. All he needed was a unicycle, and he'd have been a one-man show.

The shrill sound of a gramophone began, as its owner sung opera. A colorful cast of characters stood briefly to listen. I stopped too. Guy placed his arms around my shoulders, hugging me from behind.

"I guess affection is in your nature," I said.

"Adam, you need to feel loved at the moment. I'm just doing my job as an angel."

I smiled.

The singer hit high notes, piercing my ears. His breath control was outstanding. The record started winding down as he slowed his vocals, causing mirth amongst the crowd. A small girl with a balloon ran to the phonograph, trying to work out how to get it back to speed. She crouched beside it before her mother called her back. He sang the last verse unaccompanied as the crowd applauded.

I clapped too, but Guy kept his arms around me. His handsome profile distracted me while he stayed focused on the spectacle.

"So are all these people dead?" I asked.

"Let's talk about that in due course, Adam." He grabbed my hand. "For now, we need to talk about you and Wade."

"Yeah, I guess we do." I pointed to a candy floss stand. We strolled toward it. "Joshua's right about what he said yesterday. There's no danger of Wade and I splitting up."

"So what was the problem?"

"Betrayal, I guess."

We wandered past a man selling jewelry, and for a moment, I thought he was my husband.

"What's the matter, Adam?" The gentleman stroked a metal bracelet before slipping it onto his wrist. "Yes, he does look like Wade." He picked up an enamel bangle and displayed it to us on his palm. I shook my head politely as we continued our walk. "He's attractive, isn't he?"

"Yes, Guy, he is. He's making me long for the real Wade."

"But you said Wade betrayed you."

"Yeah, I did."

Guy stood still.

"Adam, if you surrendered to temptation with Mannix, would you have told Wade?"

I looked back at the jewelry seller.

"Probably. Maybe. I'm not sure."

"Adam, seriously?"

The man quietly observed the woman who was trying on a jade bracelet. He talked about his homemade creations as she ran her fingers over other wares, feeling their workmanship. I wanted to step to his side and press my head against his, showing the customer that we were in love. But it wasn't Wade.

"Guy, I guess I wouldn't have told him I'd had sex with Mannix. I wouldn't want him to hurt this much."

"And Adam, as Joshua pointed out, there's no danger of you splitting up."

"I know."

We continued walking.

"You got mad because you feared you'd be abandoned."

Now I stood still.

"So you're saying I was protecting my turf. How gang-like." I smirked.

"Perhaps? Could you imagine a world without Wade?"

"Absolutely not."

These words blurted from my mouth before I gave them any thought.

"He still loves you."

"Yes, he does."

"And you still love him."

"Yes, I do."

"And he's not going to run off with Mannix."

"I guess not."

"No, Adam, he's *not* going to run off with Mannix, is he?"

I glanced again at the jewelry seller. He giggled at something the woman had said. His jolly chuckle sounded like Santa being surprised by a speedy reindeer take-off. My husband never laughed like that.

"No, Guy, Wade is never going to run off with Mannix."

"And Wade *was* never going to run off with Mannix. He's madly and totally in love with you."

I grabbed my angel with both arms, forcing him against me. I didn't want him to see me cry. His arms reached around me, holding me tight. He smelled of light aftershave, clean and cultured.

As the first drop made its way down my face, I looked away, but he brought his hand behind my head and cradled my cheek to his. The market scene started fading to a blank canvas. I coughed before my tears began to stream.

"Let it out, Adam. I've got you covered."

"Where has everything gone?"

"You're seeing this place in its purest form. Just go with it."

A soft pink aura radiated from his body. He briefly looked at my face, his arresting blue eyes highlighted by the ghostly-colored hue. My crying stopped, but I couldn't stop coughing. Soon a fog spewed from my mouth. Its sooty residue sat on my lips. I stared at it, and it stared back with a pair of caring eyes.

"Now, Adam, Wade would never run off with Mannix, would he?"

The dark cloud smiled at me. I knew that expression. It was the comforting grin that my husband greeted me with every morning, before several lingering kisses. It was the grin I returned, soaking up his affection like a sponge before repaying the love tenfold.

"No, Guy. Wade loves me, and I love Wade. We both love Mannix, but neither one of us is in love with Mannix. Wade and I are in love with each other."

The mist nodded.

"And how do you know that, Adam?"

"Because like all soul mates, we fell in love the first time we met. If it wasn't at the picnic, it would have been somewhere else."

His radiant glow encompassed me, pouring love into my soul. I felt its electric charge before it slowly vanished.

The rabble of the crowd returned. Soon the markets were back to their Technicolor glory. Magnificent mystics, nimble jugglers, and flamboyant folk filled the landscape. I felt safe. My angel hugged me tighter before letting go.

"And how do you feel about Mannix?"

"Better than I did before." I took a breath. "Why did we meet him?"

Guy glanced at the candy floss stand, tilting his head briefly in that direction. We wandered toward it.

"He's part of your troop."

"My troop?"

"Not just yours. Wade and Maude's as well. You were destined to meet. You know that well-worn saying, 'Everyone's here for a reason, a season, or a lifetime.' It was time to cement that friendship again."

We stopped in front of a woman whirling sugary candy around a stick. I'd never seen such a vibrant lilac color on fairy floss before.

"Is that edible?" I asked.

"Trust me, Adam, this flavor will blow your mind."

She handed it to me. It smelled like jasmine. My tongue poked into the treat, melting it to a sticky delicious blob. Its lush taste took over my mouth.

"Guy, it's like a liqueur of some kind. Smooth and sensual."

"Like Mannix?"

He smirked.

"For an angel, you have a devilish mind."

"I'm the tool of nature. I'm just making sure your life runs on course. You have to live it to the fullest before you come back here again."

"Then I should go home and make things right."

"Not just yet, Adam. There's something else you have to do."

Chapter Twenty-Nine

ADAM

"What is that angel doing with that excuse of a boyfriend?" I asked.

"Yeah, well, love comes in many forms," Mannix replied.

He grinned.

"True. I guess I shouldn't be the one judging."

A bottle of merlot graced the table of our booth at the Pedestal. It was early afternoon, and Guy insisted Mannix and I bond before our return to the mortal world. There were only two other people in the pub—a straight couple who looked like they had seen better days. His chin was sliding off his palm, which was supposed to be holding him up, while she writhed around like a fat belly dancer to a melody that was yet to play.

"We should really eat something with this wine, Adam."

"I'm in no hurry. I'm enjoying revisiting the Afterlife, as an adult."

"It's unique, isn't it? Is this place how you remembered it as a kid?"

"I never came to the Pedestal as a kid, but I have been here recently."

"You have?"

"Yes, Guy has been visiting me lately, with his boyfriend."

"You're very special to him. Why else would he visit you as a kid? Although I did think it was a bizarre dream when you first mentioned it. I mean, really, a guardian fairy?"

"He knows what's best for me."

The writhing woman was doing handstands on the dance floor, still to no music. Her partner was almost facedown in a meal that had just arrived, before its aroma jolted him back to life.

"Okay, this mad place," I said. "How can this be heaven?"

"This parade of souls adrift? Call it the Limelight Quarter. It's where the precious keep living their dreams of stardom."

I contemplated the wall of actor portraits. Empty hearts filled each frame. The eyes that followed you around the room looked for love through applause. That missing bond when parents didn't care for their child's artistic side, so they grew up and found their own creative clique.

A shiver shot up my body. Mannix refilled my glass.

"Sorry," I said. "This place gets confronting."

"Why? You should be used to it."

"Because up until now I've only visited briefly. This time, it's becoming more real. It's becoming reality." I sipped. "Mannix, how do you feel being here?"

"I like it. It's dysfunctional. It's creative. It's where I want to stay."

"Not before your time, friend."

That dark singer was taking the stage. She watched the woman stomp around the floor, and began singing before the band set up. Her ethereal vocals filled the air. The words to "Dear Prudence" spooked my ears.

"Mannix, tell me about your love life."

"I'm not sure if I'm drunk enough."

"This place is getting weird. I need to hear something as entertaining as Guy's drugged-out mutterings last night."

"I don't think I've been in love. Well, not successfully, anyway."

"Go on."

"My two main short-term love interests were David and Murphy. Murphy had a sucking technique like someone dieting. I kept falling asleep in the middle of sex."

"You should have given him lessons."

"You're right. My face has seen more than its fair share of smile lines."

"It's not like I can tell, Mannix. You look like you've been moisturizing before you left the womb."

We sipped our wine as the singer hit some rather creepy notes. The dancing diva took it all in, working the floor like a professional wrestler.

"I also went home with a couple once," my friend said. I grinned like a teenage boy. "We daisy-chained with me in the middle."

"Was it with two other men or Ancient Roman style?"

"Two other men."

"How did it feel?"

"I felt like a piece of dental floss." He smirked.

"A new take on the Mexican wave," I replied.

We burst into laughter as Mannix pointed out our empty bottle to the barman.

"Adam, I don't know why people keep wanting me."

"Oh come on. You've got the face to inspire a thousand sonnets and a body to arouse a million dirty thoughts."

I wanted to taste his joyful lips, a marriage of wine and sex that would make a generous meal. I reached across the table for his hand. He offered it. We gripped fondly as the barman opened another merlot.

"Are we flirting?" Mannix asked.

"Seems like it," replied the bartender.

I weakened my grip, but he held on. Our barman strolled back, passing that woman who thrashed around like a dying hyena on her back. The vocalist sounded like Kate Bush with attitude as the band joined her for the last verse.

A young gay couple entered the bar, hand in hand. One towered over the other, but their mismatched physical form had no bearing on their love. They rushed to a booth and kissed sublimely.

There was Wade and I in that kiss, all those years ago. There was Wade and I in that kiss still to this day. In years to come, their bond would be a time capsule, keeping them merged forever at this age. Even when individual experience would help them grow with the world, in the center of their spirit would be the same two young men in love.

"Adam, I want to talk about our threesome."

"Why? Do you still want to go through with it?"

"I don't know. I'm a bit hesitant. Especially after what happened with me and Wade."

"Ancient history, Mannix. I've let it go."

"I don't believe you. Well, not completely, anyway."

"Trust me. I'm a lot more comfortable about it than I was before this whirlwind trip to the Afterlife."

"Are you sure, Adam?"

The singer started crooning the Rod Stewart classic "Tonight's The Night." Her vocals were softer than her previous rendition. The swarming woman stood still as her mate, with half his shirt tucked into his pants, stumbled to join her.

"I'm seeing the light, Mannix. I know what's going on. But it's not like I've been hit with a thunderbolt to knock sense into me. It's simply that the clouds have lifted."

"Melancholy is an understated emotion, Adam. Everything is in balance with hopeful clarity. Am I right?"

"That doesn't sound like something you'd normally say."

"Being here has made me grow up."

I reached for his other hand, which he presented willingly. We gripped tight.

"You're too wise, Mannix. You could be my muse."

"Adam, we all have to let our muses go so we can work things out for ourselves."

Darkness fell on the Pedestal as all voices faded. I was suddenly watching a play.

I recognized the cast. There were our ghostly doppelgangers, Allan and Warwick, onstage with Guy. He wore a sweaty wizard outfit as his wings withered. But Guy was also standing next to me, out of costume.

My dreamtime friend, Maudi, was draped in a figure-hugging dress, which propped up her bosom. She sat with two similar friends, drinking cups of tea in the audience. Francis, or Gloria's son as the angel's sketch suggested, also sat in the audience, dressed in a tie-dyed shirt.

"Where are we?" I asked.

"In a place of lessons that need learning."

"Well, that explains a lot. One minute, I'm taking your advice and chatting to Mannix; the next minute, I'm at the theater."

"Trust me, Adam, just watch."

Warwick and another woman were playing husband and wife, drying dishes in the kitchen. Another man was playing their son, wearing headphones in front of the stereo.

"No, he's not their son," said my guardian.

"How did you know what I was thinking?"

"I didn't. It's the obvious conclusion, looking at this scene."

"Shouldn't we keep quiet?"

"Don't worry. They can't see or hear us."

"Why?"

"Because they don't need to." I rolled my eyes. "Just watch, Adam."

Allan walked center stage, wearing a tacky rounded costume with a dinner suit sewn onto it. Perhaps Humpty Dumpty was off to a wedding?

"Why is he dressed like that?"

"Because he's supposed to be immortal."

"Since when are well-dressed ping-pong balls immortal?"

"Shh. He's about to deliver a monologue."

"This is just not right," announced Allan. "A loving couple support each other. They've shared their adventures and their dreams. Then there's the young idealist, searching for affection at an age when passion flows. There are more kisses to share, more fantasies to fulfill, more love to desire, but not together. Fabien, this is not a game without consequence. It's not for your entertainment. Real respect could be lost. Special memories could fade."

"But new memories could be made, special moments to lose themselves in." replied the version of Guy onstage. "A test of love that's already there. Why not share it?"

The angel standing next to me spoke into my ear. "There's more than enough love between Adam and Wade. Why cause disruption?"

"Because sometimes intimacy bonds people like no other encounter can," said the onstage Guy.

"But look at this young man," said Allan. "His future is bright, and our couple couldn't be more in love. They'll fall apart, and he'll be burnt by the incident. Fabien, why play with lives?"

"Ipan, why let life pass them by? Let the emotional become the physical. Let them share this special gift with one another."

The stage, the players, and the audience faded to white.

"Sound familiar, Adam?"

"So let me think about this for a moment. I just saw an earlier incarnation of Wade and I onstage with you, giving advice in a play about what I'm going through right now. Did you just conjure this up, or did it happen once?"

"It's a play written here in the Afterlife, and yes, we all were part of it the last time you were slumming around this place."

"It's kind of wordy. Who wrote it?"

"Francis."

"I thought so. Also known as Gloria's son. Which would make him Frankie, also known as Mannix, in my current life. Right?" Guy nodded. "And I know Maude was Maudi, and Allan and Warwick were Wade and I." Guy nodded again. "So who was Frederick?"

"A muse. Someone of this world to help people be reborn."

"And who decided Frederick had to exist?"

"Maudi brought him into existence to help her find her path back to Earth."

"And she knew this?"

"No, she had no idea Frederick wasn't mortal. She dreamed him up, unknowingly. He faded soon after her return to Earth."

"And so us mere recycled mortals run round and round in circles forever." I hugged my angel. "Guy, this is all becoming a bit too much to take in. It's making me dizzy. I need to go home."

"Adam, why hurry? I like having you here."

I let go of him.

"Because this isn't my world, yet it's becoming more real than my actual life. Confusing, but somehow, more real."

"That's the effect this place has on people. It becomes real very quickly." He looked to the nonexistent ground. "What have you learned from watching this play?"

"That there's nothing wrong with sharing passion and love, but it's not important in my life."

"So what are you going to do about it?"

"Get back to Wade as fast as possible. I need to forgive him."

"For in this life, you know it all. Wisdom collated as your journey will soon be complete."

These words echoed as the numbers on my alarm clock burned into my eyes. Its face proudly displayed one fifty-nine.

"I'm back where I started," I murmured.

"Well, I couldn't have you gone for days, could I now?"

Guy stood above me, his wings radiating their own smoky aura.

"Is that for effect? It kind of looks otherworldly. It just needs the 'Hallelujah Chorus' as a soundtrack."

He laughed.

"No, it's just what happens when I whisk myself to your world too quickly. People think it's the end of days when they see glowing wings. That's why we're not really supposed to be in your reality."

"Hey, I like it. It makes me feel like you really are my guardian angel. I feel protected. It's Hollywood effects and divine intervention rolled into one."

He leaned toward my face.

"Are you glad to be back, Adam?"

"Very glad. I really need to sort things out."

"Good. Maude has convinced Wade to pop in before work. You need to make peace."

"I'm giving him the biggest apology." I lifted my head from the pillow. "Oh no. I forgot to apologize to Mannix."

"There's plenty of time for that."

I shook my head.

"Guy, I want to thank you for everything you've done for me. Not just now, but when I was a kid as well."

"Adam, in this life, I will always be your guardian angel. Now sort out your marriage!"

Chapter Thirty

ADAM

To cut to the chase, I slept in and never saw Wade that morning. But my beautiful husband spoiled me with a bunch of flawless roses when he got home that evening.

"I should be the one buying *you* the flowers," I said.

I gave them a quick sniff before throwing my arms around him. Soon I rubbed my cheek against his and held him like he'd just returned from war. His arms reached around me, holding me tight.

"This is the Adam I've missed."

"This is the Adam that should never have gone away." I kissed his earlobe. "I am so sorry, Wade. I turned into Godzilla."

"More like Dr. Jekyll and Mr. Hyde."

The hug continued as I lost myself in my soul mate. Fear and doubt faded from our uncertain home. My lips aimed for his neck as I planted small kisses along his cheek.

"I don't know what's changed, Adam, but I like it."

"I don't think I can *ever* explain the last couple of days."

"The last couple of days? We've only been apart one evening."

"Oh yes." He pulled away and looked at me as if I'd grown a second nose. "It just seems like we've been apart for days, Wade. Oh, I love you so much." He rolled his eyes. "Come and sit down and let me explain."

I held his hand and led him to the lounge suite. We sat together with our fingers interlaced, while my other hand still held the flowers.

"You didn't go out all night, did you?" he asked. "I mean, you didn't stir this morning when I tried to wake you."

"Wade, before I go into a story that may make you want to commit me to a nursing home well before my time, can I just say how sorry I am for my stupid tirade? My mouth went into gear before I really thought about what I was saying."

"You were angry. I understand."

"I was more than angry. I was over the top."

"Adam, I'm used to that."

He raised our hands and kissed each of my knuckles.

"Wade, this is the first time you've run off to Maude's for shelter. Face it, I was a real bitch." He leaned over and planted his lips on mine. Our kiss lingered until I eventually pulled away from my addiction to his lips. "No, hear me out. I'm the one that needs to make it up to you. Let me apologize in the bedroom." I winked.

"Before you say anything, Adam, I want to say sorry for sleeping with Mannix. He caught me by surprise, and I stopped, but he was persistent, and let's face it, he's hot!"

I let out a guilty laugh.

"Yeah, I know. He tried with me, and I almost caved in."

"Why didn't you?"

"Oh trust me, it was close. But my own feelings of lust scared me more than his advances."

"So I'm the weak one."

"No, Wade, he just got you at a weak moment. Maybe if I had a drink or two beforehand, it would have been me sleeping at Maude's instead of you. Trust me, Wade, I was so close to cheating."

He took the flowers from my hand and laid them on our coffee table. I placed my hands on his cheeks and drew his face toward mine. As our lips brushed, our security buzzer rang.

"Ah, our guest is here," Wade said.

"Our guest? Oh, you invited Mannix. Good idea. I need to apologize to him as well."

He kissed me once more before he stood and took the flowers to the kitchen.

"Adam, it's not Mannix," he called as he fished around for a vase.

"Who is it then?"

"Answer the door and find out."

The buzzer sounded again, so I rushed to pick up the handset.

"Hello," I said.

"Is this the home of the Good Screw Crew?" said a screechy voice.

I covered the mouthpiece.

"Who the hell is outside?" I asked, but Wade didn't reply. "Who's is this?"

"It's Snugglepussy."

"And I thought my last few days were weird." My partner entered the lounge with the roses in a vase and placed them on the chest of drawers nearest the balcony. "Wade, what kind of talking animal is outside?"

"Well, don't just stand there. Let him in."

I reluctantly pressed the buzzer. Fast-paced footsteps thumped up the stairs.

"Wade, you didn't?"

"Didn't what?"

"Do more than just glance at the adult dating sites."

"Well, if you weren't interested, why did you let him in?"

"I couldn't leave him out in the cold."

I opened the door as our visitor reached the last step. I was about to tell him to go back home when he walked past me and placed himself between Wade and I.

"Oh darling," he said looking in my direction, "you can water my pot." His voice resembled a shrill whistle.

"Snugglepussy, do you have a name?" I asked.

"Bradley." He shimmied over to Wade and wiggled his ass. "And you darling, you can hump my grind."

"Bradley, dear, do you live far from here?"

"Why do you ask? Are we not alone?"

"I'm not sure if I'm ready for this."

"Oh, sweetheart, don't bail out on me. I've got so much candy in my piñata!"

I glared at Wade as if my eyes were about to shoot laser beams, but he simply gave me a wry smile.

"Bradley," I said.

"Oh, call me Snugglepussy."

"Okay, Snugglepussy, I don't think Wade really thought this through."

"Oh, Adam, let's give it a go," my partner said. "It will help get you-know-who out of our system."

Bradley fluttered toward me like an ostrich in high heels.

"Yeah, Adam, give me a go. Dip your dink in my ink."

"Wade, what were you thinking?"

"Adam, I did hear that right?" the visitor asked. "Your name is Adam?" I nodded. "You look stressed. I think we should start anew. Let me give you the gay handshake."

"The gay handshake?" He curled his fingers and made a masturbation gesture. "Wade, again, what were you thinking?"

"Darling, we have a guest. Be nice to Snugglepussy."

"Yes, Adam, be nice to me. Hit me with your rhythm stick."

He danced as if he was going to drill a hole through our floor. Wade gave me a sensual look, but I wasn't feeling the love.

"Bradley, we didn't mean to waste your time, but…"

"Oh, honey, let me change your mind after I prepare my body. Which way to the bathroom?" My partner pointed. Bradley headed for the door but paused to make a feline hand motion. "Purr." He wiggled his tush and disappeared.

"Wade, where did you find him? Desperate dot com?"

"I'm sure he's a nice guy. A little flouncy but at least he's entertaining."

"Yeah, like Christianity."

"Adam, do this. It will make us even."

"I won't be too long," Bradley called. "I'm just getting my blossom ready."

"Wade, this won't make us even. You slept with the class act. On our toilet is the class clown."

"Shh, he'll hear you." Wade was giving me puppy-dog eyes. "Adam, can't you just do this for me?"

"Do this for you? You just want me to appease your guilt, and trust me, you have nothing to feel guilty about. I'm okay with what happened."

At that moment, our visitor burst back into the lounge room, naked, wobbling like a baby Jabba the Hutt.

"Adam," he said, "I want to wear you like a cheap suit."

"Bradley," I replied, "you *are* the cheap suit. Ever considered less binge and more purge?" The phone rang. "Wade, you deal with this." I rushed for the handset. "Hello. Even if you're a telemarketer, talk to me."

"Is everything okay, Adam?" asked Maude.

"Oh, I'm so sorry to hear that," I replied.

"So sorry to hear what?"

"Wade, Maude needs our help!"

"What happened?" my husband asked.

"Yes, why do I need your help?" she asked.

"She's had a terrible fall. Can't feel her legs. What's that, Maude?"

"I didn't say—"

"Your house is on fire as well. We've got to get you out of there."

"Why did she call you instead of the fire brigade?" asked our nude guest.

"Because Wade and I are volunteer firefighters."

"We are?" asked my partner. I gave him a stern look. "Oh yes, Snugglepussy, we are."

"Who's Snugglepussy?" Maude asked.

"He's our neighbor's cat," I replied. "Here, Snugglepussy. Don't give me that pout."

"Adam, what's going on with you and Wade? Who's that other voice, and why is Wade talking to a cat?"

"What's that, Maude? The smoke is unbearable?" I marched into the bathroom and picked up Bradley's shirt and jeans. "Hang on, Maude. We'll be there soon."

I thrust the wannabe sex god's clothes into his chest, and he clutched them like a bear trap as I pushed him toward our front door.

"I'm still naked!" he squealed.

I shoved him outside and quickly slammed the door. Wade crossed his arms like a spoiled kid who didn't get his treat.

"Did you just throw some poor girl out of your apartment, Adam?" Maude asked.

"It wasn't a girl."

"That voice didn't belong to a girl? Was it a drag queen?"

"Not even that."

"I think I've called at a bad time. Just tell me you and Wade are all right, and we'll leave it at that."

"Blossom is hungry!" cried Bradley from outside.

"There's no room at the inn," I hollered. "Maude, everything is okay with Wade and me. Not sure about Snugglepussy, but he'll be all right."

"I know this is a story I don't need to hear."

"No, Maude, it's something you won't believe even if I told you."

"Okay. Send my love to Wade. He adores you."

"I know. He's my special man. My only man." Wade unfolded his arms as I blew him a kiss. "And he's all I'll ever need in life."

"That's my cue. Bye, Adam."

"Bye, Maude. Thanks for everything."

"Think nothing of it."

She hung up. As I put down the phone, I casually took a step toward the man of my dreams. He peeled off his jacket, let it slip to the floor, and then reached for the top button of my shirt. His fingers leisurely popped each one before reaching for my waist and caressing under my jeans.

I grabbed the back of his neck and brought his lips to my mouth. Wade's tongue answered the call and danced with mine. This was a waltz for old lovers who felt as young at heart as their first time, just with practiced steps. And each rehearsal kept adding to our lifelong grand performance.

Chapter Thirty-One

MANNIX

"What the...!"

"Mannix, everything is all right. Don't be scared, my darling."

This was the beginning of the weirdest night of my life. It was two in the morning, and I couldn't sleep. Plus a ghostly woman just happened to be standing in our kitchen with a cup of warm milk.

"Who are you?"

"Someone who's destined to help you out." She reached out with the cup. "Here, take it. It will help you write."

"How did you know...?"

She smiled knowingly. "How did I know what, Mannix?"

I seized the cup and drank half the milk.

"You knew I was thinking about writing. For the last half hour, I've been lying in bed thinking of adding lines to Maude's play. How did you know?"

"My darling, I have a confession. We all know too much about you." She gestured to the lounge room. "Just move slowly so you don't startle yourself."

I crept forward and saw two more spirits on the sofa. My cup smashed to the floor.

"We've scared the young fellow," the older ghoul said.

"Why do we bother with these mortals?" said the other.

I looked down for the shattered mug, but it wasn't there.

"No use crying over spilled milk," the woman replied.

The room started spinning, but I steadied myself.

"Feeling a little wheezy, are we?" asked the older one. "Sit down and take it all in, moment by moment."

I was shaking like a wet dog.

"I've lost the plot, haven't I? Bruce is going to find me quivering on the floor any moment now, lying in my own urine and stuttering about my imaginary characters coming to life."

"Now that I'd like to see," said the red-bearded one. "It would be more interesting than the tripe we've been putting up with from you and your scatty friends."

"Let him get his bearings before you give away too much," replied the other man.

"Here, try this." The redhead handed me a drink. I sniffed it. Scotch on the rocks. "It's better than milk."

"I've—I've seen you before," I babbled.

"Yeah, I was careless. You saw me outside the bar. I should introduce myself. I'm Fabien."

I drank.

"And I'm Farah," said the woman.

"And you're Ipan," I muttered.

"He knows us," he replied.

"Yeah, but I have no idea why. I've had odd flashes of you in my mind since childhood. But I thought you were just my overactive imagination."

I took another sip.

"Our early memories are questionable," Farah said. "It aids us to slip under the radar when the earthly world takes over a child's development."

"Then you've known me since I was a kid."

"It doesn't work that way, dear. Your destiny controls the moment you bring us into existence."

"So what are you saying? I knew you, but you didn't know me because you didn't exist? That doesn't make sense."

"We appeared at a time of growth for you, Adam, and Wade."

"What are you talking about?"

The ghosts exchanged uncomfortable glances.

"This is not going to be easy," Ipan said to the others. "Mannix, there's a terrible wrong we have to put right."

"We have to put you back on your path," Farah added.

They paused.

"No, you have to explain this to me. You've been in my memory since I was a kid. Yet you turn out to be real. Bruce has been at me to write a story about you. How can you be physically here?"

"We're here because you need us now."

"You've got a story to tell about unrequited lust," said Fabien.

"But it's based on love and respect."

"And that's what makes it hard for you, Mannix," continued Ipan. "In fact, it's what makes it hard for you, Adam, and Wade. Together, you don't know how to cross that line and what might be on the other side."

"And why that is, I don't understand," said Fabien. "You're all men. Why are you worried about feelings?"

"You sound like my inner thoughts, Fabien," I said. "But when I acted on my thoughts, I split up a couple."

"Trust me, darling," Farah replied, "all is back as it should be with Adam and Wade. They're asleep in each other's arms as we speak."

"Old lovers can't deal with drama for too long," Ipan declared.

Farah smiled at him like a girl getting a marriage proposal from a prince. I stared toward Bruce's bedroom.

"He's fast asleep, my darling," she said. "He won't wake and discover this mad scene."

"I wish he would wake up. He'll never believe this if he doesn't see it with his own eyes." I gulped a mouthful of scotch. "I still don't know why you're all here."

"You have to finish what you started with Adam and Wade," she replied.

"I can't risk it."

"But you know you want to," said Fabien.

"Oh god, yes! But why?"

"Unfinished business is a curse," replied Ipan. "If you don't resolve it, it will come back to haunt you in other ways."

"You've changed your tune, old man," said Fabien. "You were like a grumpy little weasel with no control when I started this experiment. Now you're urging everyone to the finish line."

"I'm not scared of the outcome anymore."

"It seems you've come full circle. Just like Adam did." The old man nodded. "And of course, Farah, you play carefree love like lost little Wade."

"Only when the timing is right," she replied. "But we're not here to compare. We're here to help Mannix complete his story."

"I'm even more confused now," I said. "Why are you urging me to sleep with Adam and Wade?"

"Because we've been watching this thing carry on for a while now," answered Fabien. "I wanted some excitement. All I got was sore eyes."

"Sore eyes and a morbid fascination," added Ipan.

"Well it's not my fault they were all too chicken to just get on with it."

"Fabien, it wasn't easy for me," I said.

"Not easy? All we got was a bonk between you and Wade and a badly scripted drama to follow."

"Not everyone can be as selfish as you," said Ipan.

"Mannix can, can't you, Mannix?"

"That's enough, Fabien. Let the poor boy get his thoughts in order."

"I'm not selfish," I said. "I really felt connected to these guys. I wasn't driven by personal pleasure."

"Yes, you egocentric warlock," said Ipan. "You can't blame others for your own actions."

"Oh really, you droll old man. Don't forget who I represent in this scenario." He stared at me.

"You mean me? I'm nothing like you."

"Really? Look in the mirror, Mannix. Maybe I'm the dark side of your soul. The one you wrestle with."

"Don't be harsh," said Farah. "You are not Mannix's dark side. But maybe you were the reflection of how Adam saw him, when things got out of hand."

"I'm not that dark," I replied.

"Think about it. People don't see the world as it is; they see it as *they* are. And from Adam's point of view, well, you were Fabien."

"Oh please!" said the frank wizard. "You're tiptoeing around his feelings."

"And you can be kinder," said Farah.

"You airy-fairy woman! He wrote us into existence. He knows what we might say." Fabien stuck his face close to mine. "Sweetheart, you prick teased Adam and Wade."

"I didn't prick tease." The three stared blankly at me. "It wasn't prick teasing. I was just staying in control."

I swallowed hard.

"And what do you have to stay in control about?" asked Farah.

Fabien looked away.

"Before I had sex with Wade, I was in control. I had two men fighting for my attention, and it felt good. But they were a couple. They didn't work together. Why didn't they work together? It would have made it easier."

"They were thrown into this without much choice," replied Ipan.

"Yeah, and they'd come on to me, separately. Not in a huge way. They were just..."

"Just what?" Farah asked.

"I don't know. They were just on different pages. They weren't a team. Well, they were sometimes. But other times, I felt like I had to step carefully so one of them wouldn't feel hurt. But then I did hurt one of them."

"You're not as experienced as you think you are," said Fabien.

He was still looking the other way.

"No, maybe I'm not. I can model nude, but I can't land a couple in bed."

"So you lost your bravado."

"Yeah, I did." My glass was magically refilled to the top. I drank. "I didn't really think I was worthy of them." I put the drink down. "Did I just say what I thought I said?"

"That's how you felt about David," said Ipan. "So you bought a burgundy shirt to make you appear more attractive."

"But you already are attractive," added Farah. "Both inside and out."

"I don't feel it," I replied.

"What? With people drawing your body week by week? You should."

"I can chat up strangers, or model in front of them, but when it's someone I like, it's a different story."

I wiped a tear from my cheek.

"And Adam ended up being more than a stranger," said Farah. "So did Wade."

"So how can I go through having a threesome with two cool guys when I can't even sleep with one, unless I'm really drunk?"

"You're still talking about David," said Fabien.

"Yeah, we never had sex. But I had sex with Wade, so I must be over my issues."

Fabien turned away again. The others looked in his direction, pursed lipped.

"Mannix, you found your courage with Wade," said Farah. She turned back to me. "But you have to believe you're worthy of both their affection."

"But they'll work out I'm inexperienced."

"That's just an excuse. No, it's a fear. A stupid fear, my darling."

"Mannix, don't push people away," said Fabien. He smiled sheepishly. "You can use sarcasm or a selfish personality, or in your case, fake bravado—"

"Yes, sarcasm and selfishness," Ipan interrupted. "That's your excuse."

"Please, let me finish. But, Mannix, you can't go on thinking that you're not worth loving. Even when it's just a ménage à trois between friends."

"Look at it like a start to your education," said Farah. "Or the next step in what you need to know about life in general. You've had sex. Now make love."

"But how?"

"Mannix, you already love Adam and Wade in your own way. Now give yourself permission to share that love. The rest will follow."

I laughed.

"So you're telling me to be the man-whore again and risk breaking Adam and Wade apart."

"Sex is life-affirming," she replied. "It's what you all wanted to begin with, but it has to be as a trio. Adam and Wade can teach you a lot, and not just physically."

"And you definitely can teach them something," added Fabien. "Teach them not to be so boring."

"And teach Adam to be the carefree soul he'd like to think he is," added Ipan.

"Good call, my dear lover," said Farah.

"So my role is to learn from my gay elders."

"Mannix," she said, "we all have to let our muses go eventually, so we can grow up."

"So maybe my role is to *teach* my gay elders."

"Whatever works out best," said Fabien. "Now go and seduce those two before they lose interest!"

Chapter Thirty-Two

ADAM

Amateur theater royalty strolled into the Petersham Community Hall, as if they'd just posed for paparazzi on a red carpet. They were here for the first night of *Midsummer Mayhem*, their inquisitive natures coming to observe in friendly rivalry.

I smiled at people I knew who shook my hand, congratulating me on my directorial efforts before taking their seats. Wade kissed me, standing handsome with a half beard and sexy spectacles. An opening night with my husband there was always an omen for success.

The blonde bimbo cop and her hulky sidekick entered, followed closely by Shannon. Their eyes sparkled as they greeted me.

"What happened?" I asked. "I thought you were in huge trouble."

"Adam, I have ways of working the law."

His partners in crime nodded.

"We've let him off for good behavior," said Sharon.

"And he's been behaving badly ever since," added the hunky policeman.

They chuckled before our former player took his new friends by the hand and skipped to their seats.

"You must be Adam," said an unknown woman.

"Yes, I'm the director."

Her thick cork heels clumped as she entered. She pulled the thin veil from her hair and held it in the air.

"What do you see through this piece of material?"

"Wow, there's a dramatic gesture. What's your name, and what theater group are you from?"

"I'm Monique."

"Such a mysterious name. It sounds like a femme fatale in a murder mystery."

"And behind my veil, what do you see?"

"People in their seats waiting for the play to start."

"Remember, Adam, this world of mortals and the other world of knowledge are obscured by the thinnest of veils."

Two keys were placed in my hand. I looked at them.

"The large one is for the front door of the apartment block," said Brent.

He was a friend from the theatrical society who was letting us stay at his home over the weekend while he was off to the Blue Mountains. His place was closer to the theater than ours. Plus he had a cat to feed.

"Thanks, mate."

"Just leave them on the coffee table when you leave on Monday."

Brent left as quickly as he appeared. I looked for Monique, but she too was gone. With all that had happened to me, it didn't faze me.

"Three aces or a royal flush?" Maude asked as Angela.

"What do you mean by the poker reference?" Mannix replied as Ronny.

"You seem to hold your cards close to your chest." She brought her champagne glass to her face and studied the bubbles seductively.

"How so?"

"You hint at a chance to get neighborly." She met his eyes. "Then you retract the offer when I'm willing to cash in my gift voucher."

Ronny paused.

"We're good neighbors," he replied. "We have an excellent relationship."

"But you know and I know, we both want more."

"In what regard?"

His hands fumbled as if he was about to take off a wedding ring. She kissed her glass before putting it down, and then released the top buttons of her blouse. He took a step toward her, lifting his hand as a gesture for her to stop.

"You're teasing me, Ronny."

"I need to know where I stand if anything happens. I want to hold the aces."

"Fate dictates that you can't hold all the winning cards. Not all the time, at least."

"Angela, I'm not sure that's a gamble I'm willing to take."

"My young apprentice, look at the hand you're being dealt and see if it's worth the risk. If the odds are fifty-fifty, take the chance. You may stumble. You may rise." She briefly glanced at his crotch. The audience laughed. "But you'll always regret the hand you never played."

She wandered over and placed her arms on his shoulders, before sensually blowing air on his face. He closed his eyes and bit his bottom lip.

"Don't be scared, Ronny."

They kissed. The tension in his body disappeared. He gave a carnal sigh.

End of act two. The curtains shut. The audience applauded, and some even whistled. I jumped out of my seat as the lights in the hall came on, and rushed to the Green Room.

"The crowd is lapping it up, guys!"

Maude ripped off one nineteenth-century dress before breathlessly squeezing into another. Mary did the same while simultaneously cooling herself with a fold-out fan. The men patted their faces with tissues, making sure their makeup didn't run.

"Go on, Adam, say it," said Maude.

"Say what?"

"I told you so."

"I told you so about what?"

"Mannix can act."

Our young player bowed.

"But you already knew that."

"And his extra words to that scene added so much," said Mary.

"And they were beautiful words," Maude added. "I love my lines about taking a chance when it's a two-way bet. Mannix, you can write. It's time you wrote a piece of your own."

"I'm working on it," he replied. "After I added words to your script, I began on my own short screenplay."

"What's it about?" I asked.

He looked at me like a scout, lost without a compass.

"Unrequited longing."

Maude and I grinned.

"He's a keeper, Adam. Don't let that young man stray far from you and Wade."

"I intend to have him around as long as I can."

"That's a vote of confidence," he said. "I felt like I was under the spotlight when you first met me, Maude."

"Dear, you were. But you've passed all my tests."

"What was on the exam?"

"I'll tell you later."

She blew him a kiss.

"So you're writing about unrequited longing," I uttered. "It sounds like your muses are coming to life."

"Just like Mr. Guy."

"I have the maddest urge to give you a hug, Mannix."

"Not now, Adam. I have to change my shirt." I raised my eyebrow. "And no, Adam, you're not hugging me topless."

"Oh get a room," groaned Stephen.

"You're right," I confessed. "We have a play to do. Break a leg for the third act."

Needless to say, the final act couldn't have gone better. Hearts were broken and amended. Marriages were toyed with. And the comedy of a bygone era rang true to the audience, who stood and cheered as if they had seen a Broadway play.

The first night party was just as successful, and even though a lot of the night was a blur thanks to endless champagne, many images were burnt forever in my memory. Stephen finally tongue-kissed Shannon, making me suspect the blue pills were delivered. Maude celebrated in her hooped period dress, knocking a few people over until she tumbled ass-down on the floor. I cringed at the thought of the dry-cleaning bill. Yet, she still sat poised, holding the stem of her glass between her fingers.

"A lady to the end," said Wade.

He lifted his glass as we toasted her refined public humiliation. Mannix helped her to her feet.

Some older queens whisked around the hall with old disco moves to the top-forty soundtrack. We soon joined them, trying to do the bus stop to a frenetic beat. Fists punched the air out of rhythm, and our bizarre neck movements reminded me of seagulls trying to kill fish in their beaks. But salvation was finally at hand. Someone changed the music to rediscovered house tunes.

And there was Wade and I, revisiting our youth. His funky hips swung around me like a satellite in orbit. I felt prized. My man of eighteen years was still in love with me. How lucky was I?

"Darlings, I'm going." Maude had changed into a casual gown. "Let's catch up at my place tomorrow night."

"No," Wade replied. "We're staying at Brent's. Visit us instead."

"Good idea. I'll ring you tomorrow." She looked toward Mannix. "Like I said before, keep him around. He's put a spring in both your steps. Not that you needed a spark in your relationship, but he's forced you to look at yourselves on a deeper level."

She waved away our startled looks, then walked to Mannix and gave him a huge hug before exiting. Soon our favorite younger man casually strolled over to dance with us. The joyous tunes of yesteryear made him move his hips in ways not suitable for underage eyes. Yet, his seductive display didn't throw us as, at this moment, the world belonged to just Wade and I.

Chapter Thirty-Three

ADAM

"Large homoerotic prints in the lounge are a bit of a cliché," I said.

I stood in front of gold-framed pictures of men's torsos at Brent's place. Their multiple gray shades seemed as cheap as dingy back rooms.

"Adam, they were the trend back late last century. Men's chests were on every queen's wall in the eighties."

"Antiques are one thing, but Brent should rethink his artwork."

There was a knock on the door. After I answered, a thin middle-aged man minced in with so much camp he could've upstaged Liberace.

"You're Adam, aren't you?" he asked.

"Yep, that's me."

I closed the door. In his hand was a plastic container in a peculiar shade of lime. His tight fitting T-shirt matched this lurid color. He was the man that style forgot.

"We've met before. I used to go out with Brent for a nanosecond a few years back, and you and Wade ran into us at that quaint little bookstore."

I scratched my head.

"Ah yes," said Wade. "You're Jeremy."

"No, I'm Jason. Jeremy was a couple of boyfriends before me."

"Oh."

"These are for us." He shook the container. "I've baked them for later." He winked. "These cookies will make us feel fabulous! I've just got to deal with my husband upstairs, but I'll be back in an hour or so to *share* the love." He sauntered to the kitchen, waving his arms around like an injured octopus, before placing the baked goods on a plate. "Now usually I eat cookies with milk, but I think for these delicious treats, we need something a little stronger. Hmm." His finger rested on his chin. "Well, I'll come back with something." He headed for the exit, his fingers fluttering like fish on a trawler. "Toodles."

I shut the door.

"What was that?" I asked.

"Someone being neighborly."

"We're living in Peyton Place."

"Just with gay characters." Wade sported a Cheshire grin. "He may not be a bad lay if the cookies are strong enough."

"Wade, it's been a long night. I'm tired and drunk. Plus you don't need to make up for having sex with Mannix. Just you in bed tonight is enough."

"Adam, I know you've forgiven me. I'm just suggesting something more adventurous away from home. Finish your opening night with a bang."

"No, thank you. I still have nightmares about Snugglepussy."

"At least he looks more flexible than Snugglepussy."

"Wade, he looks like a triffid who wears the discarded clothes of his prey."

There was another knock. We ignored it. Then one more, but we snubbed that one as well.

"Ah, bugger," said Mannix's voice from behind the door. "They're not here yet."

I opened the door.

"Sorry," I said. "We're avoiding one of our neighbors." Our charming friend stood with two bottles of wine, one red and one white, nestled under each arm. "That's sweet of you, but I was thinking about going to bed."

"Adam, the play was a success. You can't go to bed now."

"He's right," said Wade. "Why not make a night of it?"

I studied Mannix's sweet face.

"Oh, all right then. But only one glass, then I'm off to bed."

"Just one?"

"Just one. Now quick, get inside."

"Who are you hiding from?"

I locked the door behind him.

"Adam's freaking out about one of the neighbors."

"I'm not freaking out. It's just that he's a bit creepy."

"Well, if he's that bad, why don't you go and return his special cookies?"

I stood silent.

"What's so creepy about him?" Mannix asked.

He made his way to the fridge and popped the bottle of white on its upper shelf. I rifled around for some glasses and poured the red.

"Go on, Adam," said Wade. "Tell Mannix what's so freaky about Jason."

"Well, for one, what type of person waltzes in with hash cookies and expects sex in return?"

"One that lives in a gay apartment block," our guest replied. He lifted the plate of baked treats to his nose. "These are strong! I should leave and let you guys have some fun when he comes back."

"Mannix, I'd rather eat the cookies with you." My partner and our guest exchanged stares as if they had discovered the secret of mental telepathy. "We're not sharing the cookies now. There's a pillow in the other room with my name on it. Crash here tonight, and we'll share them tomorrow with Maude and our ditzy neighbor."

"Pour some milk," said Wade.

"Where's the cups?" asked Mannix.

"No, seriously," I said. "We can't just eat his cookies. He brought them for all of us. What do we say if he returns?"

"Hopefully, we'll all be too bombed to care," Wade replied.

He pointed to the cabinet above Mannix's head. Our guest opened them and found three Las Vegas souvenir mugs. My partner grabbed a carton of milk from the fridge. After pouring, he handed me my drink.

"I still have an ethical dilemma about eating these." Mannix handed me one of the laced delights. "Ah, smell that cinnamon. And there're raisins!" I took a bite. "I'm sure Jason has plenty more cookies. He won't miss these."

"I taste a bit of nutmeg," said Mannix. He nodded wistfully. "These are heaven."

"I can't taste the special herbs," said Wade.

"The sign of a good cook," our guest replied.

"Do you realize how terrifying it is to go to bed with an established couple?" Mannix asked.

His speech was ponderous.

"But wouldn't it be easy?" Wade replied. "We know what works for us, and we'd be inviting you into *our* world. Plus we'd be discovering what makes *you* tick."

"But what if one of you gets jealous?"

"And by jealous, Mannix, you mean me," I mumbled. "Trust me. My thoughts have changed." I lifted my wine glass. "You know they've changed. You were with me when I came to terms with it. We've spoken about this." He looked to the ceiling, expressionless. "Believe me when I say that both of you have instigated the ice breaker. The first act, if you like. This conversation is probably the second act. Let's not be scared of the third."

"Good point, Adam," said Wade. "Let's make a deal. Let's give each other permission to have a threesome."

"That's a bold thought," declared Mannix.

We gazed at each other like first-time parachutists about to jump.

"And it doesn't mean we have to," my husband continued. "We may never do it. But at least the first barrier is lifted by giving ourselves permission."

"Wade, that's why I love you," I said.

I stretched past our guest and kissed my partner fondly. Mannix tapped his finger on the coffee table.

"What is it?" Wade asked.

"Okay, permission to do it. Granted. But the two of you were going to try to spoil me, weren't you?"

"It's crossed our minds."

"Don't."

"Why?"

"Because I want to fumble through this. I want to take control even if I'm not sure what I'm doing. I need to prove to myself that I can step up to the plate with an established couple."

"Control?" I said. "Do you want me to check if anyone in this block has a whip?"

"That's why I love you both. You make me laugh." Wade and I gently leaned to kiss our guest, but he steadily pushed us away. "We've just given ourselves permission. Give me some time with that thought."

"What's the matter, Mannix?" I asked. "You don't feel like you're holding the aces?"

"That's strange," said Wade. "I thought three queens would be a winning hand."

There was a knock at the door.

"Shh," I whispered.

My finger missed my lips and brushed itself like a knife spreading jam across my cheek. Mannix almost laughed as my pointer made a second attempt at reaching my mouth. It succeeded.

"Adam and Wade, I'm here to spread goodwill to all men," said Jason. He knocked again. "Hello, darlings, are you home?"

Mannix slithered off the modular lounge and crawled toward the door. I leaped like a gazelle to grab his feet. I missed. He stopped and turned.

"Don't open it," I whispered.

I clutched my hands and pretended to beg. Wade stared at us like a shift worker trying not to fall asleep.

"Adam? Wade? Are you there?"

As Mannix began crawling again, I used my elbows to move forward and gripped one of his bare feet. He stopped, attempting to break free with as little effort as a married man trying to leave a strip club.

"They must have gone out," said Jason. "Oh well, all good things come to those who wait."

I cringed as his footsteps climbed the stairs.

"He sounds like a kid on helium," said Mannix.

I tickled his foot. He giggled.

"So do you," I replied.

He presented his other foot, so I licked his ankle. Wade began choking. I jumped to my partner's aid, picking up my glass and moving it to his lips.

"Here, drink this," I said.

"Adam, you're offering Wade wine."

"Yeah, I know."

"Shouldn't he have a glass of water?"

My man was still coughing.

"Yes. Water!" he hissed.

Mannix shot up and rushed for the kitchen sink. When he returned, he passed me the glass of water. Wade also reached out, but I took it from Mannix's hand and had a swig. Behind our guest, a flashy display of disco lights bounced colors through the furniture. For some reason, our young friend was only wearing a white pair of slacks. Neon beams ignited his creamy toned chest.

It was shore leave, and I was watching Mannix the go-go dancer smother himself around a pole at a seedy bar. My sailor suit fit my surprisingly slender body like a glove. I was wearing it off duty as a sure way to get laid.

The artiste was greased and glistening. He had moves that would make any porn director skip the casting couch and give him top billing. I rushed to the stage and placed a hundred-dollar note in his skimpy ripped denim shorts. He decided that for the price, I deserved more than just a peek.

His fingers casually reached for his fly and unzipped, lingering at the halfway mark. He looked into my eyes as his pointer waved like a metronome in front of my face, before coolly reaching down and exposing his delicious...

Wade was still coughing and snatched the water from my hand. He gulped it down.

"Adam, you're staring at my crotch," said Mannix.

"Am I? Oh, sorry."

"Adam, are you Gilligan or the Skipper?"

"That's a strange question coming from a go-go dancer."

"Yeah," replied Wade. "You're both saying weird shit."

Mannix reached out to us with both arms, which we grabbed like cut-out paper dolls trying to stand. He guided us to the master bedroom as I floated tissue-like, riding the air.

"Adam, I think you're Gilligan," he said. "You need to feel loved."

"God, yeah," replied Wade.

"And you're the Skipper. You need to be the one in charge of handing out the love."

"Just don't get us shipwrecked, darling," I said.

The humungous bed called out to us, plush and welcoming. Its pillows spied like two voyeurs ready for their next fix, while the quilt flourished like a lush tongue, ready to lick away our doubts.

"Are we scared, guys?" asked our tempting buddy.

Wade moved forward with his lips puckered, but I gently pushed him back.

"I want to say something before we start," I murmured. "Let's give ourselves permission to do this."

"But we've already done that," said my husband.

"No, listen. Imagine at this moment, the world is crumbling. All governments have fallen. Religion hasn't saved anyone. But an amazing tsunami of peace is engulfing the globe."

"So this is world's end?"

Wade and Mannix exchanged long looks.

"Well, it is, and it isn't. Like, yeah, the environment is rooted, but coming to save us is the tsunami of peace. The peace tsunami! Feel it. Breathe it. We're all part of it."

"That cookie's really kicked in, Adam."

"No, Wade, listen to him." Our friend gazed at me like a kindergarten kid being read a story. "I feel your love tsunami."

"Peace tsunami, Mannix," I said. "It's a peace tsunami."

"But if the world is crumbling, what good is a peace tsunami?" my partner asked.

"Just go with it, Wade," said Mannix. "And the peace tsunami is a good reason to just ride it all the way."

"Yeah," I said. "Not quite what I was thinking, but it sounds better than what I was going to say. Not that I remember what point I was making, but yours sounds good."

"I think what you were trying to say was that we've given ourselves permission to have this threesome." He clutched our hands tight. "Wade and Adam, hold *each other's* hands."

We did, hence forming a circle.

"I give all the permission in the world," I said. "I love you, Wade."

"I love you too, Adam," he replied.

"And I love you both," said Mannix.

"We love you too," we replied.

The disco lights of the go-go dancers' den returned. Mannix stood godlike as neon red and blue soaked his skin. Soon, the appendage that first greeted me in art class was staring me in the face. It was half-erect, rosy, and waiting for me to savor both it and this whole experience. Around us, I sensed the musky smell of males, dancing shirtless surrounding our bed.

I sat on the floor with the back of my head nestled against the mattress. I licked his joystick as Wade stood on the covers presenting his moist pride to our guest's eager mouth. We tasted and slurped like we were relishing a treat we'd never eat again. Those disco boys gave me a thumbs-up as they gyrated past in their glossy gold shorts. The bass of the thumping music kept us in rhythm.

I smelled his sweat as my mouth swallowed his shaft. My tongue cherished his first salty drop, whetting my whistle for more thrusts. We groaned and purred as the others stood in voyeuristic delight.

Mannix bent over and kissed my slimy mouth. He reached for my hand and lifted me to my feet.

Where were those gorgeous sex bunnies that were sharing this event with us? The music was still here, but they were gone.

Mannix's hands were now on Wade's butt cheeks, swaying him gently back and forth like a leather swing. My husband then stretched out like a cat, arms to the sheets and ass in the air. Our friend clutched my cock, pulling me onto the bed. The disco crowd was back again, dancing.

The slippery lube splashed onto me, soon followed by the hot lips of Mannix's butt. It swallowed me into its safe haven as he lurched forward, and I with him. His erection waiting to stab Wade, and I was here for the ride. He entered. My partner groaned. Gold shorts ripped off as the lubricant got passed around. The men copied our daisy chain.

I kissed the back of Mannix's neck, tasting his scrumptious youth. Our shared grunts and the smell of man-sex was getting me higher. I reached for his tuft of silky chest hair while watching my dick dive into bliss. All five senses were at play.

"Why did we wait so long?" he cried.

"I love you both," Wade shrieked. "Two men I absolutely adore."

"This is better than all my fantasies," I purred.

"I have both of you exactly where you should be," Mannix panted. "You're my dirty little secret. You're my own dirty little couple."

Wade and I stopped thrusting as our friend did all the work. He seesawed back and forth, gasping with each slow jab. The men watched, riding each other steadily.

I closed my eyes, intensely feeling my drill explore his luscious space. His butt cheeks slapped my balls, working us harder, frenzied and rhythmic in our private three-way worship.

He was looser. I plunged in hedonistic glory, indulging in the soft walls that gripped me. He groaned in euphoric agony, my hands firmly clasping his hips. He howled like a maniac. So did Wade.

I wanted everything his succulent hole had to offer. All the men who relished it before this moment. All that gratified it before my place in the cue. For it was my turn to feed it so it could eat me alive.

Our trigger-happy brothers panted breathlessly. They urged us on. Their creamy shots fired like shooting stars as their carnal cries echoed. They were our own chaotic chorus of deliriously spent men.

"Oh. Oh-oh." Mannix was trembling.

"Are you almost there?" I sighed.

"Almost. You've got me in the palm of your hand, Adam."

"So this is my gift to you, you beautiful man!"

He reached up, praising an ancient god. I splashed inside him. My sweat dripped down his neck. Mannix shuddered as Wade pushed back. My partner yelled like his soul escaped.

All those other men faded with their disco lights. A hundred faces sharing cheeky smirks before they were gone.

"Mannix, why didn't we just do this sooner," I whimpered breathlessly.

"Yeah, I know. This experience was well overdue."

The birds were chirping. I opened my eyes and found myself spooning Mannix. He, in turn, was spooning my husband. My arm had reached over our young companion to caress his velvety chest hairs again. His arm was cradling Wade's belly. It was the perfect moment.

"So what have you learned?" asked Guy.

As I focused on his form, the backdrop changed. We were back at the Pedestal, and that statuesque woman was back onstage singing like she'd been smoking too much. The shadows of swaying dancers added life to the muted lights, as candles flickered on every table. In front of us were the reddest cocktails I'd ever seen.

"What's this?" I asked.

He raised his glass.

"A toast to a friend who conquered fear."

"Thanks, Guy, but *what* is this?"

"An angel specialty."

It tasted crimson, if you could imagine a color having a flavor. It trickled down my throat, rich and sweet.

"Guy, I'm the calmest I've been for as long as I remember."

"You've been enlightened. The end of a chapter has that effect." His wings fluttered. "So, Adam, what have you learned?"

"That I have a strong relationship. And it's stronger than I gave it credit for."

I looked into the crowd. A hippy woman in a loose lilac gown sat with two men at a booth on the opposite side of the bar. She looked at me like a caring big sister. One of her friends wore a red jacket and seemed to stare past me before meeting my eyes and nodding gently. The other man, bearded and freckled, raised his beer. As they met my gaze, they faded like ghosts returning to the hereafter. But this was the hereafter.

"Guy, who were those people?"

"Reflections. Muses. Spirits who have played their part."

"You're not even stoned, and you're talking in riddles."

"They helped guide you, Wade, and Mannix. But their time has passed."

"Oh, I get it. Like Frederick was Maudi's muse. But he faded too."

"And those thoughts don't freak you out, Adam?"

"Not anymore. This place seems so real. But I really should be back at Brent's."

"Sorry, Adam. It's my fault. I like having you here."

Pure white washed out the background before Brent's bedroom returned. Wade and Mannix were still sleeping, cozy under the blankets. I was sitting up in bed, facing my angel.

"Thank you for everything you've done, Guy."

"That's what I'm here for."

"I sense that I'm about to lose contact with you. Am I right? What will I do without my guardian fairy?"

He smiled gently.

"I'm not leaving you yet. But look at the bed you've slept in, Goldilocks." My lovers were peaceful. "You have my messengers in bed here with you. And you also have Maude. She cared about you both when Mannix entered your lives. I can't be with you always. That's why you all have each other. Cherish your soul mates."

"And we're destined to be soul mates again and again?"

"For eternity, Adam. For eternity."

His wings lowered.

"Can I ask you something, as a friend?"

His wings twinged.

"All right."

"This Joshua thing. He's a demon. Are you making the right lifestyle choices?"

"Adam, he knows where my parents are."

"Is that...?" I rubbed my chin. "I guess that is a good reason. But it's sure to have consequences in the long run."

He leaned toward me.

"Nothing my friends and I can't handle." He met my gaze. I sensed I was one of the friends he was referring to. "Adam, I need to go before Wade and Mannix wake up. Breakfast is ready to serve in the kitchen. Just tell them you prepared it."

I kissed him. My lips tingled with pins and needles. He gradually pulled away and stood.

"Guy, when will I see you again?"

"When you're an old man. Bye, Adam. I'll see myself out."

"What? You're not going to disappear or fly out the window?"

"You're getting too used to my parlor tricks. It's time to embrace your mortal world again. Enjoy it for all its worth, and spread its riches."

He strolled to my side of the bed, sat, and gave me one last hug. I reached around his back with one arm, while caressing his silky feathers with the other. His cheek pressed to mine, soft and warm. I felt a stir between my legs before he pulled back.

"I'm looking forward to the day we meet again, Guy."

"So am I, Adam. So am I." He gestured to my sleeping Wade as he stood. "Bye, my friend."

"I love you, Guy."

"I love you too."

He carefully stepped backward out the bedroom door. I shed a tear before noting once more how settled Mannix and Wade were, wrapped in each other's bodies. How silly we were not to have done this sooner.

Here we were. Two men sharing our devotion with someone special, without fear. All had been amended in sex, love, and conversation.

The next day, all three of us greeted Maude at Brent's front door. She sported a large mischievous grin. Then she applauded. I hung my head in mock shame. We lunched at a café nearby, talked about the play, and analyzed Shannon's relationship with his new police friends. Later, Maude gave Mannix a lift home.

And that was the last time we saw our young friend. He never showed up for the next performance on Thursday night. We tried ringing, but there was no answer. We offered the audience refunds or seats for another night. But *Midsummer Mayhem* played no more.

Bruce explained it was a car crash, a story that haunted me as soon as I heard it. I held hands with Wade and Maude as we watched Mannix's casket lower. I wept into my husband's shoulder, who in turn, wept into Maude's.

"At least he didn't leave you with unfinished business," she whispered.

"And he's left a mark on our relationship I'll always remember," Wade sobbed.

"I'll drink to that," I whimpered. I lifted my head. "And boy, do I need a drink right now! Do you want to join us, Bruce?"

He shook his head as he wiped away his tears.

"But toast him on my behalf." He raised a pretend glass and gazed at the clouds. "To M. The friend I can never replace."

Maude held him as I clutched onto Wade.

"And may he share his talents in heaven," I added. "For he has so much more to achieve."

Bruce choked in grief.

"Yes. M is up there sharing his infectious grin with the angels. God bless him."

Wade and I wrapped our arms around him. Soon we strolled away from the cemetery with Maude. We looked back to Bruce as he tried to smile.

A day later, Guy visited me once more. I sat with him on our lounge in the dead of night.

"You kept this from me."

"I couldn't tell you, Adam."

"You could've given me a hint." I frowned. "And it was a car accident."

"Yes."

"Just like he told me at your place." The angel nodded. "It all makes sense now. He'd already passed on when I met him in the Afterlife, hadn't he, Guy?"

"Yeah. He had perspective on your three-way friendship. That's why I took you to my world to see him."

I smirked.

"You're a wise angel, and I'm blessed to have you."

"And you're a loving soul, Adam. I'm honored to be your guardian."

He frowned.

"What is it?"

"This is the last time we'll meet in your lifetime." I held his hand. "You have adventures to share with Wade without me interfering."

"And the strange thing is, I'm ready to let you go and live my own life without your help. But at least I know you're waiting for me on the other side, Mr. Guy."

My childhood friend wrapped his wings around me as I closed my eyes, breathing in my angel for the last time as a mortal. He kissed my lips. His sweet breath lingered before I nuzzled into his chest. I felt the confused pain of my four-year-old self preparing for his good-bye. Soon his wings wrapped tighter so I looked up at his ghostly form. He faded away as sunlight greeted me from the kitchen window.

He was truly gone. This heavenly being that I'd become accustomed to had left me alone to be an adult. Plus he had shared the secret of why we were bound to our loved ones, a vivid lesson from the Afterlife.

Wade snored, so I tiptoed into our bedroom. The morning light accentuated his beautiful coffee skin. He lovingly held my pillow as if he was cuddling me, so I snuck under the covers and watched him sleep.

Here was the man I was in love with, and the man who was in love with me. Nothing could change that. Our midlife mystery was over, and our muse was no longer here to teach us.

But together the three of us learned there's no sin in trying something new. And, personally, I learned that it's somehow okay to break our own rules. Yesterday's lessons belong to another time.

After all, life's too short to be conservative.

About the Author

Kevin lives with his long-term partner, Warren, in their humble apartment (affectionately named Sabrina), in Australia's own 'Emerald City,' Sydney.

From an early age, Kevin had a passion for writing, jotting down stories and plays until it came time to confront puberty. After dealing with pimple creams and facial hair, Kevin didn't pick up a pen again until he was in his thirties. His handwritten manuscript was being committed to paper when his work commitments changed, giving him no time to write. Concerned, his partner, Warren, secretly passed the notebook to a friend who in turn came back and demanded Kevin finish his story. It wasn't long before Kevin's active imagination was let loose again.

His first novel spawned a secondary character named Guy, an insecure gay angel, but many readers argue that he is the star of the Actors and Angels book series. Guy's popularity surprised the author.

So with his fictional guardian angel guiding him, Kevin hopes to bring more whimsical tales of love, life and friendship to his readers.

Website: www.kevinklehr.com
Facebook: www.facebook.com/DramaQueensWithLoveScenes/
Twitter: @kevinklehr
Goodreads: www.goodreads.com/author/show/4298144.Kevin_Klehr
Vimeo: vimeo.com/companionmedia/
YouTube: www.youtube.com/channel/UCcJrnpZjgSjbpCiBp-pA3Jw/

Also by Kevin Klehr

Actors and Angels Series
Drama Queens with Love Scenes
Drama Queens and Devilish Schemes (coming soon)

From Top to Bottom

Nate and Cameron Series
Nate and the New Yorker
Nate's Last Tango

Coming Soon from Kevin Klehr

Drama Queens and Devilish Schemes

Actors and Angels, Book 3

Excerpt

One

IT WAS LIKE being in a Hollywood remake of *The Jetsons*, suspended in air and surrounded by cloudless sky, with interweaving conveyor belts shifting us farther to the front.

Behind me a couple of lesbians fidgeted while peering forward, trying to see where we were going. Below, another mix of curious folk deliberately moved forward on this mechanical mess of pathways. Above me, the same.

"Do you have any idea what's going on?" asked one of the women behind me.

While she could pass for the girl next door, all made up with lips as red as a 1950s advert model, her checkered dress spoiled the effect with its huge smoldering burn mark.

"What happened," I queried.

Her partner stuck out what was left of her tongue. It too was charcoal black with a melted piercing smeared all over it.

"Let's just say, never get frisky outside while there's a thunderstorm."

She reached for her skirt and was about to lift it to prove her point. I clutched her wrist just in time.

"I get it. Your girlfriend's stud became the conductor. I don't need to see something that will haunt me for the rest of my life."

Her eyes widened. *"Your life?* Look at your chest!"

I released her arm and felt my heart. It was like someone had used too much starch while ironing my shirt. I examined a rusty brown stain on the crisp white cotton.

"I've returned, but this time for good," I muttered.

"Wha uw ya awing awout?" said the one with the brittle tongue.

"What did she say?"

"I think she wants to know what you're talking about."

I stood on tippy-toes to see farther ahead, but all I saw was a long row of people waiting patiently.

"I've been here before, I think. I'm not sure." I jumped high on the spot but still couldn't see where we were going. "I guess that's why I've got this frantic ink blot on my chest."

"Sweet cheeks, it's blood."

"Yes, I know that."

"So what's your story? How did it get there?"

I felt it again. Its sandpaper texture began to crumble. "I wish I knew." Bending sideways, I tried to steal a glimpse, but it was no use.

"Well, it's not quite how I imagined it. I'm not sure it's how you saw it either, Frida." She held her girlfriend's hand. "I was expecting tattooed angels parked on clouds with big black motorcycles ready to take us to Heaven."

Frida nodded.

"What did you expect, um, what's your name?"

"Adam."

"Hi, I'm Sue." We shook hands. "And this is Frida."

"Ice oo eet yoo."

"My pleasure."

"So, is this the way you pictured it?"

"No, I can't say it is. My partner isn't here."

"What's his name?"

"Wade. We've been together for nearly nineteen years. Or at least, we were."

"I'm sorry he's not with you."

I felt my bloodstain once more.

"Well, at least he survived, if what happened to me happened to him, if that makes sense?" I bit my bottom lip. "Actually I really don't know what I'm talking about."

"Aw leees ee awive..."

Sue raised her hand like a cop stopping traffic.

"Don't try to speak, darling. It looks like hard work."

"Yeah, but I get what Frida's trying to say. At least Wade's alive instead of here."

"A silver lining in the cloud."

"That's one way of looking at it."

Below me a young chap in a Second World War uniform peeled off his gloves. His conveyor belt had stopped. An African woman wearing more colors than a rainbow tried to speak to him, but he seemed too traumatized to reply. She raised her arms in disappointment and began talking to the gray-haired woman behind her.

"Leopard print," said Sue.

"Huh?"

"Check out the middle-aged woman in the leopard print, far behind us. Wow! She's wearing more jewelry than a 1960s movie star."

I looked. "I think she is a 60s movie star. Look at that beehive!"

"Jackie O she ain't."

"And look at the older woman next to her. A lollipop in a pantsuit."

"Adam, how can they be from the 60s?"

"Now I know I've been here before." I glanced ahead and saw the tip of a wing obstructed by the others on my conveyor belt. I couldn't hold back my smile. "Sue, let me ask you something. What era are you from?"

"Nineteen ninety-three. Why? Aren't you?"

I pointed to the man in uniform. Sue's jaw dropped steadily.

"And what country?"

"Poland. And you?"

"Australia, twenty-first century."

"You speak Polish well for an Australian."

"Sue, I'm not speaking Polish."

She shared stunned looks with Frida.

"Wha iz ee alking avout?"

"Girls, you're about to enter a world I've been dreaming of returning to since I was last taken from earth before my time."

"Maybe you should *try* Polish. I have no idea what you mean."

Frida rotated her finger by the side of her head; a gesture to make out I was loony. Sue shrugged before carrying on a private conversation with her girlfriend about the family they'd left behind.

A few drops of water splashed on my face. I looked to the moving path above. A group of teenagers also from the 60s flower-power days stood shivering, saturated to the core. One long-haired guy, with enough swirls on his shirt to send you into a trance, saw me.

"Never do your own plumbing when you're tripping, man," he called. "I flooded the apartment."

"Why didn't you run outside?"

A naked girl with waist-length long hair clutched onto his arm. "I thought I was swimming in candy floss," she replied.

"Candy floss!" he said. "I thought the sky had fallen and there was no escape."

"Weren't we in space, floating?" asked another.

I chuckled before bending sideways to look ahead. I saw half his body. My guardian angel, Guy. He acknowledged me with a kind grin. I was eager to jump to the head of the queue. I took a calm breath, stood up straight, and closed my eyes.

I already sensed his comforting hugs, letting me know I'd returned to safety. I could feel his strong wings wrap around me like an extra layer of armor. Nothing would harm me here in the Afterlife, not with him by my side.

"Adam's here," said another voice I recognized.

"Yeah," Guy replied. "There's something I need to explain."

"Mannix?" I mumbled to myself.

Many passengers later I was at the front. I stepped off the conveyor belt onto thin air, and before a word was uttered, both the angel and my old friend wrapped their arms around me. I clutched them tightly, never wanting to let go. Huge smiles engulfed us all. Behind me were bewildered murmurs, as a stray tear from Guy softened my cheek.

"I've missed you," I said to my angel. I kissed him tenderly on the forehead. "And I missed you too, Mannix."

"Welcome to the Afterlife again," said Guy.

"Why am I here?" I whispered. We stepped apart.

"I think this time you're actually dead," Mannix replied.

He sounded unsure, like a wife telling her tired husband that there might be a burglar in their house. He was still in his early thirties, just as he was the last time I was whisked off to the Afterlife six months earlier.

His sensual demeanor still warmed me in places I'm too polite to mention, even though his boyhood looks had faded slightly since we last met. A man was taking his place. A man wise beyond his years, wearing older-sexy like a stylish coat.

"Where's Wade?" I asked.

"Sadly mourning your demise, my friend," Guy said in a hushed tone. "Adam, we'll talk about that later."

I touched the dried blood on my shirt, crumbling it into tiny pieces that fell away.

"Guy, I need to know what happened."

He turned to Mannix. "I'm releasing you from welcoming duties to show Adam his new home."

"Which is where?" the young man asked.

Guy pulled out a key from his trouser pocket. "The apartment under mine." He had a devilish grin. "Adam's not the only one who needs a friend at the moment."

"So you and Guy welcome the dead?" I asked.

"Yeah, but we call them new visitors," Mannix replied. He sipped his scotch and Coke. "*I've* just started, but Guy's been doing it for ages. He got a promotion when they put in the new conveyor belts. They needed to upgrade." He looked around the room before leaning toward me. "Too many lost souls coming at once."

I had showered and changed, and was now sitting with Mannix at a lavish bar called the Carousel in the Medieval Quarter. Two drunken men in full armor jousted with plastic toy swords in the corner while a topless woman with tassels on her perfect breasts attempted to tango as she ignored their clatter. Some drinkers shared their attention between the drunks and the playful dancer, pointing and chatting as if they considered themselves boring by comparison. But to me, they were just as fascinating.

The last time I'd visited the Afterlife, I was still alive, because Guy felt the need to take me away from my earthly dramas. And once again, the supporting extras still intrigued me in this land of the dead. After all, this part of the Medieval Quarter was known as the Carnival of Lost Souls. A fitting description.

"There's something bothering me, Mannix."

"Besides not knowing how you died."

"Well, there's that, but..."

One of the armored men collapsed to the ground with a thud. A tall woman in a lime backless dress stood up and applauded. I clapped briefly before I realized that no one else was taking her lead. A barman strolled over to check on him.

"Adam, you were saying?"

"My new apartment looks a lot like mine and Wade's back in Sydney."

"We do that. I know it's unsettling at first, but it helps new arrivals fit in."

"But how did you do it? The couch is the same. My stereo is the same, just without the television. The kitchen is kind of the same, just in a lighter color."

"Adam, this is the Afterlife. We're masters of pulling things from thin air."

"But doesn't it seem odd to you?"

"I've had more time to get used to it."

"This whole place, it's like an ethereal version of Earth. There's running water. Electricity. Music collections. Food and alcohol." The waiter came to refill my glass of merlot. "But you know what, Mannix? I've never seen a toilet. Come to think of it, I didn't need one the last time I was here." The waiter nodded before going back to the bar. "And besides that, the only thing that points to this place being the Afterlife is a bunch of people hanging around bars in period costume from a hell of a lot of eras. And, of course, there's an angel. Take that away and we may as well still be alive."

"Maybe your wine is the blood of Christ?"

"Don't go there, Mannix. If it was, I'd be more enlightened."

An assortment of bizarre collectibles adorned small shelves on the walls. Some looked like rejects from a charity shop. Other's seemed too precious to be gathering dust. A detailed figurine of a girl walking her shih tzu sat next to a clay horse's head, so lifelike it seemed more a freaky attempt at taxidermy.

Each table also had an ornament sitting on it. Ours was a vintage doll with a wonky eye. I picked it up while watching a fiendish man in a leather jacket striding up to the topless woman.

"Mannix, is Guy still with that boyfriend of his?"

"You mean Joshua? What made you think of him?"

I pointed to the man who was now trying to touch the woman's tassel. She took his delinquent hand and slapped it.

"I see your point, Adam. He reminds me of Joshua too."

"Yes, with the same personality it seems."

As if written as their cue in a play, Guy and Joshua entered the Carousel that very moment. Joshua was in his angel disguise, with a slight emo twist highlighted by black feathered wings. When he was his demon self, the wings were still black, but resembled those on a bat. Small horns were also part of his natural look, but when he slummed it in the Afterlife, he couldn't get away with being himself. The only clue to his true form could be found in his reflection, as I discovered when catching a glimpse of his likeness in a drinking glass.

They headed for the bar, Josh gazing at me briefly as if I was the only witness to a murder he'd committed.

"Mannix, what does that beautiful angel see in that sarcastic demon? And why is an angel going out with a demon?"

"Between you and me, I think it has less to do with romance and more to do with the fact that Joshua knows where Guy's parents are."

"Oh yes, I forgot about that. Guy never met his folks. Something about being brought up by a fortune-teller, wasn't it?"

"Shh. They're almost here."

Guy plonked a large champagne bottle on our table before Joshua landed four glasses next to it.

"It's not peer pressure. It's peer support," he said. His black wings fluttered.

"I'll drink to that," Guy replied. They both sat. "So, Adam, how do you like your new flat?"

"It's spooking me out."

"From memory, everything spooks you out," replied Joshua.

"Only when it has dark wings and a 'try hard' attitude."

"Now, now, boys," Guy said. He popped the cork and began to pour. "I don't want my two favorite men—"

Mannix faked a cough.

"Sorry, three favorite men bickering. I need to celebrate!"

He slid my drink toward me.

"What's the deal with that cock-eyed doll you're holding?" Joshua asked.

I looked at the toy's face. "I forgot it was still in my hand."

"You've been using it to punctuate your gestures ever since you picked it up," said Mannix.

"It must be my security blanket."

"Don't worry," said Guy. "A few celebratory drinks will ease your nerves." As the champagne reached his mouth, his glass became wobbly.

"Are you already drunk?" Mannix asked.

"I just had one drink before I came."

Joshua peered down his nose.

"Okay, maybe two."

Joshua's eyes now looked to the ceiling.

"No seriously, only two."

I gazed at Mannix who nodded discreetly. I then peered at Joshua who seemed to have trouble smiling.

"Why did you start without us?" I asked.

"I want to celebrate your arrival," Guy replied. "After all, Adam, I've missed you." He raised his glass. "To an old friend becoming my neighbor."

We clinked, then sipped.

"Now that the formalities are over, can you please tell me how I died? That was a nasty bloodstain on my shirt."

"In time, Adam. I need to ask for a favor, first."

"You need *my* help this time? Of course, my angel buddy. What is it?"

He looked to his lover.

"Guy is going to meet his parents," Joshua replied.

"And I need moral support."

I reached for his hand. He grasped mine gently.

"Wow. I'd consider it an honor to stand by your side, old friend. Where are they?"

Again he looked to Joshua.

"That's a secret for now," Joshua replied.

"Why?"

The black-winged immortal shook his head so only I would see.

"He won't tell me," said Guy.

"Adam, I suggested you should be here when he meets them," Joshua replied. "I know how much he respects you."

I glanced at Mannix.

"He said the same thing to me," he declared. "For whatever reason, Joshua wanted you to be here to support Guy."

"But Guy has both you and Joshua. Why wait till I died? Are you recruiting an ensemble cast for the reunion?"

"It's difficult to explain," said Joshua. "The more friends he has here, the better."

Guy let go of my hand and topped up his champagne, then drank. He put the glass down, unsteadily. I picked up the doll and stared at its imperfect face.

"Wow, I just arrive and already there's mystery and adventure. I need Wade by my side to share it with. I'm missing him terribly. I just wish I knew how I died."

"Adam's right, Guy," said Mannix. "I think he needs to know what happened."

"The secrecy is killing me. Oh wait, I'm already dead. Okay, the secrecy is driving me mad."

"All right," Guy answered. "I'll take you to see Wade. That's all I can do for the moment."

"Can't you also tell me how my shirt got covered in blood?"

"No, I can't." He reached for *my* hand this time. I put down the doll and clasped his soft palm. "You have to work out what happened for yourself, Adam. It will start coming to you. That's the way things work here." He clasped tighter, but somehow I suspected he didn't actually know himself. "But I guess if I take you to see Wade, your healing process will begin."

"My healing process! Shouldn't I know how I died first? Why don't you tell me before we see Wade?"

"Now that you're here, you need to take one step at a time. Come to terms with your demise, calmly. If I tell you everything up front, you might find it too hard to handle."

I sighed.

"I know this is hard to take in, Adam," Mannix said, "but Guy's right. I've made the mistake of telling someone too much too soon. It wasn't pretty."

"What happened?" I asked.

"A loving parent was poisoned by his kids for the inheritance money. Years of therapy followed here in the Afterlife."

"Oh dear. I wasn't murdered, was I?"

"Trust your guardian angel. Let him guide you."

Guy stood, and as we were still holding hands, I too was lifted from my chair.

"Adam, it's time to start healing," he said. "Let's see Wade."

Also Available from NineStar Press

www.ninestarpress.com